THE TREES KNOW

Other books by Kris Lockard

Green Ridge

A Matter of Trust

Evil on the Run

Peril on the Prowl

The Coldest Case

THE
TREES KNOW

A Novel by

Kris Lockard

ISBN: 978-0-9964308-5-2

This is a work of fiction. Names, characters, places, and incidents either are the product of the author's imagination or are used fictitiously. Physical characteristics of the cities of Portland, Madras, Bend, and the Metolius River Basin have been distorted to accommodate the story line. Errors in police and legal practices and procedures are entirely my fault.

Photo credits: Cover: Author
Back cover insert: Keely K. Studios
Book design and layout: Gorham Printing
Printed in 12pt. Garamond

This book is dedicated to abuse victims everywhere.

———————— ✴ ————————

PEOPLE ASK ME what motivates me to write a book. Usually, it is an occurrence which really pisses me off. Prior to writing The Trees Know, *a domestic abuse crime occurred in Portland, Oregon in the Fall of 2021. It was a crime which made me angry and frustrated because justice for the victim was never achieved when it counted, when she was alive. I could do nothing about it but grieve for a victim I didn't even know. Consequently, I spent the next fifteen months writing this book.*

A WRITER cannot know everything needed to write a book. I must
rely on the generous cooperation of people who often don't know me.
Their knowledge, generosity, and good humor will
never cease to astound and humble me. I would like
to acknowledge the following individuals:

Lt. Andrew Copeland, Keizer Police Department,
keeping us safe in an uncertain world.

Lark Brandt, for permission to use critters from our youth.
In writing their parts, I reminisced with every keystroke.

Roseann Kendall, Tracker Extraordinaire. Everything I know about
tracking I learned from Roseann.

Greg Lies, for his good-natured willingness to let
me use his name spelled like it sounds.

The folks at Gorham Printing for making me
look good, book after book after book.

When I think I don't have it in me, these guys keep me going,
always encouraging, always there for me, chapter by chapter.
My Editors:
Janell Hales
David Lockard
Susan (Soupy) Thompson

—KRIS LOCKARD
Keizer, Oregon
Krislockard.com

The Trees Know List of Characters

Alphabetically by first name

The Geezers

Arthur Perkins—Retired banker from Baker City, Oregon/Beth Welton's husband.

Beth Welton—Author and philanthropist from Portland, Oregon/Arthur Perkin's wife.

Cal Wiggens—Semi-retired forensic pathologist from Portland, Oregon.

Conrad Wardwell—Retired Navy Commander/Phyllis' husband.

Dave—Retired Systems Analyst, Oregon State Dept. of Transportation, from Salem, Oregon/Married to Mick's sister. Dave is patterned after my husband, Dave.

Mick—Retired radiologist from Puyallup, Washington/Dave's brother-in-law. Mick is patterned after my brother, Michael Scott Campbell, MD.

Old Bowels, AKA O.B.—Retired firefighter from Camp Sherman.

Phyllis Wardwell, AKA Aunt Phil—Retired criminal defense attorney from Seattle/Conrad Wardwell's wife/Adam Carson's aunt.

Yank-um (Lewis P.) Campbell—Retired dentist from Salem, Oregon. This character is patterned after my dad, Lewis P. Campbell, Jr., DDS.

Other Major Characters

Adam Carson—Semi-retired attorney from Portland/Sophie Summers husband/Aunt Phil's nephew.

Annie Dozler—Abused wife of Luke Dozler.

Cyril Richmond—Jefferson County Deputy Sheriff, Camp Sherman.

Emily Martin—Semi-retired CPA from New York/Sheriff Gary Larkin's friend.

Gary Larkin—Jefferson County Sheriff/friend of Emily Martin.

Greg Leese—Deschutes County Deputy Sheriff.

John Hadwin—Veterinarian, from Maple Valley, Washington.

Kayla Harvey—Officer, Jefferson County Sheriff's Department.

Mazie Odom, PHD—Expert tracker, Silverton, Oregon.

Luke Dozler—Rotten husband of Annie Dozler.

Oliver—Tommy Jax's partner.

Sophie Summers—Hairdresser and Director, Performing Arts Theater/Adam Carson's wife.

Tommy Jax—Ex-organized crime figure/Oliver's partner.

Will Barclay—Sergeant, Jefferson County Sheriff's Department.

Minor Characters

Andy Evans—Police Officer, Black Butte Ranch Police Dept.

Doug Miller—Black Butte Ranch Wrangler.

Eric McElroy—Chief, Black Butte Ranch Police Dept.

Hadley Taylor—Philanthropist from Bend/Restoring the Santiam Pass Ski Lodge.

Jayden Martinez—Sergeant and K-9 Handler, Black Butte Ranch Police Dept.

Jerry Banning—Corporal, Portland Police Bureau, Homicide Division.

Shawn Avery—Lieutenant, Portland Police Bureau, Homicide Division.

Trever Kowalski—Sergeant, Portland Police Bureau, Homicide Division.

Not as many as a Russian novel, but almost. This is what happens when writing a series. The number of characters builds, I become fond of them, and don't have the heart to get rid of them.

❧ CHAPTER 1 ❧

WHO WAS SHE, this shadow in the darkness? Only the trees knew. They had heard her sob as she agonized in despair. With her arms around their massive trunks, she sought security and solace, leaving tears on their rough bark. These same trees had witnessed the agony of human suffering for hundreds of years and now shielded her from storms, covered her with their fragrant foliage, and warded off the wind and wet. She, like a lost soul hiding from hell, carefully made her way from one sheltering stand of trees to another, through a wilderness as vast as the ache in her heart.

SHE CAME BY starlight, slipping quietly among the old cabins, as though her feet were feathers. Like a zephyr, she moved from one end of the little community of Camp Sherman to the other, weaving her way in and around the Ponderosa pines, avoiding yard lights with their pools of light cast upon the ground. Even if you'd known she was there, you wouldn't see her.

Dave was outside at the time she drifted by his cabin. He did not hear her as much as felt her presence. She passed then hesitated, looking back at him. He squinted into the darkness, not sure of what he saw... or felt. Did she then disappear into the trees or, ghost-like, simply dissolve?

"Dang these old eyes!" Dave muttered, furious with the oldness of his body. His eighty years wore on him. Unable to sleep for more than a few hours at a time, he often would step outside his cabin. Quietly closing the door behind him, he would let the chill of the night envelope him. Experiencing the night as the forest creatures did, he could smell the fragrance of the trees, feel the forest more than see it, and hear the river whispering.

Dave squinted into the darkness, blinking but to no avail. He knew she was gone, whatever she was. He could feel the emptiness she left behind, like a wake in fog.

MICK WAS THE first to reach the summit of Green Ridge. With his chocolate Labrador retriever Buddy at his side, he leaned on his walking sticks, took a deep breath of the clean alpine air and gazed at the majestic Cascade Mountain Range. These mountains had been in his life for eight decades, but he never tired of the sight.

Tall and slender, Mick was a retired radiologist. He had spent his career in Washington State, and in his scarce spare time climbed and hiked in the Northern Washington Range of the Cascade Mountains. He grew up here, in the Central Oregon Cascades just outside of Bend, Oregon, hiking, fishing, and camping with his dad and sister. Mick had lost his wife not long ago and seeking the comfort of an earlier time, moved to Camp Sherman, coming home to his beloved mountains.

Puffing up the trail behind him was Arthur Perkins. The retired banker from Baker City, Oregon, was accompanied by his perpetually happy dog, Max. The dog, a huge, mixed breed was a bundle of wavey black hair. As a stray in Baker City, the dog had "adopted" Arthur and now followed him everywhere. It was as though Max was afraid if he lost sight of the man who gave him a name, a home, and unconditional love, he would disappear forever.

Arthur, taller than Mick and muscular from the years spent building his cabin and wood shop, pulled a handkerchief from his pocket and doffing his hat, wiped the sweat from his forehead, neck, and head. His head was bald except for a ring of neatly trimmed white hair around the back. The ring of hair was matched by a white mustache.

"That hill gets steeper every time we do this."

"Yup, but we'll keep doing it 'til we drop."

"We got nothing else to do and the rest of our lives to do it."

"You got it!"

The men had decided to take their dogs for a hike to the top of the ridge. Green Ridge was a volcanic fault scarp which ran north to south and bordered the venerable Metolius River in Central Oregon. It served as the backdrop for the tiny community of historic cabins called Camp Sherman. Named in the 1800s by wheat farmers from Sherman County, the area became a popular destination for the farmers who came to the coolness of the river to refresh after hot dusty harvests. The U.S. Forest Service took over maintenance of the land in the early 1900s. In the 1920s and 30s, people were allowed to build log cabins along the river. Many of the cabins were still owned by generations of the original families.

Arthur had built an A-frame log cabin on the opposite side of the ridge from the historic area of Camp Sherman. He was very much involved in the community and was a tireless advocate for Camp Sherman to keep its quaint, historic nature. Arthur had lost his young wife to breast cancer in the 1960s and he had stayed single for decades. He had purchased a few acres on Green Ridge from a lumber company and once he retired, built the cabin and planned to spend the rest of his life in these mountains.

Arthur had met his current wife, Beth Welton, when she was a fugitive from a homicidal and money-grubbing daughter. Not far from Arthur's cabin, Beth had hidden in a cave which was one of many lava tubes found in the area. While stealing corn from the man's carefully tended garden, she was caught red-handed by Arthur and Max. Max instantly fell in love with her and Arthur, knowing his dog's instincts rarely proved false, also accepted her presence and was soon as enamored by her as was his dog.

Mick and Arthur continued their hike up the spine of the ridge, following a trail which ran from one end of the ridge to the other. It started where the ridge connects to the backside of 6,436-foot Black Butte and culminated approximately six miles to the north at the wickedly ravaged volcanic cone of a long-extinct volcano. Now called Castle Rocks, the jagged formation predates the more prominent Cascade Range of volcanic peaks by several million years.

The men soon came to a small clearing separated from the trail by a copse of young trees and manzanita. With a knowing nod to Arthur, Mick let the big man cross in front of him towards the clearing. Mick followed Arthur into an area of dusty earth dominated by a small cairn of rocks.

"When I climb the ridge, I always have to come here," Arthur said as he looked down at the rock pile. "It makes me feel closer to that time in Beth's life when she was on her own here in the woods and buried her dog and her first husband's ashes under that cairn. Soon after I met her, I lost her again. She felt she had to go back to the woods to hide from that blasted daughter of hers. It wasn't until Max and I headed up here in the snow that I found her and asked her to come home with me. As if I don't already need reasons to appreciate her in my life, Mick, coming here brings it all together for me."

"I get it," Mick said simply, having lost his own life's partner. "We can never take anyone for granted."

"Nope," Arthur answered. "Well, thanks for stopping. Shall we carry on down the trail?"

"Sure, anytime you're ready."

Through breaks in the forest of mixed conifers, manzanita, and service berry, the two men could see nearly 1,500 feet down to the bottom of the Metolius River Basin. From this height, the river looked like a ribbon of silver as it skirted the ridge and wound around small islands of trees and brush on its way to join The Deschutes and Crooked Rivers, forming Lake Billy Chinook.

The dogs spotted it first; a movement among the trees, a movement unlike anything caused by one of the many wild creatures that called the forest home. Both dogs stopped in their tracks and noses into the wind, huffed and looked down the west side of the ridge to a spot about half-way down.

"Wha...?" Mick asked his dog and then he saw it too. Just a blur, a piece of color, and then it was gone.

"Did you see that?" Mick asked Arthur. "There! There it is again. Something moving. Dang, I lost it! Now, it's gone."

"No, I couldn't see it, but Max did," Arthur answered, still peering into the forest, trying to spot whatever it was his dog was fixated upon. "What do you suppose? There's no trail down there. Cliffs mostly. Steeper than shit."

"Yeah, it is. If that was a person, he'd have to be half-ape."

"I knew a lot of guys like that," Arthur commented, lightening the mood. "Most were the bank's customers. Frequently they were all in the lobby at once, each one wanting to talk to me."

Mick laughed. 'Yeah, I knew a few like that too." He then said to his dog, "Come on, Buddy, let's get a move-on."

Buddy, having his attention torn from what he had been watching, wagged his tail and, in the way of dogs, looked at Mick apologetically although he had done nothing to apologize for.

BETH SAW IT TOO, the flash of yellow against the green foliage and rough brown bark of the trees. "Not a good color to wear, yellow," she thought as she looked up the side of the ridge. She was driving their Dodge pickup home after delivering her huckleberry pies to the Camp Sherman Store. "Not a good color at all, especially when you want to hide." After a moment of thought, Beth turned the truck around and drove back to the store where she bought a sweatshirt in a camo pattern. Returning to a wide spot in the road, Beth pulled over, turned off the truck and stepped from the cab. As her feet sank into the volcanic dust beside the road, she reflected how quiet it was, the only sounds were those which belonged there; the wind in the trees, squabbling of squirrels, and the occasional screech of a red-tailed hawk. She took a parcel from the truck bed and adding the sweatshirt to it, attached a note she had written. *Don't wear yellow. Too easily seen.* She crossed the road and walked uphill into the woods. She left the parcel tucked underneath the half-burned trunk of a tree which had fallen long ago in a now forgotten fire.

Beth knew who she left the parcel for. She felt this person's dilemma deep within her soul. Beth's heart was long in tune with that of a fugitive on the run, not from the law, but from evil over which the law had no control. Beth felt it because she had been there.

❧ CHAPTER 2 ❧

GEEZER CENTRAL, CAMP SHERMAN, OREGON. The cabin belonging to Conrad and Phyllis Wardwell, octogenarians from Portland, was now dubbed Geezer Central by the community of Camp Sherman. Today, the old log structure was alive with Geezers on a mission.

The Geezer Underground, as they called themselves, consisted of elders in the community who, in their seventies and eighties, had gathered to find purpose in their lives, lives often shoved aside by a younger society. Not ready to be shelved, this group of oldsters were past business owners, doctors, lawyers, and other professionals who had found depth in their retired lives by assisting local law enforcement track suspects in criminal investigations, whether the law wanted it or not.

Using their age as well as costumes as cover, they would stalk the alleged lawless souls and, when the time was right, surreptitiously report the individual's activities to the Jefferson County Sheriff's Deputy on duty in Camp Sherman. Deputy Cyril Richmond, already beleaguered by a workload consistent with being the only deputy in this far-flung corner of Jefferson County, now had the added burden of the safety of these oldsters as they prowled the surrounding territory. Their intent was to be an asset to local law enforcement no matter how often or adamantly law enforcement pleaded with them not to.

However, today the group had gathered to discuss not a new investigation, but a fundraiser for the volunteer mountain search and rescue operation for Jefferson County headquartered in Camp Sherman.

Managed by Jefferson County Sheriff's Office emergency manager, the Camp Sherman Hasty Search and Rescue Team provided immediate response primarily to incidents in the Metolius Basin, the eastern slopes of the Cascade Mountains, and parts of the Pacific Crest Trail. Comprised of volunteers, the team included members from all over the Sisters area of Central Oregon.

The Geezers had offered to serve as coordinators for this community fund raiser. They decided a Renaissance Faire would be fun, allowing participants and patrons to dress up in period costumes. The booth raising the most money would get a prize of some sort, the Geezers, at this time, not sure just what that would be, but with shared optimism, they were positive they would think of something.

The Wardwells had added room onto their cabin according to U.S. Forest Service specifications, but it was still a cramped place when all the Geezers crowded in, especially like today when their dogs were included. Consequently, some of the happy group spilled out onto the sun-filled front yard where many gathered around a picnic table.

Taking up quite a lot of space at the table was Tommy Jax. No stranger to a knife and fork, Jax was a huge man at 6'4" and nearly 400 pounds. He dominated any Geezer gathering not only with his size but with his jovial nature. Not old enough to be an official Geezer, T.J., as the Geezers called him, provided key assistance to their investigations through his criminal contacts up and down the West Coast. For years, Jax had been a prominent figure in the murky underworld of crime until Phyllis, while she was a criminal defense attorney in Seattle, saved his substantial hide on a murder charge. She detected an obscure error in the police investigation that no amount of denial could hide.

Although King County prosecutors fussed and fumed, tore their hair and exchanged unpleasant snarls with Phyllis, Jax walked free. Phyllis threatened Jax if he didn't straighten out his life, she'd send one of several hit men after him. After all, as a criminal defense attorney, she was acquainted with quite a few. Jax knew from her reputation as a straight shooter who didn't take any guff from either prosecutors or her clients, he should take her very seriously, and so he did.

Jax and his partner, a reserved, reed-thin man by the name of Oliver, started an outreach service for the homeless in Seattle. They also provided hot meals for a nearby homeless shelter. Being computer savvy, Oliver helped recovering addicts navigate the extensive documentation required in applying for social services. The time between applying and getting an interview was sometimes weeks or months apart. Often the paperwork would get lost or damaged in the rain. Oliver kept records for all the people he helped, and they knew they could get copies from him when they needed to. When Jax and Oliver traveled, all the applicants had to do was use the phone in the homeless shelter to call Oliver and the thin man would send a PDF file of the individual's paperwork to a printer at the shelter.

Recently, Jax and Oliver had been spending a lot of time in Camp Sherman helping with Geezer investigations. So much time, in fact, that they purchased a second home at Black Butte Ranch, a golfing and outdoor recreation community not far away in neighboring Deschutes County.

Joining Jax and Oliver at Wardwell's picnic table were brothers-in-law Mick and Dave. Dave had been married to Mick's sister, a writer, for over fifty years. Dave's wife would get irritated at the amount of noise he made binge-watching football games, whooping and hollering and providing his own commentary. As a result, she would often throw him out of the cabin. She claimed she couldn't get any writing done with him around. He would not have cared had she made enough money selling books so he could buy a yacht. However, that possibility didn't appear it was going to be happening anytime soon. Mick, knowing his sister well, took pity on Dave and the two codgers spent a lot of time together in and around Camp Sherman. They met each morning at the post office and worked on the daily crossword puzzle. They claimed it took the two of them to get all the three-letter words.

"What's going on out here?" Joining the group at the table was Old Bowels, a retired firefighter who came by his nickname quite naturally. Of short stature and wiry, he had had so many hernia operations that his fellow firefighters started calling him Old Bowels or O.B. He'd been called Old

Bowels and O.B. for so long that he wasn't sure anybody knew him by his real name. His doctors had told him he needed to quit firefighting because there were just so many times they could sew him back together. They made him aware he was rapidly running out of those times. Consequently, he retired to volunteering at the fire station in Camp Sherman and kept the fire engine and equipment in top shape.

"Hi, O.B!" Jax extended his huge hand for a shake.

"Hey, T.J, haven't seen you for a while."

"Oliver and I have been doing some remodeling of the kitchen in the Black Butte house."

"Ah, not big enough for Geezer meetings?" Mick asked as the rest of the group snickered.

"No where near!" Jax answered. "We're doing lots of stuff like putting in a huge range and double ovens. Also, one of those zero-degree refriger-ator-freezers. Dang thing is big enough to put me in it." The big man then laughed. When Jax laughed, he laughed with his entire body. Rarely could anybody near him not laugh with him, whether they heard what was said or not.

Also at the table were Dr. Calvin Wiggens, a semi-retired forensic pa-thologist from Portland and his life-long buddy, Dr. Pat "Yank-um" Camp-bell, a retired oral maxillofacial surgeon from Salem. His dentist pals had given him the nick-name Yank-um because whenever they tried to remove a tooth that wouldn't budge, Campbell could always be relied upon to pry it loose.

About that time, the group was approached by Adam Carson, a swarthy-looking, semi-retired Portland attorney who also was Phyllis Wardwell's nephew. Although Adam and his bride, Sophie Summers, both hovered one side or the other of sixty years of age, they were also too young to be full-fledged Geezers. They considered themselves Geezers-in-training.

Room was made at the table for Adam, a larger version of his stocky aunt, as he said, "I was just inside," Adam cocked his head toward Wardwell's cabin, "and heard that the Geezers wouldn't compete for the prize or even necessarily do a booth but dress up in costumes and wander around the grounds, keeping tabs on what's going on. Phyllis has some ideas about doing a fortune telling booth, and the rest of us will just do whatever we want."

"I'm glad we won't be competing for the prize," Old Bowels replied. "That keeps us involved but doesn't pit us against the rest of Camp Sherman. Lord knows at our ages, there are enough challenges in life, we don't need to compete with anybody!"

Phyllis, or as her nephew called her, Aunt Phil, came bounding out of the cabin and overheard the conversation at the picnic table. "Hey, you guys, what do you think about me being a fortune teller? I'll be Madame Gorgonzola!" She started dancing around the sunny grassy clearing as though she was already wearing her imaginary gown. Spreading her pudgy arms wide, she twirled in a circle and exclaimed, "I can see me now! I'll wear this huge kaftan-type thing with big billowing sleeves, scarves all over, and use some kind of a crystal ball thingy."

"Sophie can help with costumes," Adam offered. The Geezers shenanigans had been augmented by Adam's wife and her talents at dressing them in crazy outfits. She had a seemingly endless cache of costumes from a performing art's theater in Sisters where she volunteered as director.

"Okay," O.B. said, "The rest of us can be medieval townspeople or knights. I'll bet Sophie can come up with something for us."

"This is supposed to be in the era of Robin Hood, right?" Jax said. "I could be little John!"

Oliver, who rarely said anything, picked up on the vibe and offered, "I can be the world's skinniest Robin Hood!"

Aunt Phil added, "That would be a hoot! So much easier to hide in the trees. But first, we're going to have to get this website online so folks can get info and then sign up their booth. That's what Conrad, Arthur, Beth and I were trying to do just now inside the cabin. The tech support guy who is building the website for us uses terms that mean nothing to any of us; like *back side of the website* and something called *WooCommerce*! When we ask a question, he smugly tells us to find the answer on his website's 'ticket.' What the heck is a 'ticket,' for crying out loud? Why can't he just give us the answer when we're already on the phone?"

By now, Aunt Phil was in a rage and was stomping around. She had run her hands through her short, white hair until it looked as though she had driven a car with the windows down. With her blue eyes blazing with fury, she went on, "So, like good little old people, we obediently go to his website and click on this link to our 'ticket', and discover it requires a password! Are you kidding me? Does he think we're going to hack his computer and sell copies of a video of his colonoscopy or something? All we have is a simple question and we need a password to get a frigging answer? What kind of a process is this that this guy can't use a telephone to give an answer to a bunch of old people who have never had to speak this kind of language? Has he forgotten it was someone in our generation who taught him how to tie his shoes? And did we badger him if he had trouble catching on right away? Of course not! It was getting so frustrating, I had to get outta there before I started having gaskets explode!"

Oliver then stood and in his strange, stick-like manner, left the table. He said, "I'll see if I can help. If I can find a copy of his colonoscopy video, I'll let you know." Chuckling, he headed for the cabin.

"Oh, thank you so much, Oliver!" Aunt Phil said gratefully to his back as he stiffly headed inside. "If you also find a video of his vasectomy, I'll split the profits with you!"

By now, everyone in the small clearing in front of Wardwell's cabin was enjoying a good laugh. Nearby, the Metolius River gurgled its approval. From the trees not far away, a pair of eyes were following the action. Then, the eyes melted away into the forest and disappeared.

❦ CHAPTER 3 ❦

THE JEFFERSON COUNTY Sheriff's Office in Madras, Oregon, was as far as one could get from Camp Sherman and still be in Jefferson County. The waiting room was colder than a witch. Lucas Dozler sat and fumed. He thought it must be nice, having taxpayers pay for the air conditioning. He didn't know how long he'd been sitting there but it was long enough for him to get thoroughly pissed. A well-built man in his late thirties, Dozler's patience was worn thin. He had work to do and having to wait this long to see the sheriff hadn't helped. He could have given his report to that sergeant and been out of here by now, but he wanted Sheriff Larkin, front and center. After all, Larkin should know he's an important businessman in this community and deserved special attention. Some pity and empathy wouldn't hurt, especially now.

THE DUTY SERGEANT, a burly Black man by the name of Will Barclay, filled the doorway of Sheriff Gary Larkin's office and waited for an answer. Looming behind his desk like a grizzly bear, Larkin sat, and with smoldering eyes, glared at his sergeant. Larkin was in his late fifties, had close cropped grey hair, and hazel eyes. Larkin was an honest man who had a presence about him that had appealed to voters in Jefferson County for two decades. However, as he had gotten older, he had grown more and more impatient with fools, whether they voted or not.

"Tell him I'm in a meeting."

Barclay, with his thumbs tucked into his duty belt, leaned against the doorjamb, knowing his sheriff would change his mind. Then, Larkin brushed his big hand across his face and wearily got out of his chair. "Nah, I'll come, Will. His wife's missing. That's serious, although if she did a runner, I can't say as I blame her. The guy's an ass."

Grinning, Barclay stepped out of Larkin's way and said, "Don't like him much, do you?"

Larkin's boots made a ponderous clumping sound as he headed down the hallway towards the front of the office. He said over his shoulder to Barclay, "Nope. Not one bit."

THE CONFERENCE ROOM was no warmer than the rest of the building, and Dozler was miffed that he had been relegated to a common conference room and not the sheriff's private office. Coffee also would have been nice. He thought about asking the young female officer to get some. That sort of thing is what women in offices do, right?

Officer Kayla Harvey had recently graduated with a master's degree in criminology from the University of Massachusetts-Dartmouth. The Jefferson County Sheriff's Office was her first job. Graduating at the top of her class, Harvey had received other job offers, some from big city police departments, but she had grown up in Madras and was excited to apply her education here in her hometown. She had already entered the conference room, introduced herself to Dozler and explained she was there to take notes.

Dozler thought she looked nice and curvy in that uniform. He wondered what she would look like without it on. He knew she was coming on to him. All women did. Why shouldn't they? He was extraordinarily handsome with gelled black hair and flashing dark eyes. He was rich and was a demigod in bed. So what if he slept around some? His wife was not happy with it, the bitch. Any guy this virile was entitled to exercise his God-given talents, wife or no wife.

Larkin entered the conference room, carrying a file folder. He asked if

Luke had met Officer Harvey. Dozer winked at her and wiggled his eyebrows. Without taking his eyes off Dozler, Larkin loudly slapped the file onto the table and sat down. Without saying a word, the sheriff opened the file and looked at it for a few seconds. Closing it, he folded his hands together, focused his attention on Dozler, and said, "Okay, Luke, tell me what happened."

Dozler expounded about the opening of a new restaurant in Bend. About one hour's drive to the south in Deschutes County, Bend was one of the fastest growing cities in Oregon and was a mecca for the sport minded. "You know, it's been a dream of mine to be in the big city. I want to get out of the sticks here in Madras. With the opening coming up soon, and Annie running off, well, it would not look good."

Larkin interrupted him, "No, Luke, I don't mean about the restaurant or how your wife being gone will reflect on you. Tell me what happened between you and Annie and the last time you saw her."

"Well. She can be testy, you know."

"No, I don't know. Tell me."

"Well, we argue on occasion. Maybe she fell."

"Maybe as in..."

"She slipped, Sheriff! She slipped and fell."

"Did she? Did you hit her?" After no response but a sulk from Dozler, Larkin asked again, "Luke? Did you hit her?"

"No!" *Of course, I hit her. She deserved it.*

The sheriff kept looking at Dozler while the man scowled, giving the sheriff furtive glances.

"This happen often Luke?"

The answer came quickly, "No. She just really pissed me off. She's nothing without me and forgets sometimes. She can be a bitch, Sheriff.

Look, Sheriff, I love her and am devastated by her being gone, does that sound better?"

Larkin continued to stare at Dozler as he opened the file folder and said, "Maybe. But what I see here is a report of a police call to your home in Baker City, Oregon on August 14, 2018, for a domestic disturbance."

"Oh, that."

"Yeah, that. Called in by a neighbor."

"That neighbor was senile. Nosey old hag! Exaggerated everything."

Larkin looked at the file again and said, "The police didn't think so. Neither did the hospital who treated your wife: two teeth dislodged, and right eye socket cracked. The responding officers reported that there was obvious offensive physical contact and cited you for misdemeanor harassment. What I don't understand is that neither your wife nor the county ever pursued the citation."

"It was trumped up. I told you that neighbor was senile."

Larkin was quiet for a moment while he stared at Dozler until the man squirmed. Finally, Larkin continued, "So you moved to 'the sticks' here in Madras in May of last year. Since that time your wife's been submitted to St. Charles Medical Center twice for, and I quote, "contusions, possible broken bones."

"She fell!" Dozler snarled. The once-cold office was suddenly feeling very warm.

Larkin stared at him again for an uncomfortably long time. "When did you last see your wife, Luke?"

"Two weeks ago."

"Two weeks and you are just now coming to report her missing?"

"Well, she's done this before, taken a powder. But she always comes back. They always do Sheriff. Women are lost without a man in their lives."

Again, the stare, this time with a raised eyebrow. "Are they?" It was a statement, not a question. "Does she have any family around here she could have gone to?"

"No. Her family is trash. They're all in Baker City. Squabbling squaller they are... or what's left of 'em, those who aren't in prison or stoned. I did her a big favor, marrying her outta that bunch. She should be grateful. She never would have amounted to anything without me."

Larkin let that statement go unchallenged because he could argue with this scumbag all day and it wouldn't help find Annie Dozler.

"When she left those times before, do you know where she went?"

"Nah, she just finally showed up. Looked a mess, like she'd been out in the woods."

"She never said where she'd go?"

"No. She would just always come home. I'd fuck her and things would be fine. Like I said, they can't live without their men." Dozler then turned his attention to Officer Harvey and asked, "Can you?"

Officer Kayla Harvey looked at Dozler like he had just vomited a rat and said, "That's none of your business, Mr. Dozler."

"I was just funnin' with you, sweetheart," he said and smiled with cheap but dazzling dental work. Then he turned to the sheriff and said, what you need to do is get some men out there and bring her back!"

"We'll find her, but we need this preliminary information."

"Whatever. Just find her, damnit! I have things I gotta do to get that restaurant opened in time."

When the interview was over, Officer Harvey stood to leave the room. Dozler reached out to touch her bottom and was surprised to find the sheriff's hand on his wrist like a vise. The big man moved so quickly that he left Dozler speechless. With Luke Dozler's wrist pinned to the table, the sheriff hissed into his ear, "Don't! Just don't! You will know and respect your boundaries in this office and with my staff or I'll slap a sexual harassment charge on you you'll never get out of."

If Luke had been blessed with a tail, it would have been between his legs by the time he left the sheriff's office.

"SO, SHERIFF LARKIN," Officer Harvey asked once Dozler was gone. "Why does a woman stay with a guy like that?"

"The answer isn't easy, Kayla. Sometimes they grew up in a household with abuse, sometimes the woman is convinced she did something to deserve it, mainly because that's what she's been told all her life. It sounds like Annie Dozler didn't come from the most ideal family situation. Sometimes the woman stays with her abuser because he's threatened to kill her or her kids, or her family members or pets if she leaves. All too often he goes through with it."

"Gee!"

"Yeah! When we find Annie, we'll find out more from her perspective. Do you want to be there?"

"You bet I do!"

"Good," the Sheriff smiled for the first time. "I was hoping you would feel that way. Women are more likely to talk frankly to another woman because most men in their lives have been nothing but a source of hurt and humiliation. Big city cops have more resources for that sort of thing than we do."

"Out here in the sticks."

"Yes," the Sheriff chuckled, "out here in the sticks."

⚜ CHAPTER 4 ⚜

DEPUTY CYRIL RICHMOND hung up his phone from talking to Deschutes County Sheriff's Deputy Greg Leese. It immediately rang again. He groaned in dismay at the interruption until he saw who it was, his boss, Sheriff Gary Larkin.

"Richmond."

"Cyril!" Larkin's booming voice caused Richmond to move his phone away from his ear. "Do you remember Luke Dozler? He owns a string of sandwich shops."

"Uh, I think so. I went to a Chamber of Commerce luncheon with you once. Was he the guy who was so full of himself like he had cold lips from kissing the mirror?"

"Yup."

"What's he done?"

"His wife's missing."

"Oh, crap!"

"Yeah. She may be out in the woods, so he says. When they have a spat, and I suspect he beats her, she runs away. He thinks she goes into the woods, but he doesn't know where. I think he may have fabricated a story to cover up a homicide, so we need to be looking at all angles. Since you are out there in the woods, keep an eye out. Also, let the Geezers know she's missing...just missing and may be lost. For now, they don't need to know any more than that. They may see or hear something."

"Okay. Has she ever filed for a restraining order?"

"No. I've talked to the Baker City Police Chief. When Dozlers lived there, a neighbor would call the police because she heard yelling and crashing noises coming from Dozler's home. The wife, Annie, had injuries but she never filed a complaint. The police gave him a citation for misdemeanor harassment, but it never was pursued. The Chief told me Luke Dozler's dad is a county commissioner."

"Crap!"

"Yeah. Since they moved to Madras, twice St. Charles Medical Center has informed us she's been there for injuries consistent with being beaten. At the time, our guys talked to her, but she wouldn't file a complaint."

"Damn, I hate that!"

"Me too."

Both lawmen were quiet for a moment while they reflected on the ugliness spousal abuse cases had brought to their careers. Domestic disturbance calls offer some of the most dangerous and frustrating incidents law enforcement can encounter.

"Did he supply a photo of her?" Richmond asked.

"No, the bastard! He said he didn't have one. Didn't have a photo of his wife? Can you believe it? He did give a description; she's 36 years old, 5'7", slight build, long light brown hair, hazel eyes."

"Okay, got it. By the way, I was just talking to Greg Leese. Apparently, the people who are trying to restore the Santiam Pass Ski Lodge think an unauthorized person has been staying there. Greg asked me to go with him to check it out."

"That's in Linn County," Sheriff Larkin replied. "What are they doing calling Deschutes County?"

"I dunno. I'm closer here in Camp Sherman than anybody else."

"You are. Okay. Check it out. There's a wild chance Annie Dozler may have been there. I hope so and she's not dead in a ditch somewhere."

CYRIL RICHMOND SLAPPED a cap into his head, left his office in the Sisters-Camp Sherman Fire Station, and fired up his truck. In his early fifties,

Richmond was a twenty-five-year veteran of the Jefferson County Sheriff's Office. He loved his beat in this remote south-west corner of the county and he loved the people who called Camp Sherman home. His kids had attended the tiny, two-room Black Butte schoolhouse. He had taught the kids to fly fish in the Metolius River and how to carefully release the fish unharmed back to their watery home. He taught them not only to appreciate the natural world but to be stewards of the forest and the river. Richmond's roots had grown deep into the volcanic soil of the Metolius Basin.

Since Deschutes County Sheriff's Deputy Greg Leese was stationed in Sisters, a western-themed town about twenty miles to the east of Camp Sherman, Richmond had told him he would drive ahead to the lodge and Leese could get there when he could. The two deputies from different counties had a good working relationship. Many incidents happened on their shared borders, so they often worked together. It made for a crossover of duties, but for these lawmen, created camaraderie and contributed to effective law enforcement.

On his drive up to the 4,816-foot Santiam Pass, Richmond tried to remember what he knew about the Santiam Pass Ski Lodge. The structure sat back from the north side of Highway 20 and being behind a copse of trees, was almost invisible from the road. It was built in 1939-1940 by the Great Depression's Civilian Conservation Corps. After serving as a ski lodge and then a church youth camp, it sat vacant for nearly thirty years. During that time of neglect, it suffered vermin infestation, dry rot, and water damage from rain and snow melt. If not for the heroic efforts of wildland firefighters, it would have been destroyed in the 2003 Bear-Booth Complex Fire which burned over 90,000 acres between Mt. Jefferson and Mt. Washington. Now, an enterprising couple from Bend took it upon themselves to restore the structure and acquired a special use permit from the Willamette National Forest. By using innovative methods of volunteers and grant funding, the old building was now looking forward to a new life as a winter recreation hub, the purpose for which it was originally created.

Richmond reached the unmarked track that led to the lodge, located just to the west of the summit. He then followed the short drive to find

Hadley Taylor waiting for him beside his black Acura SUV. When Richmond exited his truck, Taylor stepped over to greet him.

"Didn't expect you, Deputy," Taylor exclaimed. Taylor was a well-known entrepreneur and philanthropist from Bend who had retired from a lucrative real estate business. He smiled at Richmond from behind shaggy white eyebrows matched by an unruly mop of thinning white hair. "I called Deschutes County but sort of forgot Jefferson County had a presence in Camp Sherman."

The two men shook hands as Richmond explained that Deputy Leese had requested his assistance and that the two deputies often share responsibility where several county lines come together.

"I knew a Linn County cop would be at least an hour away," Taylor continued apologetically. "Me being a Bend guy, thought to call only Deschutes County."

"That's no problem," Richmond said pleasantly. "We're always glad to help. Deputy Leese was involved in another case but will be here soon. In the meantime, why don't you show me what you found."

Taylor led Richmond to the north side of the old structure. They worked their way around several stacks of building materials, roofing, and piles of bagged insulation covered by waterproof tarps. Taylor moved aside a bale of insulation to reveal where, low on an outside wall, a board had been pried loose.

"On the other side of this wall," Taylor said as he knocked on the old weathered boards, "Is an empty storeroom that we really haven't yet paid much attention to. We've been replacing rotten timbers on the front and south side of the building because that's where the storms come in."

Richmond squatted on his haunches and looked at the board. The screw heads were rusted, and it wasn't hard to imagine the board could easily be pried loose. At the top end of the plank, only one screw remained, so that once the bottom was unfettered, the board could swing to the side and back again. Studying the board closer, he pulled from his pocket a small evidence bag and a pair of tweezers. He tweezed a long brown hair caught in the rough edge of the board and carefully lowered it into the evidence bag.

Standing up and showing the bag to Taylor, Richmond said, "I think your trespasser left this. I suspect whoever it was, left in a hurry and didn't return the board to the original position."

"Maybe it was just now when I drove in," Taylor said, as Richmond examined the dirt for footprints. Seeing a partial boot print and then another, Richmond could tell they led away from the building north toward the mountainside.

Following Richmond's gaze, Taylor said, "The Pacific Crest Trail is up there."

"Yeah, I know. Do you have any other buildings in that direction?"

"No. There is just a parking lot for hikers and the trailhead."

"Okay," Richmond replied and then he heard the arrival of a vehicle. "I think Deputy Leese is here."

The two men returned to the front of the lodge to see Deputy Greg Leese emerge from his patrol car through a cloud of dust of his own making. Taking the car *off* would be a better explanation for how Leese exited his car. A tall and well-muscled man, Leese's shoulders were so broad he gave the impression that he was really meant to be two policemen. He ambled up to Richmond and Taylor and drawled an apology for being late. Apparently, someone broke into a coffee shop and stole all the sweet rolls and single serving bags of M&Ms.

"Look for someone with a sugar high bouncing off walls," Richmond offered with a grin.

"And working on his girth," Taylor added.

They took Leese behind the lodge and showed him the loose plank. With Leese holding a measuring tape to the boot print, Richmond took a picture of the print and explained the hair he had placed into the evidence bag.

WEARING THE NEW camouflage sweatshirt with the hood drawn down around her eyes, Annie Dozler crouched behind a thicket of manzanita. She parted the stiff branches so she could watch the three men as they walked around to the front of the lodge. Her hiding place in the shelter of the old structure had been revealed and she was going to have to get away from this place. However, the entire mountainside was a huge burn scar affording few places to remain unseen, so caution kept her feet grounded behind the manzanita.

Just because the men had gone inside, didn't mean they wouldn't spot her flitting among the shadows. The main story of the lodge sported an entire bank of windows offering a panoramic view of the very path she would need to reach the Pacific Crest Trail. She hadn't survived this long in the forest without being keenly aware to never allow an impulsive desire to flee take control over common sense. As a result, she huddled in the dirt and continued to wait.

THE ORIGINAL STAIRS of the lodge's main entrance had rotted away, leaving nothing but the concrete foundation. Temporary planks had been placed across the foundation posts and Taylor cautioned the lawmen to watch their step. Once on the main floor, they could see the extensive renovations the team of volunteers had accomplished.

The forty-foot sill plate under the windows as well as studs and headers had been weakened by decades of dry rot and carpenter ants Using cedar timbers recovered from the Holiday Farm Fire near Cougar Reservoir, the workers had replaced all the wooden members. The entire structure smelled of freshly milled cedar. Richmond drank in the refreshing, earthy aroma. He marveled at Taylor's vision and innovation by using volunteers and funding by the Oregon Cultural Trust. This treasure of President Franklin Roosevelt's job-creating project during the Great Depression would soon be restored to its former glory.

Taylor led them through piles of original flooring and paneling which would be put back in place once the supporting structure had been made sound. Taylor opened a skinny door, and the men descended a narrow staircase into a basement storage area. Over by an outside wall, Taylor pointed out the plank that had been pried loose and what appeared to be the remains of a rustic camp. A ratty sleeping bag had been left in a wad and stuffed against a wall.

"Okay, it's pretty obvious someone's been here," Leese said to Hadley Taylor. "We'll take the bag as evidence and keep you in the loop. It may be a vagrant looking for a dry stop to rest. We have a growing number of homeless here in Central Oregon."

After thanking the officers, Taylor went back to preparing for the squad of volunteers soon to arrive. Leese and Richmond returned to the parking area. Once the two lawmen were out of earshot of Hadley, Richmond told Leese of the missing person's case involving Luke Dozler and his wife, Annie.

"Not that scuz?" Leese exclaimed. "My god, what has he done to her now?" Leese remembered times in the past when he was called to St. Charles Medical Center in Bend when Annie Dozler would show up bruised and bleeding.

"We won't know until we can talk to her. This trespasser," Richmond nodded in the direction of the old lodge, "may not even be her. However, we may want to bring in a tracker to start from here."

"Gotcha," Leese replied.

Richmond added, "If Annie Dozler was here, this shows to me that she is not lost but is running away."

Leese shook his head in disappointment as he said, "From what I hear about Luke Dozler, I can't say as I blame her."

WHILE THE TWO deputies discussed her, Annie Dozler watched and listened from her hiding place. When the lawmen left, their patrol cars were soon lost in the dust of the lodge's parking lot. Annie took advantage of the dust screening her from the lodge and did what she had done before. She ran for her life.

Carrying only a water bottle and a small pack, Annie didn't stop until she reached the summit on the Pacific Crest Trail. She paused and with sobbing gasps, took the thin air into her lungs. This is what her life had become, always on the run, wary as a deer, suspicious of everyone. For years, she had thought that if she went back to Luke, try her best not to aggravate him, maybe she could change him somehow. However, this time she had finally convinced herself that changing his behavior was not in her capabilities nor was it safe to even try.

This escape from his brutality was going to be the last time. She was committed to hiding from him until she either died in the attempt or he gave up trying to find her. She learned long ago that his rage at her running away was not born out of love for her or fear for her safety, but out of his own inconvenience and the face he tried to thrust into the business community.

Luke Dozler was a charming con man and had seemed like her ticket out of the filthy trailer where she had grown up and suffered abuse from her brothers. She had no support from her drug-addled, single mother. So, as soon as Annie graduated from high school, she leapt at the chance to go with Dozler. Since then, he had used her as a punching bag and an excuse for his own failures as a human being.

She left the Pacific Crest Trail and plunged down the eastern slope into the Metolius River Basin. Remembering what the deputies had said about getting a tracker, she traveled on rocky areas and along fallen logs, trying not to leave a trail of boot prints. She found a small rivulet and just in case a scent dog was used to track her, splashed down the stream of icy water. Where its path steepened into a waterfall, she stumbled down the rocks, often falling and hurting herself. What was another bruise to a woman who had taken beatings by the man to whom she once pledged her heart?

❧ CHAPTER 5 ❧

CYRIL RICHMOND'S NEXT task was to inform the Geezers that Annie Dozler was missing and may be somewhere in the woods of the Metolius Basin. He hesitated to say she was lost, as he seriously believed she was out there on purpose. This was even more a possibility if she proved to be the trespasser at the Santiam Pass Ski Lodge. If she was in hiding, she was going to be more difficult to find. She also faced dangers in the woods not related to her unfortunate relationship with Luke Dozler, in which case she or her remains might never be found.

He knew that no matter how much he tried to present the situation as a typical search and rescue, the Geezers would quickly read between the lines. They would figure out she was running from an abuser. In past cases, their sense of suspicion always bettered his abilities to hedge. His challenge would be to discourage them from tormenting her husband. He knew this bunch well enough to know that during their various careers, they had dealt with every scumbag on the planet. Now, knowing what they did about human nature, they were not going to give a jerk like Luke Dozler one ounce of slack.

As he pulled his truck into the lane leading to Geezer Central, Richmond was surprised to find the small parking space in front of Wardwell's cabin filled with Geezer rigs: Mick's orange 1950 Chevy pickup, Old Bowels' green 1946 Ford pickup with the blue fenders, T.J. and Oliver's Bentley, Adam's Explorer, Arthur and Beth's huge Dodge Ram pickup, and Yankum's old Chevy Blazer.

Richmond wedged his truck carefully between the Bentley and a stand of small Ponderosa pines. "Egads, it's a blinking used car lot!" he exclaimed as he slid from the cab. He was greeted by laughter from the group at the picnic table.

"Make an offer!" Dave said as he approached Richmond. "I can say that because none of them are mine!"

All those at the picnic table exchanged handshakes with Richmond, including Tommy Jax. Richmond was always in cautious awe of Jax ever since he learned the Geezer's investigator had been a notorious figure in the Seattle organized crime scene. It was the "had been" that was Richmond's concern. For the Geezer's sake, the deputy stayed cordial with the big man until his suspicions that Jax hadn't really cleaned up his act morphed into more than just suspicions.

"What's up, Cyril?" Jax asked as he took the deputy's hand in his big paw.

"I need to talk to the Geezers," Richmond answered then looked around the small dusty parking space crammed with cars. "It looks like I came at the right time."

"That you did, Cyril," Old Bowels said. "I'll go inside and fetch the others. We're working on that fund raiser for the Hasty Search and Rescue program."

"Oh, good! What I have to say to them involves that very thing."

Old Bowels quickly unfolded his small, agile frame from the picnic table bench and scampered into the cabin. Soon Geezers and dogs spilled out of Wardwell's cabin not unlike a circus Volkswagen purging clowns. There were handshakes and manly back slaps as Richmond received a full-fledged Geezer greeting from Arthur, Cal Wiggens, Yank-um, Adam, Conrad, and in his stiffly reserved way, Oliver. Beth, Sophie, and Aunt Phil received sweet pecks on their cheeks and gentle hugs. Adam's two English bull dogs, Mick's chocolate Lab, big furry Max, and Wardwell's diminutive longhaired Chihuahua mix, Fido, expressed their delight with barks and tail wags until every Geezer critter received attention from this, their favorite police person.

Richmond dearly loved these people. They formed the backbone of community spirit which exemplified everything Camp Sherman meant to him. At the stage in their lives when they were unfettered by the burdens of child rearing and building careers, they pursued everything that was fun, especially if it was a meaningful contribution to the quality of life and safety in Camp Sherman and the surrounding Deschutes National Forest.

Conrad Wardwell, his military bearing carried over from a career in the U.S. Navy, quickly brought the Geezer gabfest to order. He knew Richmond couldn't spend all day here although he was quite sure the deputy would prefer to.

Cyril Richmond stood in the clearing with the Geezers gathered around him. Some were sitting at the picnic table and even on the table or leaning against the trees. Richmond could feel the warm July sun on his shoulders. He took off his cap and wiped his forehead. It was going to be a hot one today. He briefed the Geezers on the report out of Culver of a missing person, Annie Dozler, and gave her description. The report indicated that she could be somewhere in the Metolius River Basin.

"Sheriff Larkin told me to let you know. We'll post bulletins in the store and the post office as well as Black Butte Ranch and Sisters. We'll also submit an announcement for the 'Alert Camp Sherman' email. That should go out shortly. The more folks who know about this, the better our chances of finding her."

He then told of the trespasser at the Santiam Pass Ski Lodge who may or may not have been Annie Dozler. "Once we can determine the trespasser and Dozler are the same person, we'll get the Search and Rescue Boys up there to start tracking. By the way, thanks for organizing the fund raiser for the search and rescue program."

Old Bowels asked, "Gee, Cyril, if this woman is missing from Culver? That's a long way from here."

"You're right, O.B., but I understand she's been gone for about two weeks, so it's feasible she could be here."

"Two weeks?" squeaked Aunt Phil. "She's been missing two weeks and we're just now hearing about this?"

Cyril Richmond knew the Geezers were already reading more into his announcement than he wanted them to know so he hedged, "It's complicated, Phyllis. I just heard about it this morning. I want you guys to keep an eye out and an ear to the ground, okay? I'll let you know when I know more."

Mick was the next one to speak up. "When Arthur and I were hiking with the dogs on Green Ridge we, er, I saw someone moving among the trees and rocks down on the side of the ridge."

Arthur, with his arm around Beth's diminutive shoulders added, "I saw a movement, alright, but it was just a flash of color. I couldn't tell what it was. We continued on down the trail and didn't see it again."

Dave said, "Well, on a night last week, I couldn't sleep, so I went outside. I could have sworn someone, or something was out there. It went past the cabin. It was like it hesitated, then went on. I couldn't hear it or really see it... I dunno, I can't explain it very well. It was more of a presence, I guess, but then it was gone. I suppose it could have been a person."

"Good thing it wasn't a bear!" Aunt Phil exclaimed.

"Maybe it was," Conrad answered.

"Nah, he would have been eaten," Old Bowels replied.

Mick, always taking advantage of an opportunity to needle his brother-in-law declared, "Not without mustard. You'd need a lot of mustard to eat Dave."

"Probably ketchup too, don't you think?" Yank-um asked his buddy, Cal Wiggens.

"Maybe a little Tabasco," Wiggens added with a chuckle.

"Seeing ghosts, Dave?" Conrad asked.

"Maybe." Dave enjoyed the humor of his friends but knew there was something very peculiar about his experience on that night.

Aunt Phil said, "I want to come back as a ghost. That'd be fun, spooking people!"

Sophie replied, "I'd be a friendly ghost and do good deeds."

"Good ghostly deeds," Adam smiled at his bride.

Beth added, "Maybe that's what angels are."

"Good ghosts?" Conrad asked.

"Sure. Why not?" Sophie smiled with her amazing amber eyes.

"Why not indeed?" Conrad smiled back.

"Okay, you characters, I've delivered your assignment and now I gotta go to work," Richmond declared. "Let me know if you learn something."

"Oh, Cyril, do we have a picture of this woman?" Aunt Phil asked.

"No. Sheriff Larkin asked her husband for a picture, and he said he didn't have one." Richmond let that statement make its impact. Then, the deputy climbed into his truck and left, leaving small whirlwinds of dust behind his tires.

The Geezers watched him leave, then stood around shuffling their feet on the forest floor and looking at one another. A warm breeze sent the pine branches swaying and the Metolius River could be heard gurgling close by.

"What's he not telling us?" Old Bowels finally broke the silence.

"I'm not sure," Dave offered, "but there's more to this than what we're hearing."

"Yeah, what kind of guy doesn't have a picture of his wife?" Mick asked incredulously. Having lost his own wife two years ago, Mick had kept her picture in every aspect of his life, from displayed around his cabin to the wallpaper on his computer.

"If she's missing from the Madras area and was trespassing in the Santiam Pass Ski Lodge, she's not lost," Tommy Jax said, casting a glance at Oliver.

"Not by a long shot," Oliver added.

Everyone looked at T.J. and Oliver. The positivity of their statements cemented what everyone else was thinking.

T.J. added, "Many of the women at the homeless shelter in Seattle where we volunteer are trying to escape abusive relationships of some kind or the other."

Oliver added sadly, "Their stories are gut wrenching."

Aunt Phil said to T. J. and Oliver, "You think she's running away or hiding... from something."

Conrad added, "Or someone."

T.J. looked around the group, "Yeah. Someone."

Sophie noted, "The woman is reported missing from Culver. Someone had to file that missing person report in Madras. It sounds like it was her husband. If we find her and tell Cyril, then she'll have to go back to him, right?" Sophie was visibly shaken by the thought.

"Not necessarily," Adam said. Standing behind Sophie, he put both arms around her shoulders and hugged her to him. Her mane of auburn curly hair tickled his face. He continued, "But in case she's still here in the woods, we need to find her if, for no other reason, to keep her safe from whatever it is she's running from."

Dave gazed up at the trees, their tops swaying and humming in the freshening breeze. "If she is here, the trees would know. If only they could tell us." He then looked around the group of Geezers and added, "When we find her, who says we have to tell Cyril?"

✗ CHAPTER 6 ✗

DAVE'S QUESTION COMMANDED further discussion. The Geezers felt the need for privacy, so the meeting reconvened inside Geezer Central. Getting everyone in the cabin was always a bit of a challenge that didn't get accomplished without a lot of fussing and rearranging. Soon everyone found a place to settle, some sitting on pillows tossed onto the floor. The dogs always thought it was great fun and got lots of licks in on the pillow people. Today, however, the Geezers were a subdued bunch.

"Don't we have a responsibility to Cyril to be honest?" Sophie asked.

Adam added, "Keeping anything from Richmond would be counter-productive to his investigation. However, I think there is nothing dishonest about us evaluating Annie Dozler's situation and acting accordingly."

"Annie hasn't committed a crime, has she?" Aunt Phil asked.

"Not that Richmond is letting us know," Conrad answered. He was sitting at the dining table with Fido on his lap. Fido's buggy eyes were fixated on a huge plate of cookies resting on the tabletop. Uncharacteristic of the Geezers, the cookies had been momentarily forgotten.

"It could be nothing more than a simple lost person situation to me," Yank-um offered. "I think we should treat it as such until we know more."

"Okay," Mick added, "but let's look at something else. What if Annie Dozler is running from an abuser and he or she comes looking for her?"

Dave answered, "We need to be ready for him!"

"Bring on the bastard!" Wiggens added emphatically, his grey curls bouncing emphatically. "The problem is, we don't even know who he is, do we?"

Arthur, who had been sitting on the stairs leading to the cabin's loft said, "I can venture a guess."

All eyes turned to Arthur. Beth sat on the step below him with Arthur's arms protectively around her shoulders. She knew what he was going to say.

"His name is Luke Dozler," Arthur continued. "I know him from Baker City."

"And?" Mick asked, sensing there was a lot more Arthur was going to say.

"Even though I'm retired from the bank, I don't talk about bank customers because of their right to privacy. As for Luke Dozler, however, he doesn't respect anyone else so what do I care? Suffice it to say I wouldn't loan money to him for a restaurant because his credit report looked like forty miles of bad road. His father, a County Commissioner, offered to co-sign and threatened to ruin us if we didn't make the loan. I insisted that I wouldn't put Luke on the loan no matter who co-signed. I may have even referred to Jesus Christ. Anyway, the father stomped out and took his son to another bank. That was fine with me. I didn't want our bank to have any association with a deadbeat like Luke, co-signer or not.

"As it was, his dad didn't honor his commitment as a cosigner, and the lender eventually had to foreclose on Luke's restaurant. That bank got stuck with a huge bad loan on the books and a mess of restaurant equipment taken as collateral. What's a bank going to do with used restaurant equipment, open a taco truck? I don't know if it was his or his dad's idea, but Luke shortly thereafter left Baker City and went to Madras."

"They should have had Jesus on that loan," Dave snickered.

Conrad asked, "So, did his dad set him up in Madras with a new restaurant? It's the dad who owns that chain of pizza joints and sandwich shops in Jefferson County, right? Luke manages them?"

"That's right. I have no idea what funding he has," Arthur continued, "nor do I care. I'm so glad that now I don't have to deal with assholes like his dad."

"We get to deal with his asshole son," Old Bowels said despairingly.

"This might be fun," Aunt Phil said, always the optimist. "We can send

34

him off on wild goose chases."

"Send him up to the hatchery," Yank-um offered, his big blue eyes dancing with the idea. "Maybe he'll fall in. Maybe we can sort of, you know, push him. There are trout in there big enough to eat him."

"We don't have to hurt him, just drive him nuts," Wiggens replied.

"Whatever we do, we'll get him pissed at us... really pissed!" Conrad warned.

"At my age, I'm not afraid of making enemies," Arthur noted.

"Me neither," chorused the rest of the Geezers.

Tommy Jax said, "First, let's find Annie. Does anybody have a clue of where to start? It sounds like Cyril scared her away from the Santiam Pass Ski Lodge."

"What I want to know," Old Bowels said, "is why she doesn't go to the law? It seems odd to me that she prefers to stay in the woods."

Beth knew why. From her perch on the stairs with Arthur's arms around her, she finally spoke, "Because the law can't protect you from everything."

All eyes now turned to Beth as she continued, "How many times do you read in the paper or see on the news a woman getting killed by a man even though she had a restraining order against him? I didn't bother to get one against my daughter because it's just a piece of paper and is treated as such by too many abusers. Time is of the essence because the most dangerous part in a victim's life is when they make that decision to leave. Her husband is going to be furious because she's made a fool of him. Therefore, he also will really be dangerous. We must be careful."

Beth was quiet for a few moments. The rest of the Geezers watched in anticipation, knowing this soft-spoken, gentle woman wasn't through with her story. She then said, "I may be able to convince Annie to talk to us. You see, I've been supplying her with food and clothing. I think she'll trust me."

The rest of the Geezers were gobsmacked. Annie Dozler now became a very real person; a person who was trying to survive in the woods of the Metolius Basin and was escaping God only knew what horrors in her marriage.

"Beth," Aunt Phil asked gently, "How did you meet her?"

"I was up on Green Ridge. You know the spot, Phyllis, where I buried my dog in that little clearing. Arthur and I go there occasionally. One time I went by myself, and Annie Dozler was there! She was sitting on a rock looking out over the mountains, just like I did when I was running from Dana. I stepped into the clearing and said hello. I really startled her, and she moved to run away, and I asked her to wait, and that I wasn't going to hurt her.

"I could see the fear in her eyes, and I had a heck of a time convincing her I wasn't going to tell on her. I told her *my* story and I guess she believed me because she started to relax, and we talked for a long time. She told me she was running from her husband and that she wasn't going back, that she'd die first.

"I told her I would leave dried food and some warm clothing for her. I pointed to a spot further down on the ridge that would be easier for me to reach from the road. Ever since, I've been leaving things for her, and they are always gone the next time I take something. I haven't talked to her since. I just know her fear and felt I needed to do something for her."

"Did you tell her about your cave?" Dave asked. By now, most everyone in Camp Sherman knew about the lava tube on Green Ridge Beth had used as shelter during the year she was on the run from her homicidal daughter.

"Yes. I even showed it to her. It appeared to her as a trap with only one way in and out. It was just a matter of time before Luke came looking for her. His overblown ego wouldn't let her go without at least trying to find her himself. The punishment she would suffer would most likely be fatal. She felt safer in the forest where she could move about, using the trees as a shield and within their thickets shelter from storms.

"Of course, I told Arthur and he's been very supportive of my decision not to tell Richmond. T.J.'s right, we need to find her before her husband does. Also, if we told Richmond where she was, he'd have to go after her and be honest with the husband. We Geezers don't have to be honest with anyone."

ON THE OPPOSITE side of Green Ridge stood a small cabin. It was snuggled into the woods within walking distance of Arthur and Beth's big A-frame. A middle-aged woman lived there alone. Her name was Emily Martin. She was the daughter of the cabin's original owner, Wilbur Martin. Wilbur had been brutally murdered two years prior. Emily, somewhat estranged from her father over her parents' divorce and her mother's subsequent mental illness, sold her home and accounting business in New York and moved to her dad's beloved mountains in Oregon.

The Geezers, all friends of Wilbur, had adopted Emily as their own and had upgraded the rustic cabin with a new roof, thermal windows, plumbing, insulation, recalked the old log walls, and with a bit of red paint on the door and the addition of window boxes, made it a welcoming refuge.

Cyril Richmond had known his boss, Sheriff Gary Larkin, had been a single father for most of his two grown sons' lives and might be a good fit for Emily. Richmond introduced the two. Emily and Larkin now shared a comfortable relationship augmented by frequent visits from the sheriff. Larkin easily found excuses to visit Richmond's remote post for any trifling issue which could have easily been resolved by a text, email, or phone call. Larkin's trips to Camp Sherman always included a deli sandwich from the Camp Sherman Store and a visit with Emily.

As the Geezers were having their meeting at Wardwell's cabin, Emily Martin was sitting on the back porch of her cabin, enjoying a glass of iced tea and watching a Steller's jay and a Pine squirrel squabble over a fallen pinecone. Stepping out onto the porch wearing Emily's fluffy bathrobe and towel drying her freshly shampooed hair was Annie Dozler.

≪ CHAPTER 7 ≫

ANNIE DOZLER SANK onto the chair next to Emily. There was a comfortable moment of companionable silence between the two women. Annie took a sip from the glass of iced tea Emily had poured for her.

"I wish I could stay on this porch forever," Annie finally commented, feeling more tired than she wanted to reveal.

"You know you're welcome any time," Emily replied, smiling.

"Yes, I know I am, and I thank you for that... and for so much more, like letting me wash my clothes here."

"The dryer finished just a moment ago."

"Well then, I better get dressed and be on my way."

"Can't you stay for dinner? I can fix a salad and I have some great sourdough rolls I bought at the Camp Sherman store today."

Both women stood and made their way into the kitchen. Still wearing Emily's robe, Annie leaned wearily against the door jam and looked around the tiny room. Emily had transformed her dad's dreary cooking space by painting the walls a butter yellow. The Geezers had installed a modern sink, faucet, and countertops. They had cleaned the old wood stove, but also installed an apartment-sized propane three-burner stove and oven. A new refrigerator-freezer took up an opposite wall and open shelving held an assortment of pots, bowls, and powder blue dishware.

"I hate to keep taking advantage of you," Annie said.

"You're not taking advantage of me. I'm inviting you because I like your company. It gets lonely in this cabin all day." Emily wrapped the rolls in foil and put them into the oven. She then folded her arms across her chest and turned to face Annie. "Okay, I'm also doing it to help you. You're in a pickle. A huge pickle! Nobody in their right mind would turn you away."

"Well, you certainly have helped me! I don't know what I would have done if you had called the cops when I showed up on your front porch that cold night a couple of weeks ago. I knew I was going to need help and I bet everything that whoever was in this cabin would be the right person, and you were."

The two women put together a salad of vegetables, fruit, tomatoes, and feta cheese and sat down at the small, wooden table in the center of the kitchen. The cabin filled with the fragrance of warm bread. Annie tried not to show how hungry she was but paced herself to Emily's good manners.

Buttering a slice of roll, Annie looked at Emily and said, "The last thing I want to do is put you in an awkward situation with your friend, Sheriff Larkin."

"You let me worry about Gary, Annie. He's a good person and will try to help you as much as he can, but you must talk to him."

"I know how you feel about him, but he's the law, Emily! The law has never been able to protect me. Unless they can catch Luke beating me, or witness the damage within a couple of hours, they can't charge him with anything. Even if they could, they can't stop him from killing me. The whole system is so incredibly stupid..."

Emily placed her hand on Annie's to calm her. "If you would just talk to Gary. He's not like other men, Annie, or I should say the other men you're used to."

"No! I can't Emily! I'm sorry, but I just can't trust him not to tell Luke where I am." Close to tears but knowing Emily was sincerely trying to help her, Annie offered softly, "Maybe someday, but not now."

On that bitterly cold evening two weeks prior when Annie had appeared on Emily's doorstep, the two women had talked long into the night. Emily heard about the treatment Annie had suffered from Luke. The gang rape by her two abusive brothers. The resulting painful, self-induced abortion. Emily understood the sad distrust Annie had for men and the law administered primarily by men. Emily knew the best thing she could do right now is just to be Annie's friend.

The women cleaned up the kitchen. Annie dressed and bundled her clean clothes into a backpack Emily had given her. She donned the backpack, and with the bag of sourdough rolls clutched in her hand, gave Emily a hug and left. Emily stood on the back porch of the cabin and watched her go. Annie moved through the trees with a fugitive's stealth. In the waning light of evening, Annie Dozler faded into the forest and disappeared.

DEPUTY CYRIL RICHMOND strode into the Jefferson County Sheriff's Office in Madras. He had under his arm a large plastic bag carrying the sleeping bag found at the Santiam Pass Ski Lodge. He knew Luke Dozler would be waiting impatiently. Richmond had come into the building through a back entrance in order to avoid the man until he had a chance to talk to Sheriff Larkin.

"Hi!" Richmond stuck his head into the doorway to Larkin's office.

"Oh, hi!" Larkin said as he stood from behind his desk. Upon standing, the sheriff seemed to fill the room. "I'm glad you're here. Dozler is driving them nuts down there in reception. He's far too important to be kept waiting."

"Oh, really?"

"Yeah. If I hadn't told you, he would have." Larkin picked up two bundled old sleeping bags from the floor and said, "Come on, let's get on with this goat rodeo."

Richmond removed the sleeping bag from the plastic and queried, "Goat rodeo? Is that kind of like a shit show?"

"The very same."

Richmond snickered as he followed his sheriff down the hall.

LUKE DOZLER HAD learned to enjoy this devasted husband gig. People would stop him on the street, hug him, bring him food. He put on a mask of grief and soaked up the attention, especially from women who offered to relieve him from the terrible sexual tension he must be experiencing. Oh yeah, he loved it! Nobody could fake pitiful like Luke Dozler could.

He was applying these newfound charms to Officer Kayla Harvey who was manning the duty officer's desk. Dozler thought that the delectable young woman, who kept her attention focused to a project on her computer screen, must be hard of hearing because she wasn't responding to his chatter. About the time Luke was wondering how someone that hard of hearing could land a job with the sheriff's office, Larkin and Richmond entered the reception area.

Upon seeing the Sheriff and his deputy, Dozler barked, "Well, it's about time! I'm moving to Bend, and I have lots of things to do, Sheriff!"

Without apologizing, Larkin simply said, "Mr. Dozler, this is Deputy Richmond. So, you're moving?"

"Yeah. I told you I wanted to get out of the sticks."

"Oh yes, I remember. The sticks. Well, we'll need your new address. Let's go into a conference room, shall we?"

After being ushered into the room, Richmond got Dozler's new address out of him, although Dozler was distinctly preoccupied by looking at the three sleeping bags Larkin and Richmond had placed on the table. "What's this?" he said. "Are we having a sleepover?"

"We need to know if any of these bags look familiar to you."

As Dozler gawked at the sleeping bags, Larkin asked him, "Did you bring those things of Annie's I requested?"

Dozler answered, "I brought a pair of her shoes, but I can't find a picture of her."

Larkin made a point of staring at Dozler to emphasize he couldn't fathom a man, in this age of cell phone cameras, not caring enough about his wife to have a picture of her.

"Look, Sheriff, Annie and I, well, we weren't a huggy, cuddly kind of a couple, you know?" Larkin didn't know but kept quiet so that Dozler would further explain himself. "Annie was different, standoffish, rather dull. We got along well, for the most part. I brought in the money. She took care of the house with the allowance I gave her. We didn't do things together, like go places on trips and such. It worked for me. I provided for her, and she gave me sex. She owed me a lot for taking her away from that hellhole she was living in."

"Uh-huh," the sheriff responded dryly, thinking Dozler didn't think much more of his wife than a servant. What do you think about the sleeping bags?"

"What do I think? Like, I'm supposed to identify one? Well, I suppose that one on the right could be mine, but…but…"

"But what, Mr. Dozler?" asked Richmond, who had been standing by the door, quietly taking notes.

"I can look in the attic and see if it's missing. I'm still digging out things to move but she knows she's not supposed to get into my stuff."

Both lawmen gawped at him. The more Luke Dozler talked; the more he revealed of what life must have been like for his wife. Dozler's face turned red as he looked from one lawman to the other and back again. "What? Look, you two. I'm the victim here, understand? I'm the victim!" He pounded the table with his fist. His eyes bugged out like a ferret with its tail in a twist. "She walked off and left me in a world of hurt. I need help opening that restaurant and I don't need these distractions or any judgement from you! Your job is to get out there and hunt her down!"

Larkin replied with what Richmond thought was more reserve than he could have mustered, "We'll give you a receipt for the shoes and keep you informed."

"That's all? That's all you have to say? You're not going to even tell me where you found that sleeping bag?"

"No. That will compromise our investigation."

With his rage one moment away from a total blowout, Luke Dozler stormed out of the Sheriff's Office.

Richmond stepped to the window and watched him go. "He told us to 'Hunt her down.'" He turned away from the window and said, "Interesting words. He doesn't sound like he's exactly heartbroken by his wife being missing."

Sheriff Gary Larkin looked at his deputy and answered, "Nope. Just inconvenienced and really pissed."

LUKE DOZLER SLAMMED the door of his super-charged Dodge Ram pickup. With a flat black finish, no chrome, a roll bar, dual back wheels, lifted suspension system, and an exhaust pipe the size of a three-pound coffee can, Dozler's truck was a monument to testosterone. He exited the parking lot, and laid rubber as he sped down the street toward town.

Parked one-half block away in his 1947 Ford pickup, Old Bowels was squeezed into the truck's cab along with Drs. Cal Wiggens and Yank-um Campbell. With the intent to follow Dozler, Old Bowels fired up his vehicle, a feat accomplished only after a few retries and back-fires. Once the old machine chugged to life, it sent the three men jiggling on the pickup's bench seat. Campbell, his big blue eyes invisible behind aviator dark glasses, turned to the other men and commented, "You know what? We're going to follow him in an antique pickup. It's green with blue fenders. Do we really think we're going to stay incognito?"

Wiggens, his curly hair poking out from under a weathered flop hat, said, "We've followed him this far."

Old Bowels looked over at the other two men and answered, "True, but why press our luck? Once he's on to us, our whole mission is screwed."

Campbell looked at Yank-um and then at Old Bowels and asked, "Time to call in the cavalry?"

"The cavalry it is."

❧ CHAPTER 8 ❧

THE CAVALRY WAS waiting just down the street. Adam was behind the wheel of Wardwell's Volvo XC90 with Conrad beside him, Aunt Phil and Sophie were in the back seat. When Luke Dozler rocketed past them as though his tail was afire, Adam had to floorboard the SUV in order to merge into traffic behind him.

"Egad, for someone who just came from talking with the sheriff, Dozler drives like he has no fear," Conrad said, gripping the door handle with one hand and the dashboard with the other.

"Or brains," Aunt Phil added, the volume of her voice matching the acceleration of the car.

Sophie used her cell phone to call Wiggens to report that they had seen Dozler and were in pursuit. She then notified Arthur and Beth that Luke was headed their way. They were with Mick and Dave and were waiting further down Highway 97. However, Beth and Arthur didn't get to join in the chase because Luke led the Volvo only a few blocks before he abruptly swung into a tavern's parking lot. He exited his truck and disappeared into the grimy building's dark entrance.

Adam drove the Volvo to the next business, a convenience deli and gas station and parked to the side of the building.

"What'll we do now?" Adam asked.

Aunt Phil answered, "I dunno. You call Wiggens and I'll call Arthur and we can discuss it."

Using a combination of phones on speakers, the group decided that someone had to go inside the tavern and survey what Dozler was up to.

"Cal and I can go in," Yank-um suggested. "After all, we've done it before when we chased down that crooked lawyer in Portland."

"You guys don't get to have all the fun," Aunt Phil spoke up, "I'm going in with you."

"Not without me, you aren't," Conrad replied.

"Are you going in without disguises?" Sophie asked incredulously.

Mick's voice could be heard in the background on Arthur's phone when he said, "In this case, Sophie, our age is all the costume we need. Nobody pays any attention to old people and Luke has never seen any of us."

Old Bowels, Wiggens, and Yank-um rattled up in the Ford and came to a noisy stop next to the Volvo. Yank-um nodded to Wiggens and the two bailed out of the pickup as Conrad and Aunt Phil exited the Volvo. They huddled together for a few moments discussing under what pretense they were going into this tavern, not that anybody would notice aside from the bartender and maybe a couple of rats.

While the oldsters hashed out their tactics, into the parking lot came a Honda Civic born in the previous century. It had smaller wheels in the front than in the back, giving it a constantly moving downhill look. It was so loosely put together that the woofer of its stereo system made various wobbly pieces of the car quiver to the beat. The trunk lid sported an add-on spoiler which was as useless as a bra on a boulder.

Driving the car was a guy who had pimp written all over him. He wore dark glasses and sat so low in the car as to look about twelve years old. He slouched behind the wheel, vaping and blowing smoke out the windows. The disheveled little beater of a car looked like a mini volcano.

When the Civic finally shivered to a stop, two young women awkwardly removed themselves from the back seat. They wore very short skirts, patterned tights, and low-cut blouses barely covering their mere suggestions of breasts. Aunt Phil took one look and said, "Uh-oh. These little girls are trolling for sperm."

The girls didn't go into the tavern but hovered around outside the door. Luke Dozler came out, gave the girls a once-over and handed the twelve-year old look-alike in the Civic what appeared to be a wad of cash.

The oldsters, collectively clued into Luke paying for underaged prostitutes suddenly pulled out their cell phones and announced, "Selfies! Let's do selfies!" while Conrad whispered, "Get photos of Dozler and the girls! Get some of the pimp and his car, quick, before he leaves! We'll send them to Cyril!"

While all four Geezers were milling around in front of the tavern pantomiming poses; some of them grinning together, or alone, all the while capturing just about every moment of Luke Dozler paying a pimp for underage prostitutes. The Geezers remaining in their cars were also catching the scene on video with their cell phones.

True to what Mick had said about nobody pays any attention to old people, Dozler was oblivious to the attention he was getting from this small cluster of elders. Smiling like the fiend he was and while copping a feel or two, he ushered the girls into his truck and soon sped off, leaving the tavern's parking lot filled with the fumes and roar of his exhaust system.

As Conrad and Aunt Phil scurried to the Volvo and Wiggens and Yankum piled into Old Bowel's pickup, Adam had Arthur on the phone telling him that Dozler was headed his way with what appeared as underaged prostitutes.

Arthur answered, "We're all over them. They just went by."

Conrad said, "We're sending the pictures to Cyril. Have someone in your car call him and tell him where you are. We'll try to catch up."

Luke Dozler, his hormones inflicting havoc upon what little common sense he had, was so intent on the anticipatory orgy involving the nubile young girls that he was totally blind to the caravan of Geezers following him. They followed him through the town of Redmond and were soon on the outskirts of Bend.

The computer screen in the Camp Sherman Office of Deputy Cyril Richmond came alive with images of Luke Dozler's dirty deed. A phone call from Beth to Richmond told him in what part of town they were, and that Dozler had turned off the bypass and was heading into a residential district.

Richmond immediately understood what had just transpired and forwarded the images to the Bend Police Department. He was soon on the phone to a police lieutenant telling him Luke Dozler appeared to be headed to his home with underage girls in his car. "Our informant reported they are definitely not housekeepers." He then gave the Lieutenant the Bend address for Dozler obtained earlier when Dozler was in the Sheriff's Office.

When Luke had been waiting for the girls to arrive at the tavern, he had gone inside and fortified himself with several quick shots of whiskey. By the time he pulled into his driveway, even his truck was staggering as he brought it to a sudden, sloppy halt, nearly slamming into his own garage door. He flung open the driver's door, then jerked open the door to the back seat. He pulled one of the girls out roughly by her skinny arm. Just as he was pulling out the second girl, a large, unmarked SUV, followed by a black Bend Police Department patrol vehicle, pulled across the end of the driveway, effectively negating any hair-brained ideas Luke might have to escape. Inside the unmarked SUV were a man and a woman, vice cops from the City of Bend Police Department.

Luke and the two girls froze in their tracks. The lead officer, a slim and suave man in a well-tailored dark suit, slid out of the SUV. He approached Luke and, backed by the uniformed officers from the patrol vehicle, drawled, "H'lo, Luke! Who do you have with you? Hi, girls! What are your names... your real names? You have any ID? What you all doin', gonna help Luke here wallpaper his bathroom?"

The vice cops took the girls, two runaways ages 14 and 15, back to the station where they were turned over to Children's Services. The two uniformed officers hauled off Luke and booked him into the Deschutes County jail on charges of DUII and soliciting sex with a minor.

All three Geezer vehicles had pursued Luke Dozler until they saw the police activity transpiring in Dozler's driveway. The Geezers then surreptitiously turned back into the neighborhood, knowing they had done their job. Following one another, they proceeded to get lost in the area's vast system of round-abouts. Finally, they found their way to the highway and headed to Camp Sherman.

CYRIL RICHMOND, AFTER finishing a call-back from the vice officer who arrested Luke Dozler, sat at his desk and pondered how the Geezers had known where they could find Dozler and trail him into Bend. Richmond decided he really didn't want to know as he remembered the close ties the Geezers had with the former gangster, Tommy Jax.

Jefferson County Sheriff's Deputy Cyril Richmond tipped back his chair, parked his boots on his desk, and dialed his Sheriff's number. When Larkin answered, Richmond said, "Remember when we were talking about goat rodeos?"

≫ CHAPTER 9 ≪

LUKE DOZLER'S VENTURE into the world of sexual bliss with underaged females cost him $10,000 and 30 days in jail. He was required to complete a course on how not to repeat the offense which went into one ear and out the other because there wasn't much inside to stop it. For his DUII conviction, he was given a concurrent jail sentence. Luke put on his best "Poor Pitiful Me" act by pleading that he wasn't aware the girls were underage, he was set up, he was the victim, he had a restaurant to open, his wife had left him, all the tension he was suffering, blah, blah, blah. The judge saw right through it and since Luke had refused to leave the room until he got his way, she ordered him hauled out of the courtroom.

After reading about his punishment in the Bend Bulletin, the Geezers were feeling proud of themselves. It still didn't solve their dilemma of how to find Annie Dozler or what to do with her once they did find her. At an impromptu meeting in the clearing outside Wardwell's cabin, they decided that first they needed to talk to her.

"You know, Luke Dozler's sentence is only for 30 days," Mick noted. "After which, he'll be pissed and will probably come looking for her."

"That's a scary thought!" Dave agreed.

"If we can convince her to trust us, we can hide her from both her husband and the law," Arthur suggested.

"Right," Aunt Phil said. "She can move from cabin to cabin until she can feel she's free from her husband, however that's going to happen."

"So how are we going to contact her?" Yank-um asked.

Beth said, "As I told you, every few days I leave for her a little bundle of stuff. You know, like fruit, energy bars, nuts, that kind of thing. I leave it at a place on Green Ridge not far from that clearing where I buried my dog, Sadie. I'll leave her a note asking her to meet with me at the clearing and I'll tell her I have friends who can help her and would like to talk to her. If she agrees, we'll set up a time and place and see if she shows up. What do you think?"

"Sounds good, Beth," Aunt Phil answered. "Where should we have her meet with us? It will need to be somewhere no one else will notice, which means somewhere outside of Camp Sherman."

"Well, it can't be that clearing," Beth continued, "because there are other cabins on that side of the ridge, and someone is bound to see or hear all of us up there."

"How about our house?" Tommy Jax asked, knowing the home at Black Butte Ranch was now well-equipped for Geezer meetings.

Oliver said, "Since our lot backs up to BLM land, it's kind of isolated and will be easy for her to get to. She won't have to go through the resort."

"That's a long way for her to go," Adam noted. "It's five miles from here to the highway and then another two to Black Butte."

Beth noted, "But not from where I leave her stuff, Adam. It's much closer to where Oliver and T.J.'s house is. She has appeared all over, like up at the Santiam Pass Ski Lodge and then down here in Camp Sherman and then on Green Ridge. I don't think Black Butte would be too far to ask her to come. We'll offer to take her, or we'll figure something else out, like maybe a smaller group of us in one of our cabins. However, it's going to take all of us involved to protect her from both the law and from her husband."

"Our place will be perfect if you can talk her into coming," Oliver replied.

"We'll cook up a storm!" Tommy Jax exclaimed excitedly. "Then, for whatever reason she doesn't show, we can have a party anyway!"

It wasn't lost on anyone that Tommy Jax and Oliver were getting more and more involved with the Geezers. This pleased the group, as they had used T.J.'s contacts in the crime world and Oliver's computer prowess, all of which were offered free of charge. It was heartwarming for the Geezers that the two men felt like members of the group rather than merely investigators.

After the meeting, Arthur and Beth drove over Green Ridge to their cabin. Max happily rode in the pickup bed, randomly barking at things only he could see. Although tethered so he couldn't jump out, the big dog could run from side to side, not wanting to miss any of the sights and smells obscure to humans but would explain why dogs love to ride in pickup beds.

"I'm not sure I'm happy with you meeting this woman by yourself," Arthur cautioned Beth. "The first time was by chance, and it turned out okay, but... How about I go with you?"

"I appreciate your concern for my safety, darling, but I don't think I need to be afraid of her. Having you with me might scare her off, considering what she's been through. Frankly, I'll be surprised if she agrees to meet with the Geezers. She has no real reason to trust any of us."

They rumbled along in silence, the pickup tires making swirls of dust behind them.

"I could take Max with me," Beth suggested, glancing at Arthur.

"That would make me feel better," Arthur answered, watching his dog in the rearview mirror. "Max is the best judge of character of any of us."

"Plus, he protected me from Dana. When she pointed that gun at me, he charged her, sank his teeth into her gun arm, and wouldn't let go." Beth recalled with sadness that day which could have gone so very wrong. Her estranged daughter, Dana Trelstad, a convicted murderer, came gunning for Adam and instead found Beth. If it hadn't been for Max and a sharp shooting police sniper, Beth's story would have ended tragically that day on Green Ridge.

A FEW CHILLY mornings later, Beth, with Max on a leash, climbed the trail from their cabin to the ridgeline and joined the Green Ridge Trail. They continued a short way across the top of the ridge until the trail began to tumble down the other side. They then left the trail and worked their way through the small stand of young Ponderosa pines and manzanita which hid the clearing. They found Annie Dozler waiting. She was sitting on a rock and smiled at Beth. She wore the camouflage sweatshirt Beth had given her. Her face looked thin and haggard, her hair hung limply down the sides of her face, but she appeared remarkably clean and healthy considering she had been out in the woods for nearly a month.

"Hi! Thanks for coming," Beth said. "This is Max."

Max's tail wagged vigorously, telling Beth he had already made up his mind about Annie Dozler. Annie immediately went to her knees, held out her arms to him and said, "Hi, Max!" With a smile, Beth loosened the leash and the big dog plunged into Annie's arms, licking her face and trying to get as much of his big furry body available for pets. Annie laughed and hugged the dog to her, burying her hands in his shaggy mane of hair and rumpling his ears, effectively telling Beth all she needed to know about the character of Annie Dozler.

ARTHUR WATCHED THE clock. He was worried. He tried to keep busy in his shop, then he'd go inside the house for a while, and he also puttered around outside, raking pine needles. The watch on his wrist, normally ignored for most of the day, now seemed heavy, always bringing his attention to it, checking the time.

She's been gone too long. I need to go up there to see what's going on. They could be having just a good old session of girl talk. I know that's important to women, but... but what if something's gone wrong and she needs me. I can't lose her. Beth. I've waited all my life... all seventy years. I'm going up there. Now! Why did I wait so long? I gotta go now!

He slapped a cap on his head and grabbed at a jacket hanging on a peg alongside the door. Stuffing each arm into the jacket, Arthur stormed out the door and made for the trailhead to the top of the ridge. His long legs made fast time up the trail, but as the trail steepened, his breathing became labored, and his heart pounded in his chest. *Damn old age! I should be able to run up here!*

Finally, he had to stop to catch his breath… for just a half minute. Well, maybe a whole minute. He put his hands on both knees and sucked the thin air into his chest, looked up the trail at the steepness ahead, then down the trail behind him to… what? *What's that in the trail? Behind me? An animal? Bobcat maybe? Those can be dangerous! Wait! No, that's… it can't be. Booger?*

"Booger!" Arthur straightened up and bellowed at his cat.

Nonplussed, the big Maine-coon rescued by a veterinarian and given to Arthur when he and Max moved into the new cabin, plodded along up the trail. The cat occasionally sent a meow Arthur's way, for no other reason than to acknowledge Arthur's presence and send the message, *Yeah, it's me. What's your damn hurry?*

"Aw, Boogs! Whadda doin? I left the door ajar, didn't I? Well, shit! I can't take you back because Beth… Beth…"

The cat finally caught up with him and Arthur reached down to scratch his cat between the ears. "You're not safe out here, Bud. There are cougars and bears and eagles who would snatch you for lunch. Aw, damn! Now what do I do?" Arthur looked worriedly back down the trail. Taking the cat home would waste precious time.

The cat blinked his green eyes at Arthur as though it was perfectly normal to be on a hike together. Arthur scooped up all twenty pounds of cat and stuffed him inside his jacket. With just Booger's head and front paws sticking out of the top of the jacket, the animal seemed quite content to ride this way. It was certainly an effortless way to travel, and Arthur's body kept him warm. Two things cats were best at: finding warmth and doing as little as possible. Riding along inside Arthur's jacket, Booger had it made on both accounts.

Now Arthur was really starting to puff. Carrying an extra twenty pounds didn't make the trail any less steep. He had almost reached the top of the ridge when he heard women's voices coming toward him and what was that other delightful sound? Laughter? Beth had a laugh that had always warmed his heart with its tinkling sweetness.

Arthur came to a stop in the middle of the trail as Beth and Annie appeared from around a corner. Arthur felt he must have made quite a sight with a large furry cat sticking out the top of his jacket.

Both women stopped suddenly at the sight. Beth giggled as Annie cautiously watched the spectacle from over the other woman's shoulder.

"I got worried," Arthur said simply as he shrugged. Looking down at the furry head of his cat he added, "So did Booger." Booger took his cue and meowed.

"Oh, Arthur, you are so funny!" Beth smiled and then suddenly remembered to introduce Annie.

"Annie, this is my husband, Arthur Perkins. Arthur, this is Annie Dozler. And Annie, this is our cat Booger. He's our rafter duster."

Annie said hello to Arthur and smiled. Then she slowly reached out and gently scratched the top of Booger's head. The cat closed his eyes and purred. With Max prancing on ahead, the group turned downhill toward the cabin.

OVER A LUNCH of chicken salad, warm French bread, and iced tea, Annie told Arthur everything she had already told Beth. He sat somewhat in awe of this woman. She didn't appear as he would have thought a battered wife would look. He had this preconceived image in his mind of a meek and withdrawn shrinking violet. This woman who sat at his table exuded all the confidence and self-purpose of any businessperson, teacher, volunteer, medical professional, or community leader he had ever known. He suddenly had an awakening thought that anybody...*anybody* could be suffering from abuse on the inside and effectively hiding it on the outside.

They talked about the Geezers and specified how they could help her hide and would she be in favor of meeting with them. Annie didn't tell Beth and Arthur that she already knew about the Geezers from Emily Martin but said she would be glad to meet with them. A time was verified with Tommy Jax and although Annie refused Beth and Arthur's offer to drive her, said she would have no problem finding the house at Black Butte Ranch.

After dessert of huckleberry cobbler, vanilla ice cream, and coffee, Annie Dozler, her backpack filled with new supplies, waved to Arthur and

Beth as she left the cabin. She worked her way through the huckleberry garden Arthur had planted for Beth and then headed up the trail to the top of the ridge.

As they watched her leave, Arthur turned to Beth and said, "Why do you suppose she didn't want to ride with us to T.J.'s and Oliver's?"

"I don't know, Arthur. I told her about Luke being in jail, but she still feels safest on her own. I imagine she has some degree of post-traumatic stress. Whatever gives her comfort may seem strange to us, but we need to give her freedom to do what's best for her. We're not wearing her shoes."

"And glad not to be."

⚘ C H A P T E R 1 0 ⚘

TOMMY JAX WAS having fun. Getting ready for a Geezer meeting brought out the best of his culinary skills and he applied them at full throttle. He and Oliver had stumbled upon a niche with these oldsters. The Geezers had welcomed the two men into their world and given both a feeling of purpose and unconditional acceptance.

When Phyllis Wardwell went to bat for Tommy Jax in that King County court room so many years ago, she changed his life forever. He could have happily walked out of the courthouse a free man and gone back to his crime life, but her threat of bodily harm if he didn't turn his life around eventually revealed to him there was a life beyond crime.

Now he thrived on purpose. Not only in their work with the homeless shelter in Seattle, but both he and Oliver discovered they shared with the Geezers a longing to make each day count through helping, ironically, law enforcement. Today, their mission was to help someone who couldn't be protected by the law. They knew nearly nothing about this Annie Dozler, but they looked forward to learning more.

Today, their newly remodeled kitchen in the house at Black Butte Ranch was filled with the smells of Jax's now legendary vegetable lasagna and Asiago cheese bread. The big man, decked out in a white double-breasted jacket with the quintessential toque blanche squashed onto his bald head, had just checked on the progress of the lasagna bubbling in the oven when Oliver finished setting the enormous dining room table.

Jax said, "Everything seems to be ready. All we need now are Geezers."

"Good," Oliver replied. Picking up a ginger cat which was twining itself around Oliver's ankles, he said, "I'm going to take George outside for a minute."

"Okay. We brought his harness, I hope."

"Yes," Oliver answered and with a chuckle added, "He doesn't particularly like it, but that's too bad." Holding the cat under one arm, Oliver stepped out onto the deck. He took in the view which never ceased to fill him with awe; the craggy volcano, Three Fingered Jack. Like a man made of sticks, Oliver sat down on the edge of the deck. He let out George's leash which allowed the cat to explore the small clearing. Oliver watched in wonder at the intensity by which the young cat examined everything, from pinecones and rocks to tufts of dry grass as though each one had a story to tell. Oliver plucked a long piece of dry grass from the ground and shook the end in front of George's nose. The cat rolled onto his back and batted and bit at the grass with kitten ferocity.

"Hi."

Oliver looked up to find Annie Dozler leaning against a large Ponderosa pine tree growing next to the clearing. She was wearing the camo sweatshirt and she had her hands in the pockets of scruffy jeans. She smiled shyly.

"Oh, hi." Oliver got to his feet as awkwardly as he had gotten down. "Are you Annie?"

"Yes. I hope I didn't startle you," Annie said, finding it somewhat endearing watching this man play with his cat. She extended her hand for a shake.

Oliver took her small, thin hand in his boney one. "No, not at all. I'm Oliver. We didn't expect you so soon. I mean, it's fine. We're ready. Come on inside and meet T.J." Oliver picked up the cat and said, "This is George."

"George?"

"Yes. We'd taken the dogs for a walk one day, and he followed us home. He was a sickly little thing. Must have been abandoned. He gets along well with our dogs. We have three Dobermans. In fact, he bosses them around." Oliver opened the door and stepped back to allow her to enter first. He said, "The dogs aren't here. We leave them with a friend in Maple Valley, outside of Seattle, when we come to Oregon. He's a veterinarian and has a small farm and sort of an animal sanctuary. They love it there."

Tommy Jax was surprised by his quiet partner's unusual chatter and came into the dining room to see who Oliver was talking to.

Annie Dozler took in the wonderful smells of cooking, the immensity of the living space with its huge fireplace and vaulted ceiling, and then stood somewhat in awe of the enormity of Tommy Jax. At nearly 400 pounds, he looked like a giant in his chef's outfit. He approached her with a huge smile and his hand extended. Her hand was engulfed in his and to her surprise, his grasp was gentle. He offered her a glass of iced tea and she followed him into the kitchen as he fetched the brew.

"I was expecting someone older than you two," Annie said as she accepted the frosty glass. "Beth told me about 'Geezers.' You two are anything but Geezers."

"We're Geezer wannabe's!" Jax said, laughing. "Let's go out on the deck, shall we? It will be a few minutes before everyone starts arriving."

"We're sort of advisors," Oliver offered, as they went outside. George was on his favorite perch, Oliver's angular shoulder.

"You see, many years ago," Jax continued, as he offered a deck chair to Annie and then grunted into one himself, "Phyllis Wardwell, who you will meet today, was a criminal defense attorney in Seattle. I, well, got into a heap of trouble."

"T.J.'s dark years," Oliver added, chuckling.

"Boy, were they ever! My life was full of crime and heading further downhill. Well, she got me off a really bad rap and told me to shape up... or else!" Again, Jax laughed. "When Phyllis tells you that, she means business."

"So now," Oliver continued, "we do research and computer work for them."

"I have maintained a lot of connections with prior organized crime individuals. Even bad guys have friends," Jax said with a laugh and a smile. "So, when we need to find a suspect or learn something else about him, usually I can find a guy who can get some information for us."

"So, what do the Geezers do, exactly?" Annie asked quizzically, as

George flowed off Oliver's shoulder like a ribbon and sat blinking at her.

"Now don't spook at this, Annie," Jax cautioned, "because it doesn't involve you, but the Geezers work secretly for the police. They spy on known suspects in local crimes."

Annie's eyes got huge, imagining old people sneaking around corners and peeking into windows.

Jax went on, "Law enforcement, in the form of Camp Sherman's local deputy, Cyril Richmond, as well as Sheriff Larkin, usually know what the Geezers are up to, but they have fits, tell the Geezers not to do it, fear for their safety, but the group does it anyway."

"It's their way of making a contribution at a time in life when our culture expects them to just sit around and fade away," Oliver added.

Jax continued, "Not these guys! Nowhere close! They let Richmond know where to find the thugs and have helped corral quite a few bad guys... I mean, really, really bad guys."

"I see! So very interesting!" Annie replied. Smiling, she stroked George's ginger stripes as the cat climbed into her lap. "I just cannot imagine old people doing that."

Jax replied, "Well, when you think about it, why not? As they say, their age makes for the perfect disguise. Like you, who would suspect them? Old people are invisible. No one pays any attention to old people in our society."

Chuckling, Annie mused, "I'll never look at old people the same way again. Where do they all come from?"

"The Geezers have come from all over," Jax answered. "Some have been in Camp Sherman forever. Others, like Phyllis and Conrad came from Portland."

"So did Adam Carson, Phyllis's nephew," Oliver added. "He's an attorney who has semi-retired to Sisters."

Jax went on, "You've already met Arthur Perkins and Beth Welton. She's from Portland and has an interesting background. He's from Baker City."

"Beth has told me her story," Annie replied. "I thought mine was scary!"

"Yours is scary enough, to be sure," Jax answered. "That's why the Geezers want to do what they can to help you avoid your husband... what's his name?"

"Luke."

Jax continued, "Beth, like you, had to run because law enforcement couldn't protect her from her daughter. They could do nothing unless the daughter did something awful. Doesn't seem right, but that's the way it is. Now, Beth is doing very well."

"That should give you hope for your own future, doesn't it, Annie?" Oliver offered gently.

"Spending some time with Beth and Arthur and seeing their life and their love, I've had that thought," Annie answered. She looked toward the mountain and then turned to him and said softly, "That would sure be nice...first, I must figure out how to be free of Luke. If I ask for a divorce, he'll try to kill me. His pride would never survive a divorce. So, all I could do to get away from his brutality was to run away, just like Beth did. However, if he knows I'm in the Metolius Basin, he'll come here."

"The Geezers know that," Oliver went on. "That's why they also want to help you avoid Deputy Richmond. He's been given the assignment to find you. If he knew the Geezers had found you, he'd have to tell Sheriff Larkin where you are. It's his job."

"Yes, I know. I've seen the bulletins. They're all over!"

The three sipped their tea and watched George stalk a blue jay. The cat came to the end of his leash, plopped onto his belly, swished his tail and watched the bird.

Annie, having figured out the relationship between Jax and Oliver, asked, "I hope you don't think I'm too intrusive, but how did you two meet?"

Oliver answered, "I was in a homeless shelter in Seattle. My apartment building had been emptied under the pretense of an extensive remodel. Afterward, the building was sold as a luxury apartment building, and I couldn't afford the new rent. None of the prior tenants could. Then the restaurant I worked for closed."

"That's awful!" Annie exclaimed.

"My unemployment benefits got all tangled up in the massive amounts of requests for benefits, so I bunked in a shelter."

Jax finished the story. "I went in there looking for a computer guy; at least someone who could help me with some stuff. Oliver was the guy."

"That's nice," Annie said smiling.

Oliver continued, "Yeah, now we volunteer at the shelter where I stayed. There is so much need! It's quite incredible. There are many people like you, not all of them women, running from abusive relationships."

"Luke would easily find me if I went to a shelter. That's why I'm out in the woods. When I was little, I'd always run into the forest when life with Mom would get too hard to take. She was an alcohol and drug abuser, and things would get ugly. My brothers would come looking for me. For them, it was a game. They were always rough with me, and Mom was too drunk to ever notice, so I'd hide from them. I've always felt secure in the forest. Trees are easy to hide in. When it rains, I can get shelter in a thicket of small trees. I tie the tops together and use boughs to fill in the gaps. Trees have always been my friends."

Both Tommy Jax and Oliver had mental images of a lonely little girl running into the forest to escape a childhood which must have been brutal. The two men shared a look over Annie's head and without saying a word, knew they had to help this woman.

CHAPTER 11

GEEZERS BEGAN TO fill the house. They came in a bundle, noisily greeting Oliver at the door, Jax in the entry way, and George sprawled on the back of a couch. There was much fuss made over all three before somebody noticed Annie Dozler. She sat on the raised hearth of the enormous lava rock fireplace which divided the living room from the dining room. She was smiling. A crackling, hissing fire had been laid and was well on its way to warming the air and the atmosphere of welcoming affection that the Geezers brought everywhere.

Mick and Dave were first to approach her. She stood and shook their hands as they explained they were brothers-in-law and had lived at Camp Sherman since they had both retired which seemed like forever. Beth stepped up and introduced Annie to each Geezer as they filed by. Annie shook their hands, looked into their kind, warm eyes and felt a feeling of unbiased acceptance from these elders who long ago learned that to judge someone by any preconceived notion was ridiculous.

Adam Carson and Sophie Summers followed the Geezers. Sophie entered the house in a flurry of wildly wonderful curly hair, flowing sleeves and, as usual, was trailed by the fragrance of flowers. She placed a kiss on Oliver's and Tommy Jax's cheeks, then swooped George into her arms and exclaimed how much he'd grown. She captured Annie in a fragrant cocoon of a hug and said softly into her ear that she was so glad she had agreed to meet the group. Before a smiling Beth had a chance, Sophie introduced herself as a hairdresser and Adam as a semi-retired attorney. "We're

Geezers-in-the-Making or, Entry-Level Geezers, I can't remember which," Sophie announced, giggling.

"Perhaps," Annie replied, "as Tommy Jax told me about himself and Oliver, Geezer wannabes?"

"Exactly!" Adam answered, roaring with laughter.

Once everyone was finally inside and had met Annie, Jax announced that food was ready and for everyone to grab a plate and help themselves. Jax and Oliver, with Annie's help, had set up the huge island in the kitchen as a buffet. The Geezers politely let Annie go first, claiming if she waited for them, there may not be any food left. As hungry as she felt, she took only modest portions. If she'd been asked, she would have confessed she could have eaten her way from one end of the buffet to the other.

Annie sat at the table between Dave and Mick and across from Conrad and Aunt Phil. Earlier Aunt Phil had engulfed Annie in a hug, thanked her for coming, and assured her that the Geezers would do everything they could to help her.

Annie said to Aunt Phil, "Tommy Jax told me you were a criminal defense attorney in Seattle."

"That's right, and I'll never let him forget it."

Mick told Annie, "Dave's wife is a writer."

"Really? What kind of books?"

"The kind that don't sell," Dave answered.

Aunt Phil speculated, "I could write a book... a cookbook. It would be an in-depth study of can openers. Or maybe, how not to burn soup."

Dave told her that Mick is a doctor but eats potato chips until his lips catch on fire.

"That's right," Mick replied. "Just don't tell my cardiologist."

Annie giggled at the Geezers' antics. She enjoyed these easy going oldsters to the point where she briefly forgot why she was there.

Once the first helping had been consumed and Geezers were going back for seconds, Conrad leaned across the table and asked Annie, "As soon as these guys get back to the table, I think we can start the meeting. Do you mind telling us your story?"

Annie smiled at the old Navy Commander's warm crinkly eyes and answered, "Of course not."

Once everyone had settled, Conrad rapped on his glass with a spoon and announced it was time for them to hear Annie's story.

She began quietly and cautiously. If she felt inhibited talking to so many people, the feeling soon fell away. She looked down the table at the oldsters' sweet friendly faces which told her, *Go ahead, Annie. You're safe with us.* Soon her story flowed.

"Luke was the way out of my hell-hole life with my family. I thought he loved me. He was sweet to me at first, warm and loving, or so I thought. Early on, I didn't see the signs that I now recognize. He was always critical of my appearance, my hair and clothes. He never approved of my friends. When I got close to a group of other women in Baker City, he moved us out into the country. With only one car, I was isolated. My friends would come out to the house, and he'd always get angry. That's when the beatings started. It was for my own good, he'd say. I deserved it for defying him by having friends he didn't approve of.

"When his restaurant tanked, which he somehow blamed on me, we moved to Madras. The same pattern repeated and worsened. He was furious when I got close to some really nice gals. Then he moved us out to Culver. I was lonely and wanted to get a dog and he said he'd kill it. I could have left him at any time, but I thought my love could fix a terribly sick and misguided man. Instead, he just got worse. When he came home one day brandishing a handgun, I knew I had to leave.

"I left Culver with not much more than the clothes I was wearing, a sleeping bag, and a few dollars. He didn't want me to have much money. He said I wasn't responsible enough to handle it. Well, I knew I was and that I was capable of doing a lot of things he told me I couldn't.

"I knew that it would do no good to report the beatings to law enforcement. They would suggest a restraining order which he'd tear up and then beat me. I know he would! How could I file for divorce without any money or anywhere to go? He'd be able to find me. The woods seemed to be my only sanctuary.

"One day when I knew he'd be gone all day, I started to walk toward the Metolius Basin. I was able to hitch a ride with a retired couple from Washington State who were traveling to the RV Camp at Crooked River. To explain my shabby clothes, I told them I was working as a groundskeeper at the golf course and my car had broken down, but I had to get to work. They were very sweet and left me at the golf course. From there, I started walking. I did have a map, thank heavens, and I knew if I could find Forest Service Road #2055, I could work my way over to Green Ridge."

Cal Wiggens asked, "Annie, what do you expect to do? Surely, you can't live in these woods forever. It's summer now but fall comes early to these mountains."

"That's right," Yank-um added. "The winters can be brutal."

"I think Luke will give up eventually," Annie answered. "He'll get involved with his new restaurant and probably another woman and he'll move on. Then, I'll try to get to the valley. That's what I was trying to do when I got caught staying at the Santiam Pass Ski Lodge. Anyway, I've heard there is a nice women's shelter in Keizer. Maybe I can get a new start there and find a job close by. There must be businesses around there that are hiring. Since then, I've had second thoughts about the valley. I fear he'd find me no matter where I'd go.

"The only thing that really worries me right now, is that when I was at the Santiam Pass Ski Lodge, I overheard two sheriff's deputies talking about getting a tracker to find me. I stayed hidden until they left then I bolted back to the Metolius Basin. I felt that was the safest place for me to be… in the forest. If I'd kept going west, I'd have to pretty much follow the highway. Someone would surely see me."

At the mention of a tracker, the Geezers all looked around the table.

"That's not good news!" Old Bowels declared.

"Not in the slightest," Adam agreed.

Aunt Phil asked, "Annie, do we know if they have a picture of you?"

"I have no idea. I doubt it."

Conrad, knowing where his wife's mind was going said, "Disguise! They can't find you if they don't know what to look for."

Aunt Phil said, "Annie, your boots! The tracker is going to be following your footprints. We need to get you new boots! What size do you wear?"

Annie looked at her battered boots and answered, "About an eight and a half."

"Okay," Aunt Phil said, "tomorrow, you and I will go into Sisters and buy a new set of boots... something with a different tread pattern than yours."

Old Bowels piped up, "I have a good idea! I wear a men's size seven. I'll bet I can wear Annie's boots! How about I wear them and stomp around on a different trail than she came down. We'll get a map, and she can show us the trails she took. I'll head off in another direction, go through the woods, whatever. I'll make it look like she's trying to throw them off."

"Don't get lost up there, O.B!" Sophie said apprehensively.

"Nah, don't worry, Sophie," Old Bowels said. "I've lived in these mountains for decades. If I do get lost, send the tracker after me!"

Dave had drawn a map of all the Geezer cabins so Sophie could seek shelter if she so chose. Mick gave her a cell phone even though cell phone service in the basin was sketchy. He had also entered all the Geezer's names and phone numbers.

"Ok, Annie," Mick said, "don't turn this phone on until you need to use it. Cell phone service is poor in the basin. If you leave it on all the time, the phone will use up its battery looking for a signal."

Sophie offered to give Annie a new look. "This will be fun for you, Annie. We'll do something to change your appearance, just in case the tracker and the law do have a picture." Sophie looked seriously at Annie's unkept, lanky hair. "How about a cut and a light perm? Maybe even change the color a bit."

Annie started to feel a bit embarrassed as well as excited about what these plans meant for her future and said, "Gosh, you guys, you're going to too much trouble."

"Fiddle sticks!" Aunt Phil declared. "This is nothing! You'd be surprised what we get ourselves into."

As the Geezers all talked at once about what they were going to do to throw off a tracker, Beth noticed Annie looking around at the oldsters with a mixture of both confusion and appreciation on her face. "Annie," Beth said gently, "When these folks get on the move, just sit back and enjoy the show."

Annie said as she and Beth started to clear the table, "I don't know why they care, Beth. Why should they go to so much trouble for me?"

"The elderly have lost so much, Annie. They have lost people they thought they couldn't live without. They have lost their own health and vitality and a purpose for living. Their future is iffy and guaranteed to be short. Younger people who haven't yet suffered much loss and who also still have a future and all their faculties and health cannot relate to what old people go through. Consequently, they brush the elderly aside, making them feel even more useless and isolated. What this bunch has found is purpose. Purpose makes all the difference in elders' lives. You have given that to us, Annie, and we have embraced it… and you! We'll get you out of this jam. Believe in what the Geezers can do."

❧ CHAPTER 12 ❧

THE GEEZERS BUSILY went over maps with Annie to learn what trails she had used. The plan was to obliterate her boot tracks as much as possible. Conrad's cell phone rang. He noticed it was from Deputy Richmond.

"Hey, you guys!" Conrad shouted over the other voices, "Quiet, please! This is Richmond calling!"

At the name of Richmond, all Geezers suddenly cut the chatter and wide-eyed, watched Conrad expectantly. Did Richmond know they were with Annie Dozler? If Richmond asked if the Geezer's had found her, would Conrad lie to him, the deputy devoted to Camp Sherman and who had been their friend for years? They listened to Conrad's side of the conversation.

"A tracker? Oh, yeah, up at the Santiam Pass Ski Lodge. Next week? Oh, okay. Thanks for keeping us in the loop, Cyril. Bye."

Dave asked, "Did he ask if we'd seen Annie?"

"Nope," Conrad answered. "I'm glad. That way, I didn't have to lie to him."

Once their meeting broke up, the Geezers went their separate ways. Aunt Phil and Conrad took Annie back to their cabin where she would stay for a while. Old Bowels offered to take Yank-um to his cabin because Cal Wiggens, who had brought Yank-um to the meeting, said he wanted to go to the ranch's stables for a few minutes.

Yank-um asked why his friend wanted to see the stables. Wiggens explained that on a previous case, he had experienced an enjoyable horseback ride into Swallow Lake and remembered the sweet interaction he had with the little bay mare he rode. He wanted to go to the ranch's stables to see if he could find her. Yank-um just smiled at his friend's soft heart and then climbed into Old Bowel's pickup.

In anticipation of seeing the horse, Cal Wiggens first drove into Sisters where, at a farm store, he purchased a bag of carrot-flavored horse treats. Once he was back at Black Butte Ranch Stables, he got out of his old SUV and walked to the corral fence. Among the shuffling and snorting of horses, he heard a nicker, and then another. He looked over the herd of horses and out from behind the hindquarters of a big rawboned, buckskin gelding, peeked the head of the little bay mare. She nickered again. Her soft brown eyes were glued to Wiggens. There was a split second when through that horse's eyes, Wiggens connected with her soul. That was when Dr. Calvin Wiggens, MD, PhD, internationally acclaimed authority on all things forensic, lost his heart to a horse.

The resident wrangler, Doug Miller, recognized Wiggens because the wrangler had been along when the Linn County Sheriff's crime scene techs horse-packed into Swallow Lake. Linn County had borrowed Black Butte's horses for the trip. The wrangler went along to take care of the animals.

Wiggens asked Doug if there was any way he could feed the mare a treat without causing trouble with the other horses. The wrangler said, "Sure, you can take her out of the corral and put her in a stall over there. Brush her too, if you want." The wrangler remembered the attachment Wiggens seemed to have for the horse and was pleased and somewhat amused by the elderly doctor showing up and asking about her.

Doug asked, "Do you want to go in and get her or do you want me to?" About that time a palomino planted a well-aimed kick at a grey which screamed and whirled on the other horse and bit a hunk out of its hide.

Wiggens, somewhat taken aback said, "Well, maybe you better."

Doug slung a halter over his shoulder and as he opened the gate, he told Wiggens, "Horses don't generally mean to harm humans, but they are rough with each other, obviously. Horses have their own agenda and if you're between a horse and the one that pisses it off, you're going to get the kick. Also, if the horse doesn't know you're behind it, and you startle it, it may kick out and get you. So, you always want to let them know you're there." The wrangler continued to talk to each horse as he made his way over to where the mare was standing somewhat apart from most of the herd.

"There you go, Teddy. How ya doing, Missy? That's a good girl. Nope, you're not the one I want, Duke, get outta the way, please. No, I don't have any treats. There you are. Come here, Dolly," the wrangler cooed. "There's a friend here who would like to see you."

He slipped the halter over the little horse's nose and led her out of the corral and into a small stabling area. There Doug put the horse into cross-ties and showed Wiggens how to brush her. He followed the whorls of hair with the brush, used a soft brush on her face, being careful of the eyes, and used a stiff brush on her mane and tail. He also showed how to pick up and clean a horse's hoof, using a hoof pick carefully to dig out any rocks but keeping clear of the V-formation called a frog, which is sensitive.

"The best thing we can do for these animals is to make sure their hooves are clean and well cared for. No hooves, no horse."

"Gee, thanks. I had no idea you did all this to a horse. This is cool."

"Take her for a little walk, if you like, out in the pasture. Let her eat the green grass. She would probably like being able to eat where the grass is greenest without getting harassed by the other horses," Doug went on. "The horses are all in the corral for now, so there are none of them out there to bother you. Dolly's kinda at the bottom of the pecking order with this herd because she's new."

The wrangler pointed to a big bay Thoroughbred gelding with a white blaze down its face. "That horse's name is Teddy. Teddy was once a race-horse. He was retired to somebody who wanted a jumper. Teddy doesn't jump so he became a pasture pet. Dolly and Teddy were both donated to us by some folks who could no longer care for them. They also had a sheep. Since the three animals had bonded and were always together, they wanted us to take all three... so, now we also have a sheep! Her name is Sally. She goes on our trail rides with us. Our riders think it's hilarious.

"Here, let me show you how you do this," the wrangler put a lead rope on the halter and keeping the horse's head even with his right shoulder, showed Wiggens how to always keep the horse to the side and never behind him. "You know, in the wild, horses are preyed upon so even domesticated, they startle easily. If the horse is behind you and spooks, it may knock you down, not on purpose, but you just happen to be in the way."

Wiggens, fascinated, said, "That's good to know."

"Even though Dolly's small and sweet natured, she is still a prey animal and outweighs a human by a bunch. So, keep that in mind, and you'll be fine. If for some reason she bolts and tries to run away, drop the lead rope and let her go. The area is all fenced, she can't go far, but I don't expect that will happen."

"So, when should I give her the treats?"

Doug laughed and said, "Any time will be fine with her."

"Oh, okay. Thanks."

As Wiggens walked with Dolly into the pasture, Teddy, the big bay Thoroughbred, stood at the fence and watched. So did Sally the sheep.

Cal Wiggens not only fell in love with a horse that day, but he opened a door to adventures he never would have imagined.

THE NEXT MORNING, Cal Wiggens was at the door of Yank-um's cabin. The two retired doctors owned cabins on the same dusty lane which ran alongside the river and downstream from Wardwell's Geezer Central. It was a sunny but brisk morning for July. There was a light dusting of frost on the rocks lining the walkway. Sun beams working their way through the trees would soon evaporate all traces of the frost.

Yank-um came to the door in pajamas and slippers, an old plaid bathrobe tied around his ample middle. He had a mug of steaming coffee in his hand.

"Hey, Cal! Howzit goin'? Come on in! Help yourself to the coffee."

"Get dressed," Wiggens said as he walked into the tiny kitchen. Helping himself to a mug, he continued, "You need to meet the horse you just bought."

"The what?" The old dentist stood gobsmacked, his big blue eyes becoming saucers. "What horse?"

"His name is Teddy. You'll like him. Oh, yeah, there's a sheep too."

"A sheep?"

THE TWO OLD doctors bounced along in Cal Wiggen's ancient SUV. They were on their way to Black Butte Ranch's stables where they would procure the horses Dolly and Teddy plus Sally the sheep.

"Now tell me," Yank-um asked. "Why is it that we need to buy these critters?"

"The ranch doesn't want to keep them," Wiggens replied. "They took them as a favor for a local elderly couple who couldn't care for them anymore. The animal rescue bunch in Sisters didn't have room for all three animals at once so Black Butte offered to take them until they could find a better home for them."

"It seems to me that Black Butte Ranch would be the best home for them."

"Probably would for the horses, but then, there is the sheep," Wiggens explained.

"Sally."

"Sally. They have been together for years. It'd be cruel to separate them. That's the way herd animals are."

"I see," commented Yank-um, whose previous experience with animals had been with dogs and the occasional cat.

"Doug Miller, the wrangler," Wiggens went on, "also said that both the horses are getting a bit old for their purposes on the ranch. He said that right now, they have too many horses. Dolly and Teddy require special supplements for senior horses and it's hard to separate them out to feed them. Doug's idea was to keep them just until room became available at that animal rescue place. That hasn't happened."

"So..."

"Enter you and me," Wiggens grinned at Yank-um.

"Batman and Robin."

"To the rescue!"

"And just what are we going to do with them," Yank-um's eyes were still saucers, "sheep and all? The forest service won't let us keep livestock at our cabins."

"I have that all arranged. That barn right across the road from the Camp Sherman Fire Station has room. They'll keep the three animals together in a nice, grassy paddock. I've already checked it out and paid for six months in advance."

"You've been busy! All that sounds great, Cal, but what I mean is, what are *we* going to do with them? Pasture pets, I suppose. We go there and brush them, feed treats and this supplement stuff. That's not a bad deal for old, unwanted horses. I'm with you on that. We can shear the sheep, maybe. Spin a yarn?"

"Very funny. First, we're going to ride them all over the Metolius Basin and obliterate Annie Dozler's tracks. We'll also ride on Green Ridge, everywhere she'd been. That tracker will never be able to sort out all the tracks, hers, ours, plus the rest of the Geezers who will be swarming all over!"

"And the sheep will go too... Sally?"

"Yep!"

"A-ha! I'm beginning to get the picture," Yank-um said, warming to the idea. "We'll trample Annie's footprints with horse and sheep prints... poo too."

"Right!"

Yank-um crossed his arms over his belly and laughed, "That ought to blow away that tracker!"

"That's the plan, Amigo."

❧ CHAPTER 13 ❧

"IT'LL BE GOOD exercise!" Cal Wiggens exclaimed as he placed an old western saddle on Dolly's back.

"I already get plenty of exercise," Yank-um grunted while lifting another western saddle to his chest and then heaving it onto Teddy's tall back. "Every morning, I stand up, straighten my knees, stick out my chest and before I fall over, quickly sit back down. I then scratch daily exercise off my list."

"My point."

"Okay, I get it, but do *you*," pointing a finger at Teddy's nose, "have to be so fucking *tall?*"

Teddy, in the way of horses, sniffed Yank-um's hand as though it should be producing a treat.

Once the two old doctors were on their way, clippity-clopping down Camp Sherman Road, they looked a bit like Don Quixote and Sancho Panza. One rode a tall Thoroughbred and the other a diminutive Quarter horse. They soon became familiar figures on the trails in and around Camp Sherman. Their notoriety was quite possibly augmented by the woolly presence of Sally the sheep, who followed them everywhere.

Although their somewhat random appearance in the Metolius Basin seemed not to have any obvious method to it, the two were systematically cross-hatching the entire area where Annie had been, obliterating tracks coming and going. If the fact they never seemed to be going to a specific destination bothered their horses, the beasts never let on. As for Sally, she just kept following, not appearing to give a rip that they never arrived anywhere.

The only exception was when they stopped at the Camp Sherman Store so Yank-um could purchase a bottle of water. He dismounted Teddy and ran inside the store, squeezed through a group of kids swarmed around the ice cream cooler, dashed past the century-old sales counter which sat in front of a wall of snapshots, letters, and currencies from around the world. The collection was so extensive that it even lapped over onto the ceiling. He passed a cooler full of homemade salads, sandwiches, cheeses, pastries, and Beth's huckleberry pies. He hurried down the aisle of beer and pop coolers and snatched a bottle of water. He spun around to return to the sales counter and ran head-long into Sally, who had dutifully followed him inside. The other store patrons found it hilarious, and the children squealed with delight. Whether or not the proprietors were amused was left unknown as Yank-um tossed sufficient dollar bills on the counter as he scurried past, ushering Sally outside as quickly as they had entered.

He found Wiggens by a pile of firewood bundles along with a sea of children and much fuss being made over the horses. Both horses had lowered their heads to the little ones, either to better examine these miniature humans or so that the children could pet their noses.

Yank-um used a bundle of firewood as a mounting block and scrambled back onto Teddy. With a wave to the horde of little kids and their parents, the two old duffers were again on their way.

OTHER GEEZERS WERE also on the move. In pairs or in small groups and with their dogs along, they took treks here and there, as though the sole purpose was to enjoy the mountains and the soft early summer weather. At noon they would gather at the Camp Sherman Store and feast on deli sandwiches, potato salad, homemade brownies and cookies. Then they would be off again. Some swarmed Green Ridge, some ventured down river, others fanned out west into the Metolius Basin, talking, laughing, singing, as though their only care was to make sure they had a wonderful time.

As they wandered around, they shared a common intent, to examine the ground for Annie's boot prints. They would take turns looking for prints so that the whole group wasn't walking with their noses to the ground, drawing attention to themselves. If one Geezer found tracks, another Geezer would shuffle through them. After all, old people often shuffle when they walk, either because of being in pain or they're just too tired to pick up their feet. There never appeared to be a purpose to their wanderings, but not one footprint of Annie's stood a chance of surviving this bunch of determined oldsters.

AUNT PHIL AND SOPHIE had taken Annie into Sisters to Sophie's salon to treat Annie to a new shorter hair style, a soft perm, and added blond highlights. After Sophie finished blow drying Annie's hair, she added a bit of blusher to her cheeks and mascara to her eyes. Annie looked into the mirror and her hands shot to her face, her mouth open in amazement and her eyes brimming with tears. She could not believe she could look so beautiful. Even Aunt Phil teared up, knowing this was the first time this woman had ever experienced anything close to a Cinderella moment.

Annie now looked nothing like she could possibly be the subject of the flyers deputies had passed all over town. The women felt it was safe to do the next logical thing, shop for not only new boots, but a new wardrobe as well. Since Annie had left Culver with only the clothes on her back, she needed all sorts of inner and outer clothing. Like kids at Christmas, the three women had a wonderful time outfitting Annie for her new life, whatever that might be.

Aunt Phil spied a cute camisole in a shop window. Annie tried to tell her they had already bought too much, but as Aunt Phil marched through the shop doorway she insisted, "Annie, a girl can't have too much pretty underwear!"

The plan was for Annie to stay with the Wardwells and sleep in the cabin's loft bedroom. She appreciated having a bit of secure space to herself. When she was preparing for bed, she looked out the small dormer window at the star-lit night. The sparkling sky was rimmed with the tops of trees... her trees. They were still there, like sentinels, watching and keeping her safe.

She looked around the room at the shopping bags which were the proceeds of their shopping spree in Sisters. They were piled here and there on a small desk and chair. She was overwhelmed not only by the generosity the packages represented, but also by the opportunity to be under the same roof as these people who had opened their doors and hearts to her. Wearing a new nightie, she snuggled into the freshly cleaned sheets and said a small prayer of thanks for the blessings surrounding her. For the first time since she was a little girl and before her big brothers began invading her bedroom and tormenting her for sex, Annie Dozler slept without fear.

OLD BOWELS HAD been busy packing gear for his trek into the mountains. He would carry a small pack with enough emergency provisions to cold camp in case he couldn't make it back to the Suttle Lake rendezvous in one day. He also packed Annie's boots. They fit him...nearly. Being a bit narrow for him, they were uncomfortable, but he would make them do.

The next morning, he piled his pack into the bed of Mick's pickup. Already in the bed was Mick's chocolate lab, Buddy. The dog thought this entire adventure was great fun and gave O.B.'s face several quick licks to show his appreciation. With Mick, Dave and Old Bowels crammed into the tiny cab, the three codgers rattled up Highway 20 to the Pacific Crest Trailhead at the 4,817-foot summit of Santiam Pass. With Buddy's tail-wagging help, they poked around in the shrubbery of manzanita, serviceberry, and young trees until they found Annie's tracks which led away from the Santiam Pass Ski Lodge. Old Bowels then pulled on his pack and with a wave over his shoulder to Mick and Dave, set off down the trail with the plan to lead the tracker away from Annie's route. O.B. would make his way back down the mountain and meet up with Mick and Dave at the Suttle Lake Campground.

As he walked through a forest once ravished by a war with fire, he remembered the day in August 2003 when the B&B Complex Fire started by lightning. The forest was so dry, trees exploded into flames as winds drove the fire up the mountainside. It destroyed over 90,000 acres of pristine wilderness. For years after, the area seemed like a desert of white skeletal tree trunks. Some lay on the ground, overlapping each other like the old children's game of Pick-Up Sticks. Others stood as straight, stark snags against the sky.

A forest may be gravely wounded by fire, but it never dies. Evidence of life now cautiously peeked out of the rubble. Small fir, pine, and hemlock trees steadily pushed aside the debris of fiery destruction and stretched their limbs to welcome a new epoch in the ongoing life of the wilderness. The forest where Old Bowels hiked was nearly twenty years into recovery. He worked his way through many areas now lush with undergrowth. Carrying Annie's ragged shirt, he left the occasional thread snagged on twigs alongside the path.

For years, Old Bowels had been a member of the Hasty Search and Rescue Team. He had covered this part of the mountain many times. He never tired of the stunning views to the south of Mt. Washington, the Three Sisters, and Broken Top. As he traveled to Square Lake, a view unveiled to the northwest of Three Fingered Jack. Like fingers, thin spears of stone formed the western side of the old volcano. The eastern side, open like the palm of a hand, cradled a tiny lake. A field of wildflowers spilled over the crater's rim and flowed down Canyon Creek meadow. This time of the year, July, the wildflowers and flowering shrubs blanketed the mountain's slopes in a massive mosaic of colors.

Old Bowels followed Annie's tracks to Square Lake where, as she had explained, she continued north on the Old Summit Trail to Jack Lake and then made her way east into the Metolius Basin. When he reached the north side of Square Lake, he continued down the Old Summit Trail for about one hundred yards, obliterating any tracks that could have been Annie's. He also looked for tell-tale signs of her passing, broken branches, scuff marks on rocks and downed logs, and bits of cloth or threads from her shirt. Having meticulously gone over the area, he felt fairly assured he could effectively lead the tracker down the wrong trail, the trail to Round Lake.

Once back at Square Lake, he donned Annie's boots and made it look like she had cold camped next to the lake. He laid down in the grass and dirt and rolled around, crushing the grass underneath him. Then, he got up and brushed his hands through the grass, making the stiff stalks stand half-way upright. This made it appear the grass had been trampled several days ago and was on its way to recovery.

Old Bowels then headed downhill for two miles on the Round Lake Trail. The trail first covered some generally flat terrain, but lost altitude as he approached Round Lake. After passing the lake, he followed old logging roads used mainly in the winter as cross-country ski trails. The surfaces of the old roads were riddled with rocks and washouts, making walking in Annie's narrow boots agonizing. He also encountered overgrowth that choked his path and as he bushwhacked around rocks and downed timbers, he made sure a thread or two of Annie's shirt snagged here and there.

Skirting small stands of pine and hemlock that miraculously escaped the fire, he worked his way farther downhill for several miles until he could see Suttle Lake off to the right. He then followed a ridge which paralleled the highway until he arrived at the bottom of the slope. Watching carefully for traffic, he hurried across the highway and walked down a short lane to the Suttle Lake campground area. A setting sun reflected glaringly from the lake, making him squint into the brightness. A cold wind hummed through the tops of the trees and sent their branches swaying.

It was easy to spot the bright orange old pickup parked in an empty campsite. Both Mick and Dave were fast asleep in the cab. Dave's feet were protruding from the open window on the passenger side.

Mick awakened with a snort and said, "Hey, O.B., you took so long we figured you'd been in a shoot-out and lost!"

"Very funny!" O.B. replied as he took off his pack and boots and dropped them into the pickup bed. "I've had to tackle underbrush up to my armpits and fight my way through hordes of horse flies. I've rolled in the dirt to make a phony campsite and my feet are killing me!"

With one whiff of Old Bowels' sweaty, dirty body, Mick exclaimed, "Ooo-wee! You're really ripe! May I suggest you ride in the pickup bed with Buddy?"

Dave drew his feet back inside the window, shifted into a sitting position, looked at O.B., turned to Mick and drawled, "You know, that's not really being fair to your dog."

"You're right," Mick answered. "Let's let Buddy ride up here with us."

❧ CHAPTER 14 ❧

CYRIL RICHMOND WAS working late. He had month-end reports to do, and he was in a quandary as to what to say about a lost five-year old at Big Lake. His Hasty Search and Rescue team was still on the job but had turned up no trace of the child. He had talked to the anxious father, but other than the possibility his estranged wife abducted his daughter, he could offer little assistance besides giving a sketchy description of the clothes she had been wearing. The father had told his daughter to stay by the tent while he used the campground outhouse. When he emerged from the stinky, fly infested toilet and walked the short, dusty distance to his camp, the little girl was gone.

Although Big Lake was in Linn County, Richmond, in Jefferson County, was the closest authority and he didn't hesitate to act. He had immediately deployed the Hasty Search and Rescue Team and drove to Big Lake. He deployed the searchers to begin covering the forest in a grid pattern. Within an hour, Linn County Sheriff's Search and Rescue Team had arrived and had a boat and divers in the lake. By the time the search operations were underway, Richmond had put out an Amber Alert on the child as well as an all-points bulletin on the mother's car. He was hesitant to call this strictly a child custody dispute until the mother could be located. Meanwhile, there was a good chance the little girl was out in the woods. Now, the sun had just set, and the air was getting cooler. He pictured the child huddled in a hiding place, as lost children often will do, feeling the cold of yet another hungry night bearing down upon her small shoulders.

While Richmond gazed out the window of his small corner office in the

Camp Sherman Fire Station, he saw Old Bowels drive up in his rattle-trap Ford pickup. He watched as the elderly man wearily got out of his truck and walk, with a slight limp, into the Fire Station.

"Hey, O.B., what's going on?" Richmond stood up to greet this long-time and faithful employee of the Sisters-Camp Sherman Fire Department who now, in his retirement, volunteered to keep the fire engine in top shape.

"Cyril! I'm glad I caught you. When is that tracker coming to look for Annie Dozler?"

"Tomorrow morning. She comes from Silverton and says she'll be here as soon as she can get away."

"Oh, good. Would you like me to go along... another set of eyes? I know the regular team is still looking for that little girl at Big Lake."

"Sure, glad to have your help!" Richmond was surprised Old Bowels would be willing to do this, as tired as he looked. "Are you sure you're up to it? You look a might tuckered to me." The deputy searched the old man's grizzled face for whatever it was O.B. wasn't telling him.

"Oh, sure, I'm fine!" Old Bowels answered, clearly not fine. "It's just been a hard day chopping wood, but I'll be right as rain tomorrow!"

"Okay. Dr. Odom said she would call me when she got to Detroit Lake. That's about an hour away from the summit. I'll give you a call when she does, okay?"

"Okay, Cyril. See you in the morning!" Old Bowels, still sporting the limp, returned to his truck.

"Chopping wood, my ass," Richmond muttered and wondered what the old duffer had been up to.

WHEN RICHMOND HAD called Dr. Mazie Odom about Annie Dozler, he knew Odom wouldn't hesitate to be there as soon as she could. Dr. Odom was a psychologist by profession and, by passion, a dedicated expert on tracking missing people. She met Richmond and Old Bowels at the last place Dozler was suspected to be, the Santiam Pass Ski Lodge.

Odom was a solid, athletically build woman in her mid-fifties with a bushy head of silver-streaked black hair. As she swung out of her SUV, Old Bowels noticed she had a no-nonsense way about her and the keen, riveting eyes of a hawk. He hoped his attempt on the previous day to distort Dozler's trail was going to be effective against this undoubtedly relentless tracker.

Introductions were made and Richmond took Odom to the back side of the lodge where it had been determined that Annie Dozler had entered and exited the building. They then went inside and down into the basement with its decades of spider webs and packrat nests to see where Annie had sheltered. Back outside, they examined the footprints which had been roped off by police crime scene tape. The prints clearly headed east toward the Pacific Crest Trail.

The team then went back to their trucks and donned hiking boots and back packs. At this point, Odom and Richmond had no idea how long they would be on the mountain, so they had all prepared to spend at least one night. Old Bowels knew it had taken him one day to make the phony trail, but, of course, he kept this knowledge to himself. His feet still were sore from the painful episode of yesterday, and now he was grateful to be pulling on his own boots.

Once they had followed Dozler's path to the Pacific Crest Trail, Mazie Odom stopped and looked around her. She slowly turned in a 360-degree circle, her eyes taking in the topography and the type and growth pattern of the trees and shrubs through which they would be searching.

"She could be anywhere within 5,000 square miles of this spot, "Odom explained somberly. "We must narrow that area down to the most logical places. We can assume she was trying to get away from the lodge because you, Cyril, had discovered where she had hidden in the basement. These tracks we're following come to the Pacific Crest Trail and stop, as though she wondered which way to go." Odom looked closely at the ground. Dozler's footprints had been easy to distinguish up to this point, but then became confused, possibly because a frantic Annie Dozler had turned this way and that, looking at all possibilities and smearing each previous footprint.

"Okay, she went this way, and she stopped running," Odom declared, looking toward the east. "She must have felt she was out of sight of the lodge and that no one was following her. She didn't follow the Pacific Crest Trail but headed down the Old Summit Trail. See here?" Odom pointed to a tiny scrap of thread tangled onto a broken huckleberry branch. "Yeah, she went this way."

As Odom led the way down the Old Summit Trail, Richmond walked behind her, and Old Bowels brought up the rear. Old Bowels felt proud that Odom had found the scrap of thread and didn't suspect that it was left by anyone other than Annie Dozler.

Odom walked along, studying the ground as well as the shrubbery and rocks along the way. A rock kicked loose from its depression in the dusty trail and scuff marks on fallen logs told Odom a story that no one else walking this path would ever notice. "She was still in a hurry, her prints show where she slid down the steeper parts, not being careful where she put her feet."

Old Bowels remembers sliding on purpose down the steepest parts of the trail, getting his fanny filthy in the process.

I imagine she felt desperate," Richmond suggested.

"Right," Odom answered. "She may have been hungry with no idea how or when she was going to eat or shelter for the night. A person who is running away leaves a different track than someone who is lost. You can almost feel the desperation in both, but a lost person will stop and look around a lot. Particularly at this point of the trail, Annie doesn't stop. It's as though she's on a mission. By now, she knows where she's going.

They reached another fork in the trail at Square Lake, where the Old Summit Trail meets the Round Lake Trail coming uphill from the east. Old Bowels started to feel the nerves sneak up his back, leaving the shirt underneath his pack wet with sweat. This is where it was imperative they continue downhill toward Round Lake. Their entire scheme could be lost if Mazie Odom detected that Annie Dozler really had gone straight ahead on the Old Summit Trail.

Odom stopped at the junction and again looked all around her. Richmond and Old Bowels waited until Odom felt she knew which way they had to go. Much to Old Bowel's horror, she continued straight on the Old Summit Trail.

"Wait, Mazie!" Old Bowels hollered, "I think I see where she went this way," Old Bowels pointed east toward the north side of Square Lake. "Her prints go down this way and there's a thread of material on that Manzanita she must have worked her way through." O.B. was in full panic mode now as Odom continued on the Old Summit Trail and said over her shoulder, "In a minute, O.B., I have a funny feeling about this."

Old Bowels thought, *Funny feeling... it's just gas! It'll pass! Trust me! I'm an expert!"*

"Something's not right here, Cyril," Odom said to Richmond.

"Oh? What do you think?"

"This surface looks different. Look, where the dust is piled up on the edges of these rocks, almost like the trail has been swept."

Old Bowels was sweating nickels now. *That woman's good! I took such pains NOT to make it look that way!*

"Let's go a bit further," Odom said to Richmond, clearly dismissing Old Bowels' concerns that they were going the wrong way. "I'm just going to march down this way for a bit to see what we can find."

March they did, with Old Bowels scrambling to keep up, wishing, wishing, wishing they didn't find a trace of Annie Dozler. They kept going until Odom stopped dead in her tracks!

"Oh, crap!" she declared. "Look at this!"

Thought Old Bowels, *What on earth did she find that I didn't?*

Both men peered around Odom to see what she was pointing at... the hoof prints of horses. The prints filled up the trail and were augmented by a couple large piles of horse poop.

"They came up from Jack Lake, I'll bet," Odom declared, peering down the trail to the north. "Why they turned around here," pointing to the trampling of the underbrush, "is anybody's guess. Now wait, what the heck is this? A goat? See these?" she exclaimed and pointed at cove-shaped prints in the dust. "Are these goat prints or sheep? They're sheep! A goat's prints are more kidney shaped. What the hell are they doing with these horse hoof prints? Cyril, you don't have Big-Horned sheep up here, do you?"

"No. It would be an abnormality," the deputy answered. "They're mainly in the Wallowas. However, I never say never. With all the fires and drought, animals could be driven anywhere. There is always the chance somebody turned loose an animal from a private collection."

"These prints are too small for wild sheep," Odom decided, squinting for a closer look. "It must be a domesticated critter. This is just plain goofy! Nobody brings a sheep up here, nobody!"

Old Bowels turned his back and had to fight the urge to whistle and look skyward, knowing full well who would bring a sheep on this rugged mountain trail. Specifically, Old Bowels knew the sheep was not brought here, but it came of its own free will, dutifully following the two horses just like it had for years. He speculated that early that same morning, Cal and Yank-um had ridden their horses over Annie's tracks from Jack Lake and turned around when they realized Old Bowels had worked on the trail from its other end at Square Lake.

"Maybe the animal got loose, and the horsemen came to look for it," Old Bowels offered hopefully. He thought that was a pretty clever answer for being just off the cuff.

Dr. Mazie Odom huffed as though she thought the idea absurd and then stomped off in the opposite direction. "Well, they sure made a mess of the trail. Come on, you guys, let's go back to Round Lake."

Old Bowels tried to share a glance with Richmond, but the deputy was all business as he followed Odom down the trail. Why didn't Richmond mention the source of the horse and sheep prints? Surely, he knew about Cal and Yank-um, their horses and Sally the sheep. They were all over the Metolius Basin, for crying out loud? Could it be Cyril Richmond was aware of the Geezers ploy to protect Annie Dozler and was going along with it? Nah! Not a chance.

CHAPTER 15

OLD BOWELS POINTED out to Cyril Richmond and Mazie Odom a spot next to Round Lake where it appeared Annie Dozler had spent the night. He was learning to be an actor and approached the site as though he had just stumbled upon it. With a cool breeze coming off the lake, Odom went over the area with enough scrutiny to make Sherlock Holmes proud. Old Bowels thought all she needed to complete the scene was a Deerstalker hat and a magnifying glass. Much to O.B.'s relief, she seemed convinced, due to the footprints they found, including the ones where Old Bowels had squatted like a woman to pee, the camp had indeed been Dozler's. The trio then continued down the mountain following the boot prints O. B. had carefully left in the soil.

Finally, they reached the bottom of the trail and stepped out onto the edge of Highway 20. Odom again stopped and looked all around her. She looked up and down the shoulder of the road, looking for more tracks or some other sign that Dozler had passed this way. Dr. Odom was well known throughout the West Coast for her dogged success in finding runaways and lost people, so Richmond and Old Bowels just waited for her to complete her process. About the time Old Bowels was relieved that it appeared he had sufficiently bamboozled this tracking wizard, she darted across the highway to look for tracks on the road into Suttle Lake.

Oh crap! Here we go again! Would Odom see enough of O.B.'s tracks to follow them to the Suttle Lake campground? He had tried to stay on the blacktop roadway, but did he step off and not be aware? He had been so dang tired, and his feet had hurt so badly that anything could have happened! Once he had reached Mick's truck, he had immediately tugged off Annie's boots and put on his own shoes. In doing so, he would have left telltale prints. If Odom saw them, she would figure out the ruse in a heartbeat!

After thoroughly scouring the dusty edges of the roadway, Mazie Odom finally stopped in front of the Suttle Lake Lodge, turned to Richmond and said, "Cyril, has Annie Dozler been sighted anywhere other than that old ski lodge on the summit?

"No. We've posted bulletins, as you know, and the Camp Sherman folks know to look for her, but nobody has come forward with any info."

"Well then, I think your girl was picked up by someone out there on the highway. She's probably miles away by now. And, you know what? If she's running from an abusive husband, I wish her all the luck in the world. I hope that one day, she'll find happiness somewhere. That's the least life can do for her after what she's been through."

"I agree, Mazie," Richmond said somberly. "Thank you for your hard work and for coming all this way to help. We can close this chapter on Annie Dozler." Richmond looked around the deserted parking lot as he said, "Now, we need to figure out how to get back to the summit where we left our rigs. I can see if Greg can come and get us."

Old Bowels was thoroughly relieved that Odom had finally given up. Before Richmond could call Deputy Leese, he pulled out his phone and suggested brightly, "I can call a Geezer!"

"A what?" Odom looked at Old Bowels as though he had turned into a fish.

WHEN A GEEZER calls for assistance, one never knows who will show up. A Bentley Mulsanne silently flowed along the short, curvy drive into Suttle Lake and ghosted to a stop in front of the elegantly refurbished Suttle Lake Lodge.

Oliver, in his strange stick-like manner, got out of the car and shook hands with O.B. and Richmond. Richmond then introduced Oliver to Odom, who, since her first sight of the car, had her mouth hanging open.

She prudently remembered to close it and she smiled at this tall, peculiar man who was all elbows and knees.

In full chauffeur mode, Oliver opened the passenger side door of the Bentley and said with a small bow, "Please take a seat, Dr. Odom."

Simpering like a teenager on her first date, Odom obeyed. She took in the luxurious appointments of the $300,000 automobile with astonished wonder.

Richmond and Old Bowels piled into the back. O.B. turned to Richmond and said, "Fricking back seat is the size of a studio apartment."

"Or larger."

"Could be why T.J. is always so jolly."

Once Oliver pulled onto the highway, the 505 horsepower, twin-turbocharged 6.8-liter V-8 went into action. With a smooth eight-speed automatic transmission, the acceleration of the Bentley felt as one would imagine Apollo astronauts might have experienced.

For the passengers, the trip to the summit was far too short. Oliver pulled off the highway and into the Santiam Ski Lodge's parking lot. The lot was full of volunteers working on the restoration of the building.

When Richmond exited the car, Hadley Taylor broke away from a group of workers. His eyes took in the Bentley and said, "Nice wheels, Deputy! Nothing like arriving in style."

"Hi, Hadley," Richmond replied with a grin. "Like they say, it's who you know."

"Any leads on who was staying in our basement?"

"No. We followed the footprints down the mountain to the highway at Suttle Lake. We suspect the person was then picked up by someone. At any rate, they're gone."

"Okay, so we can disregard the crime scene tape?"

"Yes. I'll gather it up in a sec."

Oliver and Old Bowels said their goodbyes to Richmond and Odom.

The Bentley, now with Old Bowels in the passenger seat, pulled away and disappeared in a cloud of its own dust.

Mazie Odom watched the big car leave and said, "You have the most interesting people in your neck of the woods, Cyril."

"Don't I know it."

Mazie Odom climbed into her dusty SUV and said to Richmond, "Give me a call if you think I can help there at Big Lake. I'll turn around and come back. It sounds, however, that you have a shitload of searchers working that case."

"Will do, Mazie, and thanks again for coming."

After removing the crime scene tape from the rear of the old lodge, Richmond drove into Big Lake to check on the search for the missing child. He met Deschutes County Deputy Greg Leese as Leese was leaving the campground area. The two deputies stopped their patrol rigs with the drivers' sides facing each other. The dust from both vehicles encircled them.

Leese reported the child had been picked up by her non-custodial mother. The all-points bulletin found its way to a California State Trooper who pulled the mother over near Eureka on Highway 101.

"Sneaking along the coast," Richmond speculated.

"Or so she thought."

"The little girl, is she okay?" Richmond's thoughts went to his own kids.

"Physically, probably not emotionally. You can't really tell at that age. I'm sure she's terribly confused by it all."

"Geez! What a cruel and selfish thing to do to a kid."

"Yeah, I know. A parent using their child as a pawn in a war. I'll never understand people who do that."

"Me neither, Greg. Me neither."

ON THEIR DRIVE back to Camp Sherman, Oliver updated Old Bowels on why none of the other Geezers had been available to pick up the group at Suttle Lake. Aunt Phil had driven Annie to visit Beth, leaving Conrad with no wheels. Mick's truck couldn't carry four people unless someone piled into the pickup bed. They knew Richmond, being a lawman, would have a mental hernia over that. Dave's Prius, according to Dave, was on a hopeless book selling venture into the Willamette Valley. Arthur was in Bend buying more huckleberry plants to add to Beth's garden.

"The only Geezers we couldn't find were Cal Wiggens and Yank-um."

"I know where they were!" Old Bowels replied with a grin.

"Oh, yeah?"

"They were up on the mountain, obliterating Annie's tracks with their horses and the sheep. Sally's tracks really threw that tracker lady for a loop. A sheep was the last thing she'd expect up there."

"That's hilarious!" Oliver said with a grin then added, "T.J. didn't come with me to pick you up, obviously, because we'd never fit all of us in here."

"Has he always been so big, Oliver? I hope you don't mind me asking."

"No, of course I don't mind. He has been overweight ever since I've known him." Oliver was quiet for a moment. "You know, everyone has a response to stress, O.B. People smoke, drink, chew their fingernails, hoard stuff, take drugs, get temperamental, spend too much money, gamble, you name it. None of those things is as obvious as someone who overeats. Then that person becomes fodder for criticism from all sides, even from those who do all those other things as a response to stress. It seems terribly unfair to me. T.J. just laughs it off.

"Most of those other things," Oliver continued, "go unrecognized until they affect relationships or finances or a person's ability to work, particularly if they do drugs or drink."

"I'll bet you see a lot of those folks in the homeless shelter in Seattle."

"Boy, you bet! You know who else we see a lot of at that shelter, O.B., a lot of Annie Dozlers."

"Running from abuse?"

"Yes, and there is little law enforcement can do for them. Restraining orders and no contact orders are frequently violated. There are many, like Annie, who feel a restraining order is going to make their abuser angrier and more dangerous, so they just run. We try to hook them up with social services that can find them temporary housing and work, but they are always scared, O.B... always."

"Gee."

Oliver looked over at Old Bowels and said, "Yeah, you said it. Gee."

CHAPTER 16

AUNT PHIL WAS behind the wheel of the Volvo. She and Annie were on their way to Beth and Arthur's cabin. "You know, Annie, you're brave riding with me. Conrad would tell you I'm the worst driver ever! He said I need an ambulance following me everywhere. I say, that plus one of those pickups with a flatbed trailer which hauls porta-potties would also be nice... oh yeah, and a taco-truck. Anyway, that's why he bought this rig for me. It sees more than I do and helps keep us on the road. Before we were married, I drove an ancient Suzuki Samurai. I loved it! When I worked, the Suzuki was great because I could zip around in Seattle traffic and squeeze it into parking spots. I was always in a hurry and never stopped being in a hurry after I retired. I drove that car like the devil was after me," she paused and added with a grin, "maybe it was!

"My driving scared the crap out of Conrad one day we drove from Portland to Camp Sherman. Coming down the mountain from the Santiam Pass, I was having a ball steering that little car through those turns and Conrad was bat-shit crazy hanging onto the dashboard. He admonished me up one side and down the other about my driving. Then, he asked me to marry him. I couldn't believe it!"

"That's hilarious!"

"He said because of the way I drive; we may not live long enough for him to ask me later."

"Your driving doesn't scare me, Phyllis."

"But we're not there yet, Annie!"

Both dust and laughter rolled away from the Volvo as it headed into the woods on Green Ridge.

Once at Beth and Arthur's cabin, Aunt Phil parked next to Mick's pickup. The women then found Beth, Sophie, and to their pleasant surprise, Emily Martin. They were seated on the cabin's expansive front porch. Sprawled in the cool grass in front of the porch were the dogs Max and Buddy.

"Hi girls!" Aunt Phil exclaimed as she clomped onto the porch. "Emily, how nice to see you! Annie told us how you've helped her since that first night she came to Camp Sherman."

As the women hugged each other in greeting, Annie reflected on when she first met the Geezers. Initially, hugging seemed peculiar to her. A child who is never hugged doesn't know what hugging is about. Annie's mother was so lost in her own addictions that showing affection to her children was never a concept for which she had any inclination.

With the help of these women, Annie was getting used to hugging as a joyful way to express affection without transmitting anything sexual. As a woman who had been sexually abused from the time she was barely older than a toddler, hugging to display affection was an aspect of closeness that was new and refreshing to her. These women were teaching her oh, so much! This is what she would have wanted for her own mother. If only...

Beth interrupted Annie's thoughts with a request they all go inside for lunch. The women trooped inside the cabin along with the addition of Max and Buddy. The two canines had happily bounded onto the porch and followed the women inside. Beth quickly shooed the dogs out.

"You two go outside and help Mick and Arthur plant huckleberries. Go on now, git!"

The dogs charged back outside just as eagerly as they had come in. In a few minutes, however, they were back, coming in the doggy door from the garage, through the kitchen, and bursting into the great room with all the happy-faced, tail wagging enthusiasm their canine hearts could muster.

Beth was on her feet. "Okay, enough! Oh, look at your muddy feet! Out, dogs, out! Now!" she escorted the two villains back through the kitchen and the garage. She accompanied them outside where she said to Arthur who was digging holes in the garden alongside Mick, "Arthur! Could you keep these marauders outside, please?"

Arthur leaned on his shovel and hollered to his dog, "Max! Come 'ere!" Max, with Buddy galloping behind him, tore out to the garden where they were greeted with mild scolding accompanied by ear rubs. Both men told their dogs to lie down and stay while the remainder of the huckleberries were planted.

Muttering at the wet and muddy tracks the two dogs had left across her kitchen floor, Beth apologized for the disruption as the other women were smiling and laughing at the doggy high jinks. Beth, with Sophie's help, loaded the table with a huge bowl of chicken salad, hot sourdough rolls, and iced tea.

The women tucked into their lunch while they discussed what was the best strategy for Annie now that the tracker had been thwarted. It wouldn't be long before Luke Dozler's jail time would be concluded, and it was most probable that he would come looking for her.

"Adam told me he'd help me file for a divorce from Luke," Annie explained. "That was nice of him to offer but Luke would be able to find me if I did that."

"Not necessarily," Beth commented, "because we can hide you, Annie. That won't be a problem." The other women nodded their approval.

"I seriously doubt he'll even recognize you, now that Sophie has done your hair," Emily added encouragingly.

"I can't stay here forever," Annie replied. "Although the thought is most tempting."

"I wish you'd talk to the Sheriff," Emily said. "Gary Larkin is a good man, and he can give you options that we may not have thought of."

"Well..."

"We know you don't trust the law," Sophie commented.

"No, I don't. Besides, Luke said he'd kill me if I talked to them. So did my brothers. They said the law doesn't care about women like me because I'm just trash. They said the police would 'negotiate' protection for me in exchange for sexual favors."

The women were silent for a moment as they exchanged eye contact. Beth said gently, "I'm so sorry, Annie. Most men aren't like that. Trust me."

"They lied to control you," Aunt Phil said. "That's their way. I've had to defend those bastards in court and there is no defense for the way they treat women or anyone else they abuse, either physically, sexually, or emotionally. Some defense attorneys would try to appeal to a jury's sympathies by outlining abuse the offender suffered as a kid or whenever. There is no excuse no matter what shit they suffered. To abuse another person, just like any other crime, is a choice. I'd tell them I'd get the best deal I could for them but that their punishment was a result of their own lousy choices."

"Also, Annie," Sophie added. "You're not trash! You're an intelligent and gutsy woman, but you need to believe in yourself."

"Well..." Annie said slowly, "Okay. I'll think about talking to the cops... er, Sheriff Larkin or Deputy Richmond. "Give me a... a bit of time, please. It's a huge step out of my comfort zone."

"Take all the time you need, Annie," Aunt Phil replied. "You know we're here for you."

Beth then asked, "What would you like to do, Annie, after you're finally free from Luke?"

"I don't know, Beth. Years ago, a middle school teacher told me that if I ever wanted to go anywhere in the world, I needed to understand the English language and speak it correctly. She told me to take all the English literature and grammar classes I could. She told me I needed to sound educated when I talked. I think she was trying to get me to shed the primitive speech accents of my upbringing. So, I read everything I could get my hands on. I'd go out into the woods with a book, find a tree to climb and spend the whole day there. It was an escape for me as well."

"You got some good advice," Aunt Phil said, "from a teacher who cared about you."

"Phyllis," Annie asked, "what made you become a lawyer?"

"Annie, back in my day, in the 1950s and 60s, women were expected to get married, stay home, have babies, raise children. If your family was wealthy enough, you could go to school to become a teacher or a nurse. My dad told me to be a nurse, then I'd know how to take care of all the babies I was supposed to have.

"So I did! I went to nursing school but flunked vomit and bed pans. I became a lawyer instead, not that the experiences I've had were much different. I'd work part-time and go to school or go to school part-time and work full time. It seemed to take forever, and often I wanted to give up, but didn't, and I finally made it. Today, women can be anything they want."

Emily, being a CPA, noted, "It's still can be tough for women because some men have that good old boy thing going. They see women as competition in what they think is a man's world."

Sophie added sagely, "If stupidity was painful, there would be even more equality between men and women and among races as well as cultures. We need to do what we can to make things better for each other, and I'm including all people. Somewhere in the cosmic scheme of things the way we treat each other and the other creatures on earth is some kind of a test."

"If you pass, that's good! If you don't..." Aunt Phil ran her finger across her throat, stuck out her tongue, and crossed her eyes. They all laughed.

The group then talked about the upcoming Renaissance Faire fund raiser. Aunt Phil reported that many Camp Sherman residents had already signed up their booths and folks were getting excited.

Generously buttering another piece of bread, she said, "People were able to navigate the web site, which I find amazing, as hard as it was to get it up and rolling. Let's see, so far there will be a juggler, belly dancers, a blacksmith, a strolling minstrel, several food carts, hair braiding, face painting, I'll have my fortune telling tent, and I'm not sure what Tommy Jax and Oliver have up their sleeves. Everyone knows to be on the lookout for Luke." The women all agreed that was a good idea.

Beth then asked, "Don't Renaissance Faires have jousting, with knights and horses and stuff? What are we going to do about that?"

"Cal Wiggens and Yank-um are working on something, I'm not sure just what," Aunt Phil answered.

"Will Sally the sheep play a part?" Emily asked and giggled, remembering how the sheep followed the horses everywhere.

The women all looked around the table for an answer. Annie offered with a chuckle, "Maybe she'll be the squire."

"I cannot imagine Cal and Yank-um charging at each other on horseback," Aunt Phil exclaimed. "If so, we all better have 911 on speed dial."

"I guess we'll just have to trust them to come up with something," Beth said.

Beth had no more than gotten those words out of her mouth when in through the doggy door, again charged the two dogs. They were all wags and huffs and then, as quickly as they had appeared, galloped back outside.

Beth, in a moment of uncharacteristic exasperation said, "What the hell..."

"Ack! What was that?" Aunt Phil suddenly stood and motioned towards the great room.

"What?" The other women chorused as their eyes followed to where Aunt Phil was pointing.

"That! Right there! Now it ran under the couch... or hopped under the couch. Oh, there's another!"

The women all looked wide-eyed at one another and again said, "Like a frog?"

"Yes, it looked like a frog, a little bitty one." Aunt Phil was now on her elbows and knees, her fanny in the air, as she peered under the couch.

"Those dogs! I knew they had to be up to something!" Beth had grabbed a flashlight and scurried beside Aunt Phil to also look under the couch. "Oh my!" was about all she could say when she spied several sets of buggy frog eyes reflecting her light.

Years ago, Arthur had a well drilled at the lowest spot in the garden. The well tapped into one of the many springs that were found on the east side of Green Ridge. Because of snowmelt, the well usually overflowed in the early part of summer, creating a boggy area popular with mosquitos and frogs. It also was a favorite with dogs who like to get wet and muddy. Max and Buddy went for this bog like flies to horse poop.

The frogs were Cascade frogs, *Rana cascadea*, less than two inches in length, and were normally found in wet soggy meadows and bogs on the eastern slopes of the Cascade Mountains of Oregon and Washington. These hopping little creatures proved to be an additional attraction for the canines. For some peculiar reason known only to the dogs, they carried the frogs in their soft retriever mouths to dump them in the cabin's great room.

By this time, Arthur and Mick, still planting huckleberries, had noticed the dogs were gone again. The two men hurried back into the cabin to find all the women on their hands and knees chasing frogs around the great room. The dogs were also into the act, assuming this was a fun new game.

Booger the cat didn't think so. With the tip of his furry tail twitching, he stayed planted on his rafter over the great room, watching with disdain the pandemonium developing below.

Adding Mick and Arthur into the mix made for seven humans on all fours scrambling around the floor. The great room took on the look of a super-sized game of Twister with the added obstruction of two very happy dogs. Occasionally someone would capture a frog and with a whoop of success, trot the little beast outside for release into the woods.

LATE THAT EVENING, Beth and Arthur were snuggled under the eiderdown comforter in their loft bedroom. Exhausted from a day of play with Buddy, Max was sprawled on the floor at Arthur's side of the bed. Booger was on his back between the two humans and softly snoring.

Beth said, "What if we didn't find all the frogs?"

Arthur, used to his wife's worrying after going to bed said sleepily, "We'll hear from it sooner or later."

"I wouldn't want Booger to catch it," Beth continued, "that would be awful for the poor little thing...the frog, I mean."

"Booger hasn't caught as much as a house fly since the vet handed him to me years ago and said, 'Here, you need this cat!' Besides, I'm sure we found all the frogs. There were certainly enough of us looking."

Both Beth and Arthur dozed off but were soon awakened by a very audible "Croak!" coming from downstairs.

Arthur didn't hear so much as a stir from his dog, so he opened one eye to see that Booger was still fast asleep. From the depths of the comforter, Arthur smiled, closed the eye, and commented, "Booger, frog killer, hard at work."

CHAPTER 17

"HEY, JER! GUESS who's in the slammer in Deschutes County?" Sergeant Trevor Kowalski of the Portland Police Bureau, the biggest policeman Aunt Phil claimed she had ever seen, looked over the wall of his cubicle to where his partner, Corporal Jerry Banning, was also busy on his computer. Their office was in the Justice Center in downtown Portland. The two men were working yet another homicide, one of a multitude of gun-related deaths that currently plagued Oregon's largest city.

"Let me guess," the long-legged and lanky Banning drawled, his red hair brightening up the dark corner of the office. "Uh, Phyllis Wardwell?"

"Ha! Only because she hasn't gotten caught... yet! Would you believe it's Lug Nuts?"

"Dozler?"

"The very same."

"What's he done?"

"Solicited sex from two minors, ages 14 and 15."

"Shit!"

"Likes 'em young, he does."

"He keeps showing up, doesn't he?"

"Like he's attention deprived. We have him listed as a witness to a mess of incidents," the big Sergeant scanned his computer screen. "Let's see... two shootings over drug deals, three street racings, and two bar fights, one in which knives were involved. The other fight was with guns."

Banning leaned back in his chair, "It seems odd he lives over by Madras but is in Portland so often… and at crime scenes! He must be doing something here other than spectating."

"You think? Oh, whoa! Here's another filing, Jer! Dang, we've been so busy with guys shooting one another, I haven't kept up with this stuff. There's a filing out of Jefferson County. Dozler reported his wife missing."

Kowalski and Banning shared an alarmed look. Banning stood and said, "Let's see what Avery has to say about this."

Banning and Kowalski found their Lieutenant buried behind a pile of papers and files. Shawn Avery was not a manager who was so good at getting other people to do things that he never had anything to do. He took on the responsibility of being where the buck stopped and meticulously poured over each case file until he was sure it was complete. He fully understood it was often the details that broke a case and sent a killer to prison.

As disheveled as his desk, Avery, with his tie askew, the top button of his shirt undone, wrinkled sleeves rolled up, and the few hairs he had left on his head wind blown, looked like he'd just crawled out of a laundry hamper. He looked up as Banning and Kowalski burst into his office and reading their eyes asked, "What now?"

"Lug Nuts."

The Portland Police Bureau referred to Luke Dozler as "Lug Nuts" because each time he had been interviewed as a witness, he was driving his Dodge Ram 3500 pickup with dual back wheels, hence multitudes of lug nuts. The police kept lists of witnesses of crimes and periodically reviewed the lists looking for consistencies among the individuals. Someone who continued to show up as a witness to crime scenes might know more than they are telling and might even be involved in the crime or crimes of a certain type. The fact that Dozler, from Central Oregon, appeared consistently in Portland, put him on Kowalski's radar.

"What's he done now?"

When Banning told Avery what they had learned about Luke Dozler, the lieutenant picked up his phone and said, "Let's see what Cyril has to say about this."

Richmond was in his office when he took Avery's call. He had been waiting for Sheriff Larkin who was coming to Camp Sherman for lunch. The Sheriff loved the deli sandwiches and potato salad at the Camp Sherman Store. Richmond also knew his boss would most likely visit Emily Martin. When the Sheriff's reason for visiting Richmond was rather non-consequential, like having lunch, Richmond knew the major reason Larkin would come to this most remote outpost of all of Jefferson County was to see Emily.

Richmond thought it was terrific. Larkin had been a single dad for nearly twenty years, raising his two boys when the family was abandoned by Larkin's wife who decided she preferred joining a religious sect over being a wife and mother.

Now a doting grampa, Larkin had found another sunny spot in his life in his friendship with Emily. Just how much of a friendship the two shared was anybody's guess, and did folks love to guess! Larkin was a popular man, and the Camp Sherman community was thrilled he had developed a relationship with Emily, their newest resident.

Just as Shawn Avery's call came into Richmond's office, Larkin pulled up in his county issued SUV. Carrying a file folder under his arm, he swung out of his rig and headed for the fire station.

"Lieutenant!" Richmond bellowed. "How nice to hear from you! When are you and those two henchmen of yours going to come over and do a little fly fishing?"

"I don't think we'd ever get Trevor into that cold river again, Cyril, and he's too big to throw in," Avery laughed. "Actually, we're doing some fishing of another nature."

"Oh yeah? Who are you looking for?"

"Dude by the name of Luke Dozler. You have a missing person on his wife, and he's currently incarcerated in Deschutes County for solicitation of underage sex."

"Yup! Hang on a sec, Shawn. Sheriff Larkin just came in and he'll be interested in this conversation. I'm putting you on speaker."

Larkin had entered Richmond's small office and had pulled up a chair. Cyril had written "Lt. Shawn Avery, Portland PD" on a sticky note and showed it to his sheriff.

As soon as Richmond put his phone on speaker mode, Avery said, "Good morning, Sheriff Larkin! How are you today?"

"I'm doing well, Lieutenant! How are things over there in Portland Land?"

"As you know, people are shooting each other. It's the mode du jour of expressing one's dissatisfaction with whatever it is that's pissing them off. But that's not the reason I'm calling. We have a bit of an interest in Luke Dozler."

Larkin's eyebrows shot to his hairline as he looked at Richmond. The Sheriff then moved to the edge of his chair. 'Oh? How so?" Avery explained how Dozler had repeatedly shown up on their list of witnesses when they noticed, not only the arrest involving underaged girls, but also the missing spouse report.

Larkin said, "Well, let me recap what Jefferson County has on Dozler. He came to us about five weeks ago to file a missing person report on his wife. He didn't have a photo of her, which we thought rather odd, but we posted bulletins with her description in Jefferson, Deschutes, Wasco, Crook, and Wheeler Counties and sent out other notices state-wide. Dozler wouldn't come right out and admit to beating his wife, but we have had reports from the local hospital as well as over in Baker City where they once lived that she'd been treated for injuries consistent with having taken a beating. Investigating officers could never get her to file a complaint against her husband. She would offer other reasons for her injuries like falling from a ladder or a stool, tripping, you know the script. Dozler said that when he and his wife would argue, she would often run off and be gone for several days. He suspected her of hiding in the woods but, this time, she had been gone longer than usual.

"At first, we looked at it as a ruse to cover a homicide. However, there was a couple traveling in a motor home who saw one of the bulletins at a campground near the Crooked River Golf Course. They reported giving a ride to a woman who fit Annie Dozler's description. She had been walking from Culver and going west toward Green Ridge. She was wearing a backpack. She told them she was employed at the golf course and that her car had broken down. Luke Dozler later told us his wife didn't have a car. The campers dropped her off at the golf course. We investigated with the pro shop manager who said they didn't have Annie Dozler in their employ nor anyone who fit her description. Since she appeared to be heading west, Cyril notified the Camp Sherman people to be on the lookout for her.

"Next, she was suspected of sheltering inside the old Santiam Pass Ski Lodge. It's being restored and I guess some workmen spooked her. She ran off leaving a sleeping bag which Luke Dozler claimed could have been his. She also left a strand of hair which was the right color and length and boot prints which were her size. Richmond arranged for a tracker who followed her trail from the ski lodge down the mountain where they lost the trail at the highway. We suspect, as did the tracker, that she was picked up by someone on the highway near the turnoff into Suttle Lake Lodge. That determination was made just yesterday.

"As for Dozler's current incarceration at the Deschutes County jail, City of Bend police were informed of Dozler picking up two young girls outside a tavern on Highway 97. The informers had cell phone pictures and videos of him helping the two girls, 14 and 15 years old, into his car and also of him paying off a pimp. The informers followed Dozler to a house in Bend where Bend Police jumped him before he could get the girls inside. The house, by the way, is registered to his father. A search warrant revealed nothing suspicious other than the Bend house didn't look like it was really lived in and was used primarily to entertain sexual partners. The two girls were turned over to Children's Services. The girls spilled details about the pimp who drove them to meet Dozler. Bend Vice is dealing with him."

"Wow!" Avery exclaimed, "You have a memory like a vault, Sheriff!"

Larkin laughed and said, "I also have Luke Dozler's file right in front of me. Cyril and I were going to review it over lunch." With a wink towards his deputy, the Sheriff added, "Cyril's going to buy me one of the Camp Sherman Store's colossal deli sandwiches."

Avery, who had put his phone on speaker mode, said, "Sergeant Kowalski heard all of that. He remembers those sandwiches. As a matter of fact, he is salivating all over my desk!"

THE CAMP SHERMAN STORE was the center of activity in the community. In the busy summer months business ebbed and flowed through the parking lot and over the little bridge across the Metolius River.

On this day, the store's huge rough-hewn wooden deck teamed with activity. There was a rack of Camp Sherman tee-shirts, cards, and stacks of books written by Dave's wife. Folks were feasting on lunches purchased inside the store and were seated at picnic tables on the deck as well as scattered about the surrounding lawn. Relief from the hot, mid-July sun was provided by a grove of mixed conifers. It was a happy hubbub of campers, hikers, locals, fishermen and tourists with kids and dogs everywhere. Larkin and Richmond shared a small, pine-hewn table and bench positioned on the deck in the shade of an enormous fir tree.

"What do you think of what Avery said about Luke Dozler showing up at crime scenes in Portland?" Larkin said as he turned his ham sandwich this way and that, looking for the best place to take a bite without the whole sandwich exploding.

Richmond tucked into his own sandwich which swelled with enough cheese to put him in the hospital. He then said around the bite, "I think there is a lot more to Luke Dozler than we originally thought. It makes me want to rethink our conclusion that Annie Dozler has fled the area."

"Back to the homicide aspect?" Larkin bit into a pickle and looked at his deputy.

"It's as good as any."

"The Geezers have had no success in locating her?"

"They haven't said a word. Old Bowels went with Dr. Odom and me when we followed Annie's tracks down the mountain to the highway. We all felt positive about our conclusion, but now I'm not so sure." Both lawmen chewed on their sandwiches as well on the possibility that Annie Dozler had been murdered.

"So why do you think Luke goes to Portland and shows up at crime scenes?" Richmond asked.

"It could be all sorts of things. He's a weirdo, that's for sure," Larkin remembered nearly throwing Luke out of his office over Dozler's sexual hit on Officer Harvey. "He also could know some of those guys involved in the crimes and manages to appear all innocent when the cops show up. Plus, he could be doing business with them."

"As in..."

"Drugs. Guns. Sex trafficking. Any or all of the above. He could be delivering illegal marijuana to Portland. Lord knows we have enough illicit growers out there in the desert."

"Do we have enough for a warrant to search his house in Culver? Now would be a good time to do it with him incarcerated."

"No, 'fraid not. This is all speculation and hearsay... so far."

Richmond finished off his sandwich and looked at his Sheriff, "You didn't tell Avery who the informers were who followed Dozler and took pictures of him picking up those girls."

"No need. It might not make any difference in this case. However, down the road our position could be compromised if it becomes known we're aware those old people have been snooping around. By no means should it ever be construed that we put those oldsters up to any of their shenanigans."

"We'd be screwed if so construed, correct?"

"You said it!"

❧ CHAPTER 18 ❧

SHERIFF GARY LARKIN concluded what little other business he had with Deputy Richmond and then made his way to his SUV. As though the vehicle had a mind of its own, Larkin soon found himself on the dusty road which led over Green Ridge and to Emily Martin's cabin.

Emily's cabin was tucked into a hillside shaded by a thicket of Mountain hemlock, Lodgepole and Ponderosa pines. Sword ferns carpeted the earth and lined the steppingstone pathway to the cabin. As Larkin parked his rig and approached the porch, he saw the white cyclamen he had given her had been planted into one of the two red window boxes gracing both sides of the door. Annual begonias in a kaleidoscope of colors had been added, softening the front of the weathered old structure.

As he stepped onto the porch, Larkin never failed to appreciate the joy Emily Martin had brought to his life. He softly knocked on the door and listened to the sound of her footsteps from inside the cabin. She opened the door and he walked into her arms. With a sweet kiss and enveloping embrace, Gary Larkin travelled into a world that gave him eternal Spring.

"ANNIE WANTS TO talk to you, Gary."

"She what?" Larkin nearly choked on his coffee. They were sitting in Emily's sunny yellow kitchen enjoying Beth's huckleberry pie. With a chuckle, Emily confessed to buying the pie from the Camp Sherman Store.

"How do you...?"

"We've been talking to her," she took a sip of coffee, knowing the sheriff was mentally wrestling with what she had just said.

"We've...?"

"The Geezers and I."

"Ah!" Larkin remembered what Richmond had said about not hearing a word from the Geezers regarding Annie Dozler. "So, they were protecting her from her husband and... us?"

"In a way, Gary, but not in a bad way. She has reasonable fears of the police because of lies Luke and her brothers have told her. She's been isolated from the real world her whole life."

"They were able to keep her from reporting the abuse they were dishing out?"

"Correct."

"Geez!"

"Yeah. It's sad. She was scared to death you'd tell Luke where she was. Trust is very hard for her. I'm no psychologist, so I don't know how to fix it, but we're making inroads by just being..., oh, I don't know, just by being her friends. Does that make sense?"

"Of course. You and the Geezers have earned her trust by being kind. As a result, she's willing to meet with us. That's a huge step in the right direction."

"It was her decision. She asked us to give her some time to think about it and a couple of hours later, she said it was okay! It surprised all of us! We were crawling around on the floor looking for frogs when she announced it."

"Crawling around on the floor looking for... frogs?"

"Yes," Emily giggled. "With the Geezers."

"Tell me why I'm not surprised."

"It was rather fun, actually."

"Sounds like it. I wish I had been in on it," Larkin smiled as he enjoyed the mental images of Geezer antics. He then added, "Would someone be bringing her into Madras?"

"I think she'd be more comfortable meeting with you here, Gary. Will that be a problem?" Emily hoped this wasn't going to be a stumbling block in getting Annie the help she needed.

"No, not at all," Larkin answered. "Do you think she'd mind if I brought a colleague with me? We have a new officer who wants to specialize in abuse cases and victim advocacy. She's smart and a very nice person. She'd appreciate the experience, that is if Annie would be okay with it."

"Golly, I'm not sure she won't be overwhelmed," Emily thought for a moment then said, "Oh, heck, if those Geezers couldn't overwhelm her, it might be okay. Why don't I ask her the next time I see her? She drops in from time to time. I'm sorry, but she doesn't keep a schedule."

"That's okay. She comes in out of the woods?"

"Yes. Plus, she's been staying with a few of the Geezers, off and on."

"I'm glad to hear this," Larkin said as though a weight had been taken off his shoulders.

"Even the part about hiding her from the law?"

Larkin sat back in his chair, briefly looked at the ceiling as if to find the answer there. He said, "Instilling confidence in the police is something we work on all the time, Emily. In some cases, the unconventional works. With victims who are severely traumatized, it comes slowly, if at all. Whether on purpose or not, you and the Geezers stayed on her side until she could see that trusting you was the right thing to do. Now she's willing to make the next step... trusting us, the police. I'm no psychologist either, but that's the way I see it."

Emily looked into the kind eyes of this big lawman and thought she couldn't love him more. Caring was the unsung side of law enforcement, the side which is rarely noticed.

"Also," Larkin went on, "it could take me an hour to get here. Make sure she understands so she doesn't think I'm taking my own sweet time and she's been put on my back burner, so to speak. I will do everything I can to get here promptly when you tell me she's ready to talk to us."

Larkin heaved himself to his feet, saying, "I have to go." He smiled and said, "Thank you for the pie."

They paused on the porch for one more embrace. He loved the sweet smell of her and how perfectly she fit into his arms. He was getting used to Emily's life being part of his own. There would come a time, he was certain, that he wouldn't have to come and go but could think of this old cabin as home.

He again took notice of the flowers cascading out of the window boxes and asked if deer ate her flowers.

"The deer don't seem to like the begonias or the cyclamen, but the squirrels sure do! I whip up a batch of peppermint oil, cayenne pepper, and dried red pepper flakes and sprinkle it in the flower boxes. It seems to work, so far."

"Did you get that recipe from the Geezers?"

"Why of course!" She answered, laughing.

Gary Larkin stepped off the porch, and as he was leaving, looked over his shoulder and said, "Someday, you're going to have to tell me more about those frogs."

LARKIN'S HEAVY FOOTSTEPS in the hallway of the Jefferson County Sheriff's Office telegraphed the boss was back in the building. The Sheriff stepped into his private office and without sitting at the desk, called Sergeant Barclay and said, "Will, can you come to my office? Bring Officer Harvey with you please."

Once seated around the Sheriff's small conference table, Larkin filled the others in on what he had learned about Luke Dozler's wife and what the Portland Police Bureau knew about Luke showing up in Portland at various crime scenes and serving as a witness.

"What do you suppose he's doing over there?" Barclay asked, his distaste for Luke Dozler clearly showing on his face.

"Attention deprived?" Kayla Harvey suggested with a sly smile.

"Could be," Larkin replied. "I also suspect he's running something back and forth."

"Do you think those two girls he picked up were to be part of the cargo?" Barclay asked.

"Anything's possible with this guy. What we know about the underage girls and the beating of his wife may only be the surface of his activities. We don't have enough for a warrant yet, but the good thing is, he's still in jail. We may want to keep an eye on him after he's out."

"What about Annie Dozler? Is she okay?" Kayla Harvey's concern was obvious.

"I don't know yet, Kayla. I haven't seen her, but she has agreed to talk to us. We can thank the Geezers of Camp Sherman for that. They have been, shall we say, keeping an eye on her. When we get the word that she's ready, do you want in on it?"

"You bet!" The light which lit up Officer Kayla Harvey's face held hope for the future of abuse victims in Jefferson County.

Larkin turned to his sergeant, "Will, Officer Harvey and I may have to leave at a moment's notice when we hear Annie Dozler is ready to talk. We can't take a chance that she'll change her mind and disappear again. Be prepared to cover, okay?"

"You got it, Boss."

ANNIE DOZLER WALKED along a forest floor soft with moss and ferns. Sunlight flickered around tree boughs swaying in a warm breeze. Her thoughts traveled from the first time Luke knocked her across the room, "for her own good," to the day Emily Martin and the Geezers took her into their hearts. So much had happened to transpire despair into hope. Would this next step, talking to the police, deliver a final blow to Luke and end her suffering or would she be again fleeing into the forest? She didn't know, but she had to take yet another chance.

Annie stepped out of the woods and onto Emily Martin's front porch. Today was the day.

❧ CHAPTER 19 ❧

THEY MET ON Emily's shaded back porch. It was quiet and private. There was a soft breeze rustling through the trees and, in the distance, a nuthatch called. Emily introduced Annie to Sheriff Larkin and Officer Kayla Harvey. Annie had worn a clean pair of jeans and one of her new short-sleeved blouses. She appeared friendly but cautious as she shook hands. They took seats around a small table and then Emily excused herself to give them privacy. On the table she had left glasses and a pitcher of lemonade to cool off the warm afternoon.

In the cabin's living room, Emily joined Adam Carson who was sprawled on the couch in front of the cold fireplace. As Annie had requested, he had drawn up a Petition for the Dissolution of Marriage terminating her marriage to Luke Dozler. It was waiting in his briefcase on the floor. Annie hadn't signed it yet but wished to talk to the police first. She was afraid of a violent reprisal from Luke.

Adam quietly asked Emily, "What do you think?"

Emily didn't answer but held up both hands with fingers crossed. She picked up a throw pillow from a chair and sat briefly in the chair, holding the pillow to her chest. She then stood, clutching the pillow, and paced the room once. Reversing her direction, she paced the room again, sat down, still holding the pillow, and began to stand when Adam gently placed his hand on her arm.

"It will be okay," he said.

"I feel as though I'm waiting for a baby to be born," she said, her voice barely above a whisper. "Ever since Annie came to me that very first night and told me her story, I have been waiting for this moment. At that time, she refused to talk to Gary, and I wondered how the heck I was going to make it happen."

"And it did happen," Adam said, smiling. "Thanks to you."

"With a lot of help from the Geezers," Emily smiled back. "I don't know what would have become of Annie without them."

Adam sat back into the soft cushions of the couch and nodding toward the back porch said, "Now, she's getting advice from the best people to give it to her. The important thing is what she'll do with it. It's entirely up to her."

ANNIE PICKED UP a cool glass of lemonade and without sipping from it, held it in both hands. With her finger, she wiped at the condensation running down the glass. The drops were like her, running away.

Larkin gently said to her, "Annie, tell us your story."

So, she did. It took a long time. There were no tears, but Annie told her story matter-of-factly from her life in the trailer park with her drug-addled mother and wild brothers, to the abusive relationship with Luke. She told about the time he came home with a gun. That was when she knew she had to leave for good. This was not just Annie's story, but that of countless women who fall victim to abuse.

When she finished, Larkin outlined the process once a victim reports abuse. "You can file a restraining order, but if Luke were to contest it, you'd need to be prepared to present evidence of the abuse or testimony from a witness. Depending on the court's schedule, the hearing may be right away, so it's important to be ready."

"My say-so isn't enough even though his say-so that it didn't happen is enough." It was a statement, not a question.

"No, I'm sorry." The many times in his career he said he was sorry, he meant it to the depth of his soul.

"Too many disgruntled lovers making false accusations, I suppose."

Larkin was somewhat surprised by Annie's calm insight. "Yes. Unfortunately, it happens all the time."

"I understand. So, what should I have done? In Baker City, there was an old lady who lived across the street who reported things she saw and heard to the police, but nothing ever came of it."

Larkin was aware of the influence Dozler's politician father had in Baker City but merely said, "I can't speak for what happened there, Annie. I'm sorry, but I wasn't in on it. However, here in Jefferson County, with a restraining order in place, and the police have evidence like fresh injuries and/or testimony from a witness, the police will seek out the abuser and make an arrest. There will be a hearing and he can get jail time, probation, or a fine, depending on the circumstances. If he violates the order again, he'll get a longer jail sentence."

"But he has to violate the restraining order first."

"Yes. I'm sorry."

"This is why..."

Harvey said, "Annie, a restraining order is better than nothing. It brings attention to your situation and makes a record of it. The District Attorney's office has a victim's advocate who could help you find adequate housing, employment, anything to help you be on your own. You can find links online to file for help..."

"I had no access to a computer or even a phone," Annie interrupted. "Luke took the truck every day, so I had no way to drive to the D.A.'s office. I was isolated from any contact with other people. Whenever I'd make friends in a new neighborhood, he'd move us again. I was alone. I am also alone in the woods, but it's the only place I feel safe. He could hunt me down anywhere else. Even if I were in a huge city, he'd find me. It's a matter of pride for him. If he doesn't feel he's in charge, he'll beat me until he feels victorious. Dominance and power are the only concepts Luke understands. He's a very shallow man, Sheriff, and he's also relentless."

"Being in the woods is not a long-term solution," Larkin replied.

"Since I had no witness or fresh injuries, you couldn't have gone and arrested him, could you?"

"No. Like I said…"

"I'd have to suffer another beating, or worse. Filing the order would make him furious. Luke is scariest when he's angry." Annie's eyes were riveted on Larkin's. She knew law enforcement's hands were tied in so many ways.

This was the point where Kayla Harvey thought they had lost Annie Dozler. Annie's fear and the fear of every other abuse victim made sense. From a victim's perspective, the abuser's rights seemed sacrosanct. What would she do now? Would she bolt into the woods and be lost to them forever? That Annie felt safer dealing with hunger, thirst, exposure to the elements, plus deadly predatory animals rather than dealing with evil of the human kind, said a lot about the inadequacies of protecting abuse victims. Kayla studied the other woman's face. She was looking for a clue… anything that could tell her what she needed to say or do. Could compassion alone keep Annie in their court?

Annie looked off into the woods. She was remembering what she had been told as a child and again as Luke's wife. Luke had impressed upon her the police couldn't be trusted. That substantiated what she had been told since she was little, when her brothers and a succession of their grimy friends violated that special place between her legs that left her torn and bleeding. "Yeah, but the police are grown-up, Annie. They're big… really big! They'll hurt you a lot more than we do!" Then, they would laugh at her tearful despair.

Annie's eyes turned from the forest to Kayla's face. The policewoman's eyes told Annie something else, something that touched her core. Like the Geezers and Emily, this woman cared for her. Along with Sheriff Larkin's quiet strength, Kayla's eyes told her these officers could have her best interests in mind. To trust or not was the dilemma. She had never been able to put faith in anything except that cruelty would happen to her. Something needed to change.

Annie took a sip of her lemonade and put the glass back onto the table. She clasped her hands in her lap and said, "Where do we start?"

KAYLA HARVEY HAD brought with her the restraining order Annie needed to sign. Annie looked it over, asked a few questions, then filled out the document as the officers quietly waited. When Annie finished, Officer Harvey walked to the living room to tell Adam they needed him to notarize Annie's signature.

Adam grappled up his briefcase and dashing a grateful look at Emily, bolted through the kitchen and out onto the porch. Annie smiled at him with affectionate humor and said, "You don't have to rush, Adam. I'm not backing out now."

Relieved, Adam smiled back and sat beside her. He patted her hand and said, "You have a pen?"

"Right here," she held up the pen and signed the documents that would deliver her from hell.

SHERIFF GARY LARKIN marched into the Deschutes County Jail to serve Luke Dozler with both the divorce decree and restraining order. He was accompanied by his sergeant, Will Barclay. It was unusual for a sheriff to serve papers, but this case went straight to that part of Larkin's spirit which lost patience with those who rain misery upon the least able to defend themselves. Larkin's professional reserve went right out the window where Luke Dozler was concerned. After his meeting with Annie at Emily's cabin, Larkin had taken the documents straight into a judge's chambers for approval, then headed for the jail.

It was cold in the interview room. Dozler sat shivering in his jail issued jumpsuit and sandals. Larkin entered the small room and sat down at the table opposite Dozler. Barclay stood at the door; his arms folded across his chest, his dark eyes never leaving Dozler's face.

When given copies of the divorce and restraining order, Dozler shook the documents and exploded, "So you've seen her! You know where she is! Why don't you drag her back in here, Sheriff? That's your fuckin' job!"

"No, it isn't."

"She can't do this to me! I reported her missing and this is what I get? She's nothing without me, Sheriff! Nothing!"

Larkin leaned toward Dozler with a presence which made Luke instinctively shrink. When Larkin was within two feet of Dozler's cowering face he said, "Actually, she's quite a lot without you, Luke."

As Larkin rose to walk away, Dozler gained confidence by the Sheriff leaving and said to his back, "You son of a bitch, Larkin! You can't do this to me! You'll pay for this! My dad knows people. He'll see to it you never win another term!"

As Barclay held open the door, Larkin paused and turned to face Dozler. He said, "I'm not afraid of your daddy, Luke. Or you either." The clomping of Larkin's boots was drowned out by Dozler's curses.

CHAPTER 20

"GIT OFFA MY FOOT!"

"Oh, sorry! I thought that was your head."

"Very funny!" Dave grunted as he and Mick wrestled with a banner for the Renaissance Faire. They had driven the banner to a large common area west of Camp Sherman Road. The five-acre meadow was partially wooded with a beautiful view of the mountains. It would make a perfect setting for the festival with plenty of room for booths along with enough shade for picnic tables.

The two old duffers had managed to drag the banner out of the pickup bed. The huge bundle dropped with a dusty thud onto the forest floor. They extracted the vinyl sign from its packaging and stood puffing over the huge wad. "How the heck are we going to get this thing mounted between those two trees?" Dave looked aghast at the height of the trees.

"Not without a lot of luck… or help."

"Teddy to the rescue!" Yank-um clopped up on his horse. "Give me yon corner of the banner. I think I can reach yon branch there."

As Yank-um stretched to tie one corner to the branch, his horse nibbled at a shrub at the base of the tree. Teddy, in his youth, may have taken the opportunity when his rider was preoccupied and off balance, to abruptly change directions and gallop gaily off, leaving his rider either on the ground or hanging from the branch. No one can say a horse doesn't have a sense of humor. Those days were long over for Teddy and in the way of horses, he seemed content to put up with whatever nonsense his portly rider had in mind.

"There! That ought to do it. Now, gimme that other corner." Yank-um nudged his horse over to another tree. In dragging the corner, the banner unfolded revealing, CAMP SHERMAN RENAISSANCE FAIRE JULY 11-12.

"Now, Yank-um, how are you going to get it to stay up there?" Dave put his hands on his hips to survey the tree. "There is not another branch to tie it to."

"Fear not, ye minions!"

Dave and Mick looked at each other, pointed at the other's chest and exclaimed, "Ye minion!"

"Yea and verily," Yank-um expounded, "forsooth and forthwith cometh my faithful companion, Squire Wiggens! Who has-eth answers to everything."

Cal Wiggens came plopping up the road riding Dolly, the horse not expending any more energy than necessary. Sally the sheep followed close behind.

Wiggen's grey curls poked out from under his flop hat as he brought Dolly to a halt. Taking in the spectacle of Yank-um trying to tie the banner to a tree from the back of his horse and the other Geezers milling around, Wiggens shook his head and sighed. Then Dolly shook her mane and sighed. Wiggens said, "Ever since we started work on this Renaissance Faire, Yank-um's been driving me nuts with this medieval lingo jazz."

Yank-um twisted in the saddle to say to his friend, "Well, we gotta be ready! How are we going to tie-eth this banner to yon tree?"

"We can't reach yon tree. We're on horses, not elephants and I haven't seen an elephant anywhere around here. Besides, the side that you've tied to that branch is not high enough. It's going to have to be seen from the road. Mick, I think we need to get a ladder. If we have to, we'll put it in the bed of your truck and pray for your life as we watch you climb it."

"Who says I'm going to climb it?" Mick asked.

Dave said, "My cabin is closest. I'll go get a ladder." He then strode off through the woods.

Yank-um swung his right leg over Teddy's back and then slid to the ground. Leaning on his horse, the old dentist declared, "Oh, man, am I getting creaky!"

Always the doctor, Mick asked, "What is it, your leg, knee, hip?"

"My ass."

"Creaky ass? Sorry, I didn't study that in medical school."

"Flunked asses, did you?"

"Shall we say that proctology was not a favorite."

"Can't blame you for that."

Wiggens turned Dolly towards the post office and said, "I'm going to get Conrad and Old Bowels. Tear them away from their crossword puzzle. If we can't use the manpower, at least we'll have witnesses to the fricking disaster."

With Wiggens and his horse trotting off down the road, Mick turned to Yank-um and said, "How many old people do you need to hang one banner?"

Yank-um counted off on his stubby fingers, "Well, lessee... one to hang it, another to have 911 on speed dial, a couple to take selfies, at least one to toss a few prayers skyward, and one more to direct the coroner."

"Six! We'll have six. That ought to do it."

Sally amused herself by nibbling on Mick's shoelaces. Soon Dave came crashing through the underbrush lugging an enormous step ladder.

"Whew! I'd forgotten how heavy this thing is!" Dave propped the ladder against the tree then looked up at a branch. "Dang! It's still not tall enough."

"Let me back my truck in there." Mick scrambled into the cab of his pickup. Sally, upon the abrupt exodus of Mick's shoelaces, now nosed at Dave's. By the time Mick had maneuvered the truck with Yank-um and Dave both shouting directions, Cal Wiggens and Dolly had made it back to the Faire site. Rattling up behind were Conrad and Old Bowels in O.B.'s truck. Conrad was carrying Fido in the crook of his arm.

By the time the truck and ladder were positioned underneath the tree, Cyril Richmond drove by on his way to his office in the Fire Station. He saw the ladder in the back of Mick's truck with the Geezers milling about and thought, *"Oh, boy!"*

He put his elbow out his window and said, "Somehow, I know better than to ask you boys what you are doing."

Before long, Beth and Arthur drove by and saw Mick's pickup with the ladder in the bed. Richmond was on the ladder wrestling with the banner, and Geezers were gathered around, holding the ladder and offering all kinds of advice.

Arthur rolled down his window and said, "I've always felt that if you think you are not going to like the answer, don't ask the question."

Through hoots of laughter, Arthur said he'd be back in a minute to help. He and Beth continued into the historic area of Camp Sherman. The women were gathering at Wardwell's cabin to plan costumes for the Faire. At the cabin, Beth kissed Arthur and slid out of the cab. As he closed the door, she said, "Please stay off that ladder, Arthur."

"IF I LOST ten pounds, I could wear this...well okay, 20 pounds." Aunt Phil was online to a medieval costume website. Looking over her shoulder was Sophie. Sophie's mane of curly red hair softly tickled Aunt Phil's cheek.

Sophie pointed to the dress and exclaimed, "Oh, that's really pretty! Why don't you get it Aunt Phil?" Phyllis was thrilled that Sophie called her the endearing nickname Adam had given her when he was a teenager.

"I'm to be a fortune teller. Is that what a medieval fortune teller is supposed to wear?"

"A fortune teller can wear anything she wants, don't you think?" Emily was trying on a peasant blouse that was too small. "They were gypsies, right?"

Beth looked at the screen over Aunt Phil's shoulder and exclaimed, "Buy the dress! It's gorgeous! We'll throw a bunch of jewelry on you and a few scarves and you're...Madam Gorgonzola!"

Sophie had brought an array of costumes from the Sister's Performing Arts Center. The collection was in a heap on the couch. Beth pawed through the clothes looking for a larger blouse for Emily.

"Oh, look!" Aunt Phil was stabbing at the screen again. "Here's one for

Adam... Friar Tuck! He'll be perfect!"

Annie was thoroughly enjoying being here in this rustic cabin with these women doing fun girl stuff. She drank in the acceptance these women had for her as well as for each other. She could feel that her future was just starting. These people were the beginning.

She had plunged into the pile of clothes to help Emily look for a blouse when she said, "T.J. and Oliver are going to be Robin Hood and Little John. I can't wait to see that!"

"I can guess which one will be Little John," Beth giggled.

"Oliver was afraid that in leggings, he was going to look like a beanstalk." The women all stopped and looked at each other.

"Oh, really?" Beth was the first to speak. "That's sad! Poor Oliver!"

Aunt Phil commented. "I'm a bit surprised he even voiced a concern. He's so dang quiet, but there is a lot that can dwell within a quiet person."

Annie continued, "He told me this when I helped him set the buffet for your meeting last week. He and T.J. discussed what they were going to wear and that's when it came up."

Aunt Phil then looked at Annie and said, "To mention that to you, he must feel comfortable with you... and safe."

"Maybe he can tell I feel safe with him."

Aunt Phil smiled, "That has a lot to do with it."

Emily suggested, "Well, we can put a cloak on him. That will help."

"Here's a tunic!" Sophie had rummaged in the pile of costumes and pulled out a man's tunic. "I knew this was in here somewhere. This is long and will come past his knees. Top it with a cloak. Add a hat with a gorgeous feather, and with a quiver and bow he'll be a stunning Robin Hood!"

Beth asked, "Do we have a Sheriff of Nottingham?"

All the women smiled at Emily and said simultaneously, "Gary Larkin!"

"Oh, I'm not sure that will work," Emily said apprehensively. "I can't speak for him. He may have to be on duty or something."

"Arthur can be the sheriff!" Beth declared. "He'll think that's fun. We're retired, we don't have to be on duty anywhere. Then, if Gary can come, he can just relax and enjoy the festival."

"Sophie, as Queen Elizabeth I, you need a nobleman escort," Annie announced. Everybody looked at her in pleasant surprise. She continued, "In the books I read as a child, queens always had lots of courtiers around her."

Aunt Phil was still on the computer looking for costumes for the guys. "Conrad! Lord Wardwell! Lord Wardwell in tights!" Aunt Phil laughed, clapping her hands together. "That'll be a hoot!"

With everyone gathering around to look at her computer, she went on, "Here's some costumes for courtiers. Oh my, look at these jackets, I guess they are called doublets. They are really something! This website says the richer the guy, the more elaborate and poofy the doublet was. Here's a blue one that's downright square!" Pointing at the image, Aunt Phil asked, "Do you think Conrad will wear this?"

Sophie answered, "Sure he will! I've found, through my work with the theater, people love wearing costumes. They can really lose themselves inside a costume."

"Okay, here goes!" Aunt Phil jabbed the 'add to cart' button. "If he doesn't like it, we'll fall off that bridge when we come to it."

"What are Cal and Yank-um doing?" Emily slipped into a blouse that was a better size.

"I don't know," Sophie answered. "I asked them, but they hedged. I think they have something up their sleeves they don't want anybody to know. Mick and Dave agreed to be guards for the queen. I have some things that will work for them."

Annie added, "Oliver also said some neighbors in their cul-de-sac were going to dress like Robin Hood's Merry Men."

"Did somebody say Merry Men?" Conrad, with Arthur behind him, burst into the room. The rest of the guys crowded in, all talking and laughing at once.

"Did you get the banner hung," Beth gave Arthur a smooch then added with a giggle, "without getting hung up on the ladder?"

"Cyril hung the banner. He insisted. He is the Great Protector of us all, you know."

"Bless him! Does it look okay?" Aunt Phil asked.

"It looks great!" Mick said, then added somberly, "One thing he reminded us, Luke Dozler gets out of jail in three days."

Everyone looked at Annie.

CHAPTER 21

THE DAY BEFORE Luke Dozler was to be released from jail, Dave and Mick drove Annie high into the mountains. They bounced up the rutted, washboard gravel road which terminated at the trailhead into Jack Lake. The Geezers, along with Tommy Jax and Oliver, had discussed with Annie options for her protection. Each one offered haven for however long it took. She insisted that since Luke had a handgun, no one was safe if she stayed in Camp Sherman.

There was something of the soft wind in the trees, the hush of the river, the grace of a bird in flight in Annie's countenance. But as delicate as she appeared, she also possessed a fierce determination. The Geezers knew she could care for herself in the wilderness. It was the wilderness in Luke Dozler's mind they couldn't understand. How anyone could brutalize another person was beyond comprehension. So, as painful as it was, the Geezers let her go.

They had pooled their camping gear and equipped her with a backpack, a tiny backpacking tent, camp stove, cooking pot, dehydrated foods, binoculars, hiking boots, hat, clothes, and fishing gear. Mick charged the battery in her phone. An arrangement was made that Mick would carefully monitor his phone every evening looking for a message. In an area with, at best, sketchy cell service, it was the only thing they could do to keep in touch.

At the Jack Lake trailhead, Annie gave both Mick and Dave a quick hug and a peck on the cheek. She then hitched up her pack, cast one last smile over her shoulder, walked into the forest and soon disappeared.

Dave and Mick stood and watched the spot where they last saw her, hoping for one more glimpse of the young woman who had occupied the lives of the Geezers these past few weeks and carved a permanent place in their hearts. Without seeing any more of her, the two men looked at each other, shrugged sadly, and returned to the truck.

ANNIE STARTED UP the trail with long, confident strides. She took the northern fork of the Canyon Creek Loop with plans to intercept the trail to Wasco Lake. From there she could connect with the Pacific Crest Trail. This was the time of year when wildflowers poured out of the mountain meadows, but Annie showed no interest in their striking beauty. She was on a mission to get as far away from Luke as possible. Perhaps the day would come when she could return here and soak in the majesty of these mountains. For now, her only thought was to pursue sanctuary in the shelter of the forest.

Within a couple of miles, she had climbed to a plateau at the elevation of 5,200 feet. She paused at a spot where she could see through the trees the expanse of the Metolius Basin spread below. They were down there somewhere; the little band of elders she never would have met had she not fled her husband. Now she would never forget them. She stood for a moment, feeling the sunshine warm on her shoulders. She said a silent prayer not for herself, but for the Geezers' welfare.

Since she was a little girl hiding in the woods surrounding the shabby trailer park where she grew up, Annie had always been in tune with the creatures which called the forest home. Hearing a marmot whistle in the rocks above her, she whistled back. With a smile, she continued along the trail.

ONE CAN NEVER say the Geezer Underground is not organized. In anticipation of Luke Dozler leaving Bend when he was released from prison, the Geezers planned to fan out and cover all major highways out of the area. Old Bowels would position his pickup near the intersection of the north-south corridor of US97 and east-west US20. Further north, Conrad and Arthur would be in Wardwell's Volvo at the intersection of US97 and OR126 which led west to Sisters and Camp Sherman. Oliver and Aunt Phil would be parked in the Bentley in Sisters where they could see Dozler coming either on US 20 or OR126 where the two highways merge just east of town. Beth and Sophie would be in Sophie's Subaru in a shopping center parking lot on US97 south of Bend. Mick and Dave, plus Wiggens and Yank-um were going to conceal themselves in Dozler's neighborhood, watching his house. So, early on the day Dozler was turned loose, the Geezers had all the bases covered. The only way Luke could escape unseen was to fly.

Once out of prison, Dozler was thoroughly pissed. He had many things to do, and this is what he got; the few belongings confiscated when he was arrested and a long wait for a taxi ride into town. Shit! He'd been in jail thirty days, and he had places to go and people to see. If he couldn't supply what they wanted, they'd go elsewhere, get other contacts, make other arrangements. Then there was the restaurant to deal with... and Annie.

His house in Bend sat forlornly in an unkept yard of parched weeds. Dead needles from a thirsty pine tree had been strewn everywhere by the wind. Heat from the concrete driveway rose in wavey beams adding to the yellowed, scorched look of the dwelling. Luke struggled with the key in the lock but finally was able to open the door to an inside as hot and dismal as the outside. Mail shoved through a slot in the door was strewn on the floor. The first one he noticed was from the electric company. He tore into the envelope which revealed a final notice of a past due utility payment and a warning that unless the account was brought up to date, services would be cut off on Wednesday...one week ago. Shit... again!

Luke stomped into the kitchen and yanked open the refrigerator only to be nearly bowled over by the stench of rotting food. He slammed shut the refrigerator and with his blood boiling, fled to the garage where he fumbled in the dark to open the garage door. He fired up his truck and in a cloud of diesel smoke, roared out of the garage and down the street right past where, in the shade of a big pine, a Toyota Prius was inconspicuously parked a half-block away.

"Damn! He's in a bit of a hurry, don't you think?" Mick looked over to Dave who was behind the wheel of the Prius.

"It would appear as such," Dave calmly replied. "Must be fussed at something."

"Shall we follow?"

"Why, of course!" Dave floored the Prius, and in the way of electric cars, the two duffers quickly caught up with Luke just as he was entering the on-ramp to the bypass. Once on the bypass, he exited at NE Revere Avenue, worked his way over to Neff Road where he blasted through a school zone and then a hospital zone as though rules didn't apply to him. He zipped through a roundabout at Powell Butte Highway and continued out Alfalfa Market Road. It was all Dave could do to keep the big pickup in sight. Luke passed other cars in no passing zones and drove as though he did not have a brain in his head, which, of course, he didn't.

Mick had Cal Wiggens and Yank-um on the phone. They were in Wiggen's old SUV and had been parked at the opposite end of Luke's block from Mick and Dave. Now, they were trying to catch up as Dozler steamed further into the desert.

About the time Mick and Dave thought they had lost him, Luke's progress was reduced by three huge pieces of farm equipment laboring along the road. Traffic was backed up for a good quarter of a mile, making the line too long to pass even for Luke. By the time traffic had thinned out, Luke was so far out Alfalfa Market Road, Mick and Dave joked that surely, they would soon see the Idaho border.

Suddenly, Luke slowed and abruptly turned onto a rough dirt road which wound through juniper trees and disappeared over a rise. Mick and Dave, noticing the road was unmarked, continued past until they could pull over. Before long, Wiggens and Yank-um pulled alongside.

"Okay, so now what?" Dave had lowered his window so he could talk to Yank-um. The pungent smell of the junipers drifted in on the wind.

"We can only wait and see what happens," Yank-um said and held up his phone. "A map shows the road goes in about a mile and quits. Since it's unnamed, it's probably more of a driveway than a road. If Luke doesn't come out by dark, we all may as well go home."

"Sounds good, I'll call the others and tell them what's up," Wiggens said, pulling out his phone.

"I'm concerned we're gonna starve," Dave said, clutching his throat and sticking out his tongue.

"No fears. I'm always prepared!" Yank-um pulled from behind the seat a grocery sack full of munchies, M&M's, donuts, soft drinks, and three packages of garlic-cheese rolls. So equipped, the guys happily settled down to wait.

Two hours of waiting were augmented by several bags of chips, two six-packs of pop, half the M&M's and numerous excursions into the junipers to pee. Mick finished off a maple bar and said, "Remember when Richmond was on the ladder tying up our banner, he mentioned something about Portland Police were also interested in Luke?"

Dave replied, "Yeah, something about him being a witness to several crimes. I had no idea the police kept track of crime witnesses."

"Well, I did," Cal Wiggens said, who had worked with police departments for decades. "Sometimes the perpetrator will show up while the police are investigating because they like the attention and feeling of importance. They can also throw off the police by telling lies about what happened."

"Sick!" Dave exclaimed. "It sounded to me like Luke is a suspect in some pretty shady stuff. Cyril told us to stay away from him."

"Ha! Fat chance that'll ever happen! He knows us better than that," Mick replied.

"Yes, it's his duty to tell us although I'm sure he knows he might as well be talking to Annie's trees," Dave said as he sank his teeth into a garlic-cheese roll. Suddenly he sat up and pointed to a cloud of dust coming towards them on the dirt road. "Do you think that's Luke?"

Yank-um popped a handful of M&M's into his mouth and said around the mouthful, "What?"

"That cloud of dust that looks like a whirlwind of doom coming toward us."

"Oh, yeah!" Yank-um squinted against a setting sun. "I see it. Geez! We better get into position."

Yank-um and Wiggens scrambled into action. Firing up the old SUV, they drove past the dirt road and down the highway towards Bend. They soon found where they could park unnoticed behind a thicket of junipers. Dave and Mick stayed where they were in case Luke headed east. They all peered through the shrubbery as the dust cloud grew. Soon the cloud was accompanied by the roar of the truck's engine as Luke burst onto the highway and with squealing tires, charged west towards Bend. Wiggens and Yank-um let him go past them, then pulled out of their hiding place and followed at a discrete distance.

Mick and Dave watched them leave. Dave, still working his way through his garlic-cheese roll said, "I wonder what's down that unmarked dirt road."

Mick chomped on the last roll in the package and answered, "Wanna find out?"

"Gee, you think that's safe?"

"What's safe, at our age?"

"Nuttin'. We could die on the toilet."

"So, let's go check it out."

As they turned onto the rough road, Dave commented, "If there are creeps like Luke in here, we'll be lucky to leave with all our teeth."

"No problem," Mick said, bouncing his head off the ceiling as the Prius launched itself off a ragged cluster of tree roots. "Yank-um's a dentist. He'll know someone who does implants."

"Or, they'll find our bodies in a ditch. Implants won't help us in a ditch."

"They won't do that to old guys. We'll just act demented and lost."

"That won't be hard."

The road twisted up and around large clumps of junipers and rocks. The junipers, being invasive, had pretty much taken over undeveloped areas of the desert. The roots of the thirsty trees made humps and bumps, adding to the rocks in the road. The primitive track wove and curled through the trees. Mick and Dave drove slowly, not wanting to raise dust to announce their approach. They crested a rise in the road and looked down upon what could only be called a fortress.

Enclosed in a razor-wire topped fence was a huge compound of several long, low-roofed barns. The entire complex covered nearly five acres. A massive wooden gate, looking as though it could keep out the armies of Charlemagne, stood guarded by two burley men holding AK-15's across their chests.

Dave and Mick looked at each other, Dave saying, "Oh, shee-it!" He slowly drove up to the gate, lowered his window and said, "Hi!" with a particularly strong exhalation of breath. The garlic fumes made the gun-toting guard take a step back and turn his head away.

"We're lost!" Mick exclaimed out his window to the other guard who also stepped back. Chewing on a mouthful of garlic roll, Mick held up his phone, pointed at the screen and added, "We're trying to find the High Desert Museum." He then looked nearsightedly at the phone map, holding the phone a scant inch from his face.

"Well, Pops, you're way off. Go back to the main highway and go south. You'll see the signs." The guard waved them off, or perhaps he was merely swatting at fumes.

"Oh, okay! Thanks!" Dave threw the Prius into reverse and spun the little car around. He raised a considerable amount of dust as they charged back up the road.

"Stupid old fools!" one guard said disgustingly to the other.

"Shouldn't be allowed to run around loose," said the other, spitting into the dust.

Holding onto the dashboard, Mick said, "This reminds me of a word Mom used to use."

"Oh, yea? What's that?"

"Skedaddle."

"Good word! Let's do it before those guys change their minds. They nearly scared the crap outta me."

"Me too. However, I did get a few pictures to send to Richmond," Mick said, holding up his phone.

"Damn, you're good!"

CHAPTER 22

WHILE MICK AND DAVE, along with Wiggens and Yank-um, were pursuing Luke back towards Bend, the rest of the Geezers stayed at their posts and kept in contact on their cell phones. Luke was too much of a loose cannon to relax their watch. As Conrad had said, "This day isn't going to be over for a long time."

It was difficult to keep up with Dozler. His truck wove in and around traffic as though he was going to a fire or escaping one.

Yank-um, hanging on to the dashboard said, "Geez! He's acting like an orgasmic moose with a hard-on and looking for a place to put it."

"Where is a cop when you need one?" Wiggens exclaimed as he peered at the traffic ahead, trying to keep his eye on Dozler.

When Dozler reached US97 and headed north, Yank-um said, "I'm calling Bowels. At the rate Dozler's driving, he should be getting really close to where O.B. is parked."

Old Bowels answered on the first ring. "O.B. here, Yank-um! Is Dozler driving that big, dark truck with darkened windows, a roll bar and dual everything?"

"That's a pretty accurate description."

"I see him coming, changing lanes, cutting in front of people and being an ass. Whoa, here he comes... Egads, he went past me like I'm a dirty shirt. Heading up 97 toward Redmond like a house afire! I'll let Conrad and Arthur know he's coming their way."

"Ok! We'll fall back because we can't catch him."

Arthur and Conrad were parked where US97 splits to go through Redmond. Arthur enjoyed driving Conrad's SUV and Conrad was happy to let him do it. If Luke had turned west toward Sisters and Camp Sherman, they could notify Oliver and Aunt Phil waiting on the outskirts of Sisters. However, Luke stayed on US97. When he charged past the Volvo, it rocked as though hit by a hurricane.

"Whew! What the hell was that?" Conrad exclaimed.

"Luke," Arthur answered casually as he pulled into traffic behind Dozler.

"Oh, good! I thought we'd had an earthquake," Conrad quickly called Aunt Phil to tell her Luke had stayed on US97 and was not heading to Sisters.

"Yup," Arthur commented with a disgusted tone to his voice. "That was ol' scumbag Luke. He hasn't grown up any since I threw him and his daddy outta my bank years ago."

"Had he served aboard one of my ships, he would have grown up pretty fast," the old Navy Commander said.

"Sink or swim, huh?"

"Swim fast or feed the sharks."

Arthur laughed out loud. He thoroughly enjoyed these surveillance gigs, especially with Conrad. Both men served in the military during the Vietnam conflict. Although Arthur was in the Army, the two old soldiers had a lot in common and many stories to share. As they talked, the Volvo was being swept along in the thick stream of cars which flowed through Redmond. They were soon disgorged on the other side of town and headed north.

Conrad noted, "As we predicted, Luke appears to be going to Portland. We can let the rest of the crew give up their posts and go home. Maybe we'll find out what Dozler does when he's been spotted as a witness at crime scenes, like Cyril explained."

"Witness, my ass! My intuition tells me there's more to it than that. I'll bet he's in on a lot of it."

"Is that the same intuition which told you Luke and his daddy would default on a loan before they cleared the doorway of your bank?"

"Yes. Banker's nose, I call it. I saw the guy only twice in three years and that was five times too often."

"Maybe we'll find enough about him so Portland P.D. can nail him."

"That would get him outta our hair. Annie's too."

Conrad looked at Arthur, "Yeah, Annie's too. Poor sweet Annie."

LUKE FINALLY LOWERED his speed when he spied the flashing lights of a State Trooper who had a car pulled over. Dozler, however, remained unaware he was at the head of a convoy. The Volvo followed him at a discrete distance and Yank-um and Wiggens were behind in the Blazer. Bringing up the rear were Dave and Mick in the Prius. Every thirty miles or so on the long trip into Portland, the Geezer car right behind Luke would pull off at a rest area, restaurant or some other appropriate spot and the next Geezer car would take over. In this leapfrog manner, the posse kept behind Luke without attracting his attention.

Of course, Luke wasn't paying attention anyway. His thoughts were on the payoff for the drugs he was hauling as well as for the human contraband he would bring back to Bend stuffed into the cramped compartments built into the bed of his truck. Illegal Chinese immigrants who were promised a job and a pathway to citizenship, were smuggled into the country by drug dealers and then parceled out to what amounted to slave labor at marijuana grows. The Chinese, their hopes for freedom and citizenship dashed under tons of backbreaking work, never saw a salary or promises fulfilled. They were captives within compounds like the one Luke had just left.

AMONG LAW ENFORCEMENT, Portland is known as a transshipment hub where illegal drugs are stored in warehouses and storage units as well as residential properties. Bulk supplies of drugs, like the marijuana Luke was carrying, could be broken down into small quantities. With the proximity of an international airport, Interstates 5 and 84, plus train and bus lines, drugs could be quickly and easily moved into other areas of the Pacific Northwest and delivered to dealers on the streets.

It was getting seriously dark with a sky threatening rain when Luke turned off in the direction of Portland International Airport. The Geezers thought for sure they would lose him in the airport complex. If he headed into a gated parking facility, they couldn't all trail in behind him like puppies behind their mamma. Instead, he surprised them and turned into one of the many dark and indistinct warehouse facilities which lined the roadway into the airport. It appeared he had a code to open the gate, and as the gate closed behind him, the Geezers could do nothing more than drive past. Luke's truck was quickly swallowed by the blackness inside a yawning warehouse door. In the fading light, Mick got a quick phone video of the truck just as the warehouse door came down. Whatever Luke had been hauling would remain a mystery, at least for now.

DEPUTY RICHMOND WAS studying the pictures Mick had sent of the compound in the desert. He was sharing them with Deschutes County Deputy Greg Leese at the Black Butte Ranch coffee shop.

"What do you make of it, Greg?"

"He said it was out Alfalfa Market Road about seven miles past the hospital?"

"Yeah. He said they thought Luke would never stop."

"I dunno what to think. It sure looks like a marijuana grow and I doubt armed thugs would be guarding tomatoes. I'll show these pics to the tri-county drug enforcement guys. They know there are a lot of illegal grows out that way. It seems that once they discover one and destroy it, five more pop up somewhere."

"Sort of like Whack a Mole." Richmond downed the last of his coffee.

"For sure! The tri-county guys are compiling intel on the local movement of drugs. They are planning a raid, something big…really big! They may already be aware of this operation, but then again, there is a lot that can be hidden in that desert."

The two deputies reflected for a few moments on what seems like futile attempts by law enforcement to wipe drug peddlers completely out of business.

"By the way," Leese said, getting all six foot, five inches of himself to his feet, "the guys who took these pictures...I mean, they were *close...really close!* They'd have to have balls of steel to get that close."

"For sure!"

CHAPTER 23

CYRIL RICHMOND'S PHONE chirped, alerting him to an incoming attachment. He had already worked late, he was tired, all he wanted to do was go home. He thought, *Egads, what now?* When he saw it was from Mick, he quickly brought up a video of the back end of Luke Dozler's truck as it entered the dark warehouse at Portland International Airport.

Richmond's first thought was, *What are those Geezers doing at PDX?* His next realization was, *You mean to tell me they followed Dozler all the way to Portland?* Cyril Richmond rolled his eyes and felt there was nothing left that could make him feel any older.

Although he was sure it was Dozler's truck because of the flat, dull finish to the paint, the dual rear tires, roll bar, and the lack of any chrome, he quickly texted back, *Dozler?*

Receiving an affirmative, he quickly texted back, *He may be on to you. Get the hell out of there!*

We're trying! Mick responded, prompting Richmond to put his face in his hands with the thought, *Herding cats...Geezers... it's like herding cats.*

Portland's airport has a unique boomerang approach to terminal traffic management. An approaching driver needs to make one of three quick choices, either pick up a traveler, drop off a traveler, or enter a parking garage. The driver has a split-second to pick the appropriate lane and exit and there is no default option. Once the arrival or departure or parking duty is achieved, the driver and his car are then expelled out the far side of the terminal and is headed back out of the airport in the direction he came from. If he missed his preferred exit, the hapless driver must maneuver around the hordes of cars, pedestrians and luggage carts to get through the terminal, then journey nearly one-half mile before he can turn around and start all over.

After the Geezers lost Dozler to the depths of the mysterious warehouse, their posse of three cars was helplessly flushed along by a stream of traffic headed toward the terminal. With no avenue of escape, Mick and Dave dove for the exit marked Arrivals. Arthur and Conrad took their chances with Departures.

Wiggens and Yank-um didn't like the idea of shuffling through the masses of either comers or goers so to avoid that mess, charged into a parking garage. It took a bit of thrashing around inside the massive structure before they finally found an exit. It cost them three dollars to get out but felt it was money well spent as they were able to join the other two Geezer cars as they were finally spit out the far side of the terminal. Merging in a tire-squealing version of a galloping rodeo drill team, the Geezer Underground did as Richmond had suggested; they got the hell out of there.

Meanwhile, Richmond had called Shawn Avery to report the picture of Dozler's truck. He also sent pictures of the desert compound east of Bend along with an explanation Dozler was followed there and, a couple of hours later, was observed leaving and immediately going to Portland.

Avery said he had no idea what the warehouse at PDX was used for or who it belonged to but suspected that the Drug Enforcement Unit would be very interested. He would turn all the information over to them.

LUKE DOZLER REMAINED inside the dark, cave-like warehouse for, in his opinion, way too long. Here he was, a vital link in this operation and these thugs were taking forever to clear his cargo. It infuriated him that they treated him like shit although he provided a regular pipeline of marijuana and transported illegal aliens back to growers in the desert. Someday, these goons will bow down to Luke Dozler! He envisioned himself at the head of the entire operation. This was a major drug distribution center, and it was right under the noses of authorities. He would be king of the entire operation.

For years, Luke had admired the power of Organized Crime figures. For him, the sun rose and set over people like Al Capone, Jimmy Hoffa, John Joseph Gotti, Jr., Carlo Gambino... he had read anything and everything he could find about them. They were all meaner than shit and swaggered with power. It was the power they held over underlings that gave Luke admiration bordering upon awe. All he had ever done to feel powerful was to knock the hell out of women, particularly Annie.

Dozler again tried to engage the goons in small talk as they nit-picked his cargo. He wanted them to know he was one of them, but they ignored him. Bastards. They'd be sorry someday. He'd make them sorry...would he ever!

When the quality of his load was finally approved, they paid him in cash and sent him on his way. This time, they had no smuggled Chinese immigrants for him to transport back to Central Oregon, so he made his way down to Marine Drive which ran along the south bank of the Columbia River. He had hoped to catch up with some illicit gun dealing buddies who hung out at a tavern in the area. He emulated them as well and they were happy to take advantage of his gullibility, often supplying him with particularly hot stolen guns they didn't want to get caught with. He would launder the guns on a black market which flit in and out of the shadows in Central Oregon.

He pulled into the gravel parking lot of the No Holds Barred tavern located on Marine Drive. The lot was swamped with blackberry vines, used needles and empty beer cans. The inside of the building was a hotbed of rats, mold, and prostitutes. The fumes of stale beer penetrated his nostrils as soon as he had cleared the door. After asking around for some of his grimy crime chums and finding none, Luke ventured on into east Portland to amuse himself with a street race. They weren't hard to find. Then he could show off his truck. Maybe he'd find some female willing to give him sex in the back seat. If she wasn't willing to give him the sex he wanted, he'd just take it.

WHILE CYRIL RICHMOND spent the evening worrying about the Geezers, Mick and the rest of the posse couldn't have been more comfortable. They were firmly ensconced at Cal Wiggen's favorite dining establishment at River Place on the banks of the Willamette River in Portland. King Tide Fish and Shell was in the Kimpton River Place Hotel. The skies had cleared revealing a canopy of stars and the guys were lounging on the hotel's deck enjoying the evening. Mick was gorging himself on an appetizer of oysters on the half-shell.

Dave watched horror struck at Mick and commented. "Gag! Sorry, I can't do phlegm."

"Yum!" Mick continued to goad his brother-in-law as another oyster slid down his throat. "You put enough melted butter and garlic on anything, and I'll eat it."

"Obviously."

Cal Wiggens had his feet on an ottoman and his hands clasped across his belly. "That was a bit of fun, chasing old Luke, don't you think?"

Yank-um was sucking on a beer and answered, "Sure was! Now, what do we do?"

"Cyril told me he'd send those pictures to Shawn Avery, so we don't do anything at this point," Mick said, smacking his lips and wiping his mouth on a napkin.

"The police aren't going to want a bunch of old vigilantes getting in the way," Arthur added.

"This old vigilante doesn't *want* to get in the way!" Conrad said as he smothered a huge yawn. "So, we spend the night in town and head back to Camp Sherman in the morning. I called Phyllis and told her."

"You are all welcome to stay with me," Wiggens said. His condo was just down the promenade from the hotel. "I have two bedrooms, one hide-a-bed, and lots of floorspace."

"Mick and I talked about getting a room at this hotel," Dave said. "That is, unless Mick snores."

Mick gave him a look of hurt indignation and said, "Me? Snore?"

"Your sister does. Snores the shingles right off the roof. I thought maybe it was genetic."

"Well, dad could do that, so maybe it is. I dunno. Buddy never complains. I promise I'll do what I can to keep that from happening." Mick winked at the others, knowing full well he couldn't help snoring if he tried.

"I invited Arthur to stay with me in the cottage Phyllis and I bought from Adam. It's off Burnside in Old Town."

"Yes, I remember where it is," Wiggens replied. Nice place. That's your home away from Camp Sherman now that Adam has sort of retired and moved to Sisters, right?"

"Right."

"Keep your doors locked. You may need a bullet proof car just to get there. This isn't the same Portland it was just a few years ago," Wiggens said sadly, recognizing his town was now tainted with unrest. "My wife and I liked to drive around the older parts of town, looking at the historic buildings and homes but one wouldn't want to do that now."

"Think the police and city fathers will get a handle on it?"

"I don't know," Wiggens replied. "They squabble as to how to fix it. I hope they figure it out or the city won't be worth shit. Nothing but homeless people and the drug addled. Gang bangers shooting each other and not enough police to put them down."

Dave took the last sip from his wine glass as he said, "I'll bet Avery, Kowalski, and Banning have been kept busy. You read in the papers and see on the news that every night, there are several shootings. I don't know how they keep them all straight, let alone solve any."

"The crooks have more rights than the citizens do. And we wouldn't want to step on those rights," Conrad added sarcastically. "Portland isn't alone. Downtown Seattle is about the same. Almost unrecognizable. We never should have kicked all those mentally ill people out of state institutions. It was stupid to think they could manage their own mental health. They can't or they wouldn't have been institutionalized in the first place. Now they are wandering around ill, too sick to apply for help, resorting to illegal drugs to try to relieve their mental monsters. So now they battle drug addiction on top of mental illness. It's not their fault they are sick. They were cursed with a screwy gene which creates a chemical imbalance in their brain, and they are not capable of helping themselves. People seem to think you can tell the mentally ill to just snap out of it. That attitude takes ignorance to a whole new level. This non-approach to mental illness is not fair to those who are ill and it makes them dangerous to themselves and others. We should be helping them, not dumping them on the street.

"And then there is the proliferation of drugs and guns, and thugs running around destroying businesses and shooting real bullets at one another as if the entire town was a huge paintball venue. It is just awful! I don't understand it!" Conrad seemed somewhat exhausted by the emotion behind his statement.

"You got that right, Conrad," Yank-um replied. "Add to that the Luke Dozlers of the world, damn him all to hell!"

"You can say that again," Mick added, remembering Annie walking all alone into the woods.

Wiggens said, "I hope we all live long enough to see things change or get back to normal... at least the normal we used to know. I'd hate to go out knowing our world has been totally trashed with little, if any, hope of recovery."

A waiter stepped out onto the deck and announced the posse's table was ready. The six oldsters got to their feet slowly, as each one let their respective kinks straighten out, kinks that were caused as much by emotional fatigue as physical. They followed their waiter inside.

❧ CHAPTER 24 ❧

THE SUN TOOK its usual morning path up over the backside of Mt. Hood. Cal Wiggens stood at his condo's front window and watched the day unfold. He loved seeing the birth of a new day and got up early so he wouldn't miss it.

Mt. Hood, at 11,250' elevation, is a stratovolcano in the Cascade Range and is Oregon's tallest. Called Wy'east by the Multnomah Indians, the mountain had been in Wiggen's life since he was a child. He grew up skiing and hiking on its slopes. Now that he was nearly 80, anytime he could see it backlit by the rising sun, the spectacle still took his breath away.

Yank-um joined him at the window. He was sipping a mug of coffee and handed one to his friend. "Cool view, Cal! Now I see why you bought this place."

"Yeah, it's worked out great for me." Wiggens took the warm mug and held it in both hands. "When I worked, I could come and go and not have to worry about it. If I had to travel on the job, my wife could be safe here with lots of folks around and things to do. By the way, did the freeway noise bother you last night?" He gestured to Interstate 5 which swooped off the Marquam Bridge less than one-quarter mile away.

"Nope! Not a bit. It sounds very much like the ocean when you stay at the beach. So, when are we supposed to meet the rest of the gang?"

Wiggens looked at his watch which read almost 5:45. "The restaurant doesn't open for breakfast until seven."

"Well, what'll we do? Do you want to take a walk?"

"Sure. We'll probably run into Dave. He'll be looking at the boats."

"At this hour?"

"At any hour."

Dave was indeed looking at the boats. A marina floated at the foot of the River Place promenade and anytime Dave would be in the vicinity of a marina, it wouldn't be long, and he would be strolling the docks. He knew every model of boat by sight, years of production, what engines it had, and whether the hull was wood or fiberglass. A bit of woodwork or deck fitting in need of a good polish would garner a heart-felt "tisk-tisk." Yes, Dave was a boat guy. He waved at Wiggens and Yank-um as the two old doctors set out along the promenade in front of the hotel.

Mick came striding up a trail leading from the water's edge. Long-legged and athletic, Mick loved to walk and never shirked a new adventure whenever he was in Portland. "Hey, you two! Good morning!"

"Good morning!" Wiggens said. "Meet you at Little River in an hour?"

"Sounds good. I just called Conrad. He and Arthur will be at the restaurant by seven." Mick then set off toward the hotel.

Little River Café was tucked into a small space along the promenade with a view of the Willamette River. Talking all at once, the six Geezers crowded around a table and perused a menu chock-full of delectable breakfast choices. They felt relaxed and happy and were looking forward to getting back to Camp Sherman.

LUKE DOZLER WAS anything but relaxed and happy. He woke in a strange bed with grimy sheets that smelled of the sex he had had the night before with…someone. He couldn't remember her name. Maybe he never bothered to ask. It didn't matter because she was gone, leaving him with nothing but a roaring headache, the remains of the drinking binge he went on last night.

He lay on his back hoping the room would stop spinning. He had to get up and get back to Bend. The guys in the desert compound were going to want their money. They'd kill him if he was late…*the money! Where is it? I left it in the truck. Under the seat. I have to see if it's still there. Did I lock the truck last night? I can't remember… mind is full of fog… Gotta get up. Gotta check the truck. Where are my pants?*

Luke staggered outside, still pulling on his jeans. His feet were bare and cold. There was his truck. He had parked it crazily in a slot close to the door of the motel room. The truck's driver's side door hung open. The seat cushion was askew as though someone had known where the money was hidden. Luke plunged his head and arms into the cab and riffled around under the seat cushions, under and behind the seats, in the glove box. He leaped into the truck bed and looked in all the compartments built in and around the wheel wells… everywhere. The money was gone… every stinkin' dollar! There had been thousands!

Damn it, damn it, damn it! What the hell? Now, what am I going to do? Was I set up? Did someone at the warehouse sic that woman on me? My life now isn't worth shit. Fuck-ups don't live long. I need to run…get as far away from Portland as I can before they sense anything is wrong. Maybe Alaska. I can't go back to Bend even though the restaurant is waiting. That entire project had to be put on hold. I'll have to kiss it goodbye. It's Dad's money so it's no big deal. No, wait! I still gotta deal with Annie! She can't get away with leaving! If she'd stuck around, I wouldn't be going to some whore. Yeah! This is all Annie's fault. She needs to pay, and to pay big!

But where did she go? The police know. They've talked to her, for God's sake! They're not going to tell me, though, damn them! She must be in Jefferson County somewhere or that Sheriff wouldn't have served me the divorce papers and shit. She liked the woods. She must be the woods somewhere! Lots of woods in Jefferson County. She always talked about the forest, the trees and animals and shit. Wouldn't shut up about it. I remember she watched a rerun of the movie Brigadoon about some magical village in Scotland that appeared every 200 years or something. She said it was like paradise and that she'd heard Camp Sherman was kind of like that, only real. It was out in the woods, and like Brigadoon, stuck in a time warp of a hundred years ago. She wanted me to take her there, just to see it. I said it's all a bunch of crap and that I didn't want to hear any more about it. She cried. Stupid to cry over something like that.

So maybe I'll check out Camp Sherman. It wouldn't hurt. However, it's best to wander around the state for a while first. Like, I'll go south down the coast and take a couple of days. Make it look like I'm not going back to Central Oregon but to California or somewhere. To throw them off, I'll sneak back to the north and come into Camp Sherman from the west over the Santiam Pass. I'll look around. Talk to some folks. Somebody will know something. That's where she must be. Yeah. She'll pay, all right. Then I'll bring murder to Camp Sherman. That'd be a kick! So much for Annie's Brigadoon! Then, I'll hit the road before those thugs or the law know what happened and come looking. Alaska sounds good. A man can hide in Alaska.

HIGH IN THE CASCADES on the Pacific Crest Trail, Annie Dozler rolled up her sleeping bag and tied it to the bottom of her pack. She said her goodbyes to the two hikers she'd travelled with the past few days. They were a young couple from Seattle and had been trying to get in as many miles as possible of the Pacific Crest Trail before the end of summer. Then it was back to school for them at the University of Washington.

Annie told them she wanted to spend a day at Olallie Lake and rest for a bit. She had lied so she wouldn't have to explain what she had decided to do; return to Camp Sherman. For the past several days she had experienced a nagging worry. The sheriff had been correct when he said she can't run forever. Winter would come in a few months. Winters were harsh in Central Oregon. In the mountains, winters were deadly. The urgency she felt had more than the threat of winter behind it. Luke presented a threat of a totally different kind.

She questioned the wisdom of leaving Camp Sherman at a time when Luke might come looking for her. At first, she had felt the Geezers would be safer without her being there. However, as she trod the trail through the mountains, she had been having second thoughts. What if Luke were to go to Camp Sherman and couldn't find her? He might take out his rage on the Geezers or somebody else. She knew he was cruel enough.

As soon as her hiking companions disappeared over a rise in the trail to the north, Annie shrugged into her pack and struck out to the south.

She was still several days away from Camp Sherman and had to make up as much time as she could.

THE GEEZER POSSE was safely back in Camp Sherman. Joined by Beth and Aunt Phil, they were gathered around a table outside the Hola! Restaurant and sharing two pitchers of margaritas. The talk centered on the upcoming Renaissance Faire. Members of the community were readying their booths and perfecting their costumes and décor. The entire population of the area was getting involved.

Mick's phone pinged. "Hey, Gang!" Mick announced. "This is a text from Annie!"

All discussion stopped as everyone waited breathlessly for Mick to read the text.

"She says she's coming back! She's worried about Luke coming to Camp Sherman and if he doesn't find her, he'll take it out on us. She says she's hurrying and is two or three days out." Mick looked up at the rest of the Geezers. They were stunned by Annie's change of mind.

"That's crazy," Dave finally said. "We've lived this long, surely we can handle Luke... the bastard."

"Wait," Mick said. "There's more. She said she used to talk to Luke about Camp Sherman and that she always wanted to go there but he would never take her. Since he hasn't found her any place else, she thinks this is where he'll look."

"Well, she's probably right about that," Conrad replied.

"Should we let Richmond know?" Beth asked, looking up and down the table.

"I'm calling him right now," Arthur answered.

CYRIL RICHMOND MADE his way through the restaurant. He was wearing jeans and a denim, long-sleeved shirt. Wait staff carrying impossibly huge armfuls of plates laden with exotic Mexican and Peruvian dinners did a remarkable job of avoiding collisions with Richmond as well as with each other.

"Okay, you scamps!" Richmond pulled over a chair from an empty table, spun it around backwards, straddled the seat, and rested his arms across the back. "Let's be clear before we go any further... you are not, repeat, not to chase Luke Dozler all over hell and gone!"

Dave replied with feigned innocence, "We didn't. Just to Portland."

"We know what you are saying, Cyril," Conrad added. "We don't want to get you in trouble, but this is about Annie."

"Yes, I know it's about Annie," Richmond said. "However, I thought you'd be interested in what the Central Oregon Drug Enforcement Team was doing last night while you were chasing Dozler. They conducted a massive raid on known drug dealing operations... including the compound you guys discovered out east of Bend. By the way, they did not know about that compound until you told us about it. This was the biggest drug bust Central Oregon has ever seen. There will be a lot of people who will go to prison for a very long time. There were also several illegal aliens who were working hard labor at those marijuana farms. An interpreter learned they had been smuggled in, promised jobs and a pathway to citizenship, and then worked, basically, as slaves. They were turned over to the local U.S. Citizenship and Immigration Service.

"Gee, life is hard enough for those people and then to be taken advantage of by crooks is unconscionable," Mick said sadly.

"Yeah," added Dave. "Welcome to America."

"In addition," Richmond went on, "Multnomah County Sheriff's Office, the FBI, and Port of Portland Police conducted a similar raid on that warehouse at PDX, recovering bales of dried marijuana, thousands of counterfeit oxycodone pills containing fentanyl, a device for making the pills, and huge quantities of methamphetamine and fentanyl powder. Thousands of dollars in cash, guns as well as high-end SUVs, probably used for transporting the drugs. That warehouse proved to be a major distribution center for the entire Pacific northwest. As for the perps, there were hardly enough sets of handcuffs to go around."

"Yay!" Aunt Phil clapped her stubby hands together and nearly knocked over her margarita. Conrad grabbed it out of her way.

Wiggens asked, "How about Luke? Did they get him too?"

"Nope. No Luke. We have no idea where he is."

"That's why we called you, Cyril," Arthur said.

"We've heard from Annie," Mick explained. He went on to say Annie had left for the mountains but had a change of heart and was on her way back to Camp Sherman. "She was afraid Luke would take it out on us if he couldn't find her here."

"She knows he's armed," Yank-um added. "Apparently, long ago, she'd heard so much about Camp Sherman she was fascinated with the place. She had asked Luke to bring her here, but he couldn't be bothered."

Richmond shook his head and said sadly, "That's too bad!"

"But that's why she's positive he'll look for her here," Beth added.

"We'll keep that in mind and try to be ready for him."

"The Renaissance Faire opens in two days," Aunt Phil reminded him. "There will be people swarming all over Camp Sherman."

"We can get deputies and scatter them around. I'll talk to the Sheriff and we'll work on it." Richmond stood up to leave and added, "We'll keep in touch. Oh, and thanks, again." He flipped a wink to the Geezers and walked away with a new admiration for Annie Dozler. She was willing to come back and take a bullet for the Geezers.

CHAPTER 25

IN ANNIE'S HASTE to return to Camp Sherman, she traveled both day and night, taking short naps along the way. The moon and stars dimly lit her path. Although she had been in the mountains for a long time and knew these trails well, she watched the ground carefully for roots and rocks. A misstep in the dark could result in a dangerous injury.

She could hear the soft feathery sounds of an owl on the hunt and then the squeal of its prey. Bats flit through the moonlight to disappear into shadows. A coyote yipped in the distance and was answered by a chorus of howls from a ridge far away. She was not afraid of the creatures that prowled the dark. Humans were much more dangerous.

She tried to think positively and look forward to a life without Luke and the engulfing fear he generated. She was going to have to earn a living somehow. She couldn't... wouldn't live off the generosity of the Geezers any longer. She owed them everything. Perhaps she could clean house for them while she went to school. She could become a hairdresser and work with Sophie. Even college was not out of the question. Surely, she was still young enough. The possibilities were endless.

Annie's heart swelled with enthusiasm as she trod through the night. The urgency of her mission reflected in the speed of her progress. If only she could get to Camp Sherman before Luke did! There was too much at stake not to.

THE MORNING OF the Renaissance Faire broke bright and breezy. For the small community of Camp Sherman, the transformation of the meadow into a medieval pageant was astounding. Flags and banners waived in the wind. The cheery notes of a flute filled the air. Camp Sherman residents were almost unrecognizable in their costumes. There were peasants, knights, merchants, farmers, milkmaids, and blacksmiths. There was a troop of belly dancers, a juggler, a roving minstrel, as well as a Celtic harpist. There was a booth putting on puppet shows for the kids. A few young rat catchers raced around the grounds.

Food booths stood ready for the crowds and offered an enticing array of burgers, hot dogs, wraps, curly fries, shaved ice, meat pies, kettle corn, and even Mexican food. The pavilions offered all sorts of merchandise from costumes, jewelry, metal works, Celtic harps, pottery and hair braiding. A booth favorite with little as well as big girls did face painting and sold fairy wings. There was even an outdoor tavern. Visitors would be transported back in time as the meadow took on the air of a summer market festival in an Elizabethan Village.

Mick had offered his cabin to serve as a dressing room for the guy Gee-zers. Sophie had stopped by and left a pile of costumes for them to sort through. Buddy the dog had the time of his life wagging about and helping the humans.

"How on earth does Sophie do this?" Adam asked, pulling out a monk's robe.

"I don't know," Conrad answered, "but she had lots of help from Phyllis. She was online ordering all sorts of costume stuff. She was up until the wee hours every night. I never interrupted her because I know better than to interfere when she's shopping. She had a blast doing it!"

"If it were left to us," Arthur commented, "we'd be walking around with signs taped to our chests saying, "Guard" or "Sheriff" or "Rob-in Hood" because we don't have the imagination the girls have."

"That's for sure!" Dave exclaimed, finding two guard costumes and hand-ing one to Mick.

By the time the guys had sorted through the pile of costumes, Oliver was decked out as a convincing Robin Hood. His jackboots came nearly to his knees so the boney legs he had been concerned about barely peeked from below the long tunic. A hooded robe hung to the ground and a quiver of arrows was strapped across his back. The arrows had suction cups for arrowheads. He wore a green suede woodsman hat with a jaunty feather stuck in the band. Tommy Jax was similarly dressed but because of his size, he was an obvious Little John. He also carried a long wooden staff.

Arthur, as the Sheriff of Nottingham, wore a black velvet tunic with striped sleeves and long leather gloves. Dark trousers, boots, a sword hanging from a belt, and a black beard and mustache completed his sinister look.

Mick and Dave were dressed as the Queen's guards with identical color-block tabards which fit over their heads and were cinched around the waist with heavy leather belts. They wore hooded shirts of phony chain mail and carried spears.

Tommy Jax took one look at Mick and Dave and said, "Hey, you guys look great, but how do we tell you apart?"

Dave deadpanned, "I'm the handsome one."

Mick added dryly, "And I'm the one with his eyes rolling."

Conrad, as a nobleman, wore a nearly square but elegant blue brocade doublet with padded shoulders. The shirt he wore underneath the doublet had ruffles at the neck and end of the sleeves. Below short and puffy Tudor breeches, his legs dangled in blue hosiery. Flopped upon his head was a blue crushed velvet Tudor hat with an ostrich feather swooped to the back. He tossed a grin at his reflection in a mirror and said to the group, "I'm ready to take my noble self outside and dazzle people!" Although no one was going to tell him, Conrad looked less like a nobleman and more like a blue *Sponge-Bob Square Pants*.

Adam had donned a brown hooded monk robe of a rough wool fabric and for a belt, tied a rope around his waist. A wooden cross hung from his neck. He wore sandals and on his head was a wig with a tan colored bald patch and tonsure hairstyle. Adam asked Arthur, "Well, do I look like Friar Tuck... all holy?"

"As holy as you can get and still be you," Arthur quipped.

Mick's cabin then emptied itself of Geezers dressed as though they had just stepped out of the sixteenth century. The guys made their way to Wardwell's cabin where the women were finishing up with their costumes.

INSIDE GEEZER CENTAL, Sophie tugged on Aunt Phil's corset.

"Oof!" Aunt Phil exclaimed. "Hey, easy on the merchandise, girl! I gotta breathe somehow."

"You can breathe, Aunt Phil. This is the way women dressed in those days. We must make it tight, so your boobs poof out over the top of your bustier."

"Listen, my boobs haven't poofed since the first lunar landing."

"You're exaggerating."

"Well, maybe a little. Nobody my age has poofy boobs. Our boobs point towards the ground and look like two toads run over by the same truck."

"Well, you'll have poofy ones now!" Sophie gave one last tug on the corset.

"Yikes!" Aunt Phil yelped. She then looked in the mirror and her eyes nearly popped out of her head. "Wow! Are those mine?"

"See, I told you," Sophie giggled as she tied off the corset.

Aunt Phil put her hands on her generous hips and turned this way and that, admiring her new profile. "I now have the oldest poofy boobs in all of Jefferson County!"

"Go out there and flaunt 'em, honey!" Beth laughed as she shrugged into a marvelous green velvet gown. She was to be a Lady-in-Waiting to Queen Elizabeth I, played by Sophie. Emily Martin, dressed as a milkmaid in a long skirt, peasant blouse and bustier, helped Beth with a velvet beaded cap which matched her dress.

All the women then assisted Sophie with her Queen Elizabeth I costume. The gown was a heavy gold brocade with beaded embroidery. She wore all kinds of gold rings, necklaces, earrings and bracelets that jangled when she walked. By the time she got all the components of the costume together, Sophie was resplendent as "Good Queen Bess."

Elizabeth I, who reigned from 1558 to 1603, was the second child of King Henry VIII. His second wife, Ann Boleyn, was her mother. She was one of the most successful and popular monarchs in English history. Her reign was known for peace, hospitality, and prosperity. She made her own decisions regarding the affairs of state. She defeated the Spanish Armada and established Protestantism in England. She was known as the Virgin Queen because she never married. She claimed she was married to her duty as the Queen of England. The scandal at the time suggested she had borne a child by Robert Dudley, Earl of Leicester. How she was able to hide a pregnancy for nine months is left to the imagination.

WIGGENS AND YANK-UM had been busy at the stables outfitting themselves as Don Quixote and Sancho Panza. Yank-um wore a suit of flimsy armor purchased online from a costume website. Over the armor was a ragged hooded grey cloak. He sported a Van Dyke beard with a mustache that curled elaborately at the ends. He carried a shield fashioned from a child's beaten-up round snow sled, found at a junk dealer, as well as a not-so-frightful lance made of cardboard and tin foil. With the bottom of the sled full of dents and the lance weakly flopping about, he looked appropriately shabby and hopelessly unqualified for a joust with either a knight or windmill.

Wiggens wore a billowy-sleeved collarless shirt under a loose leather tunic. Along with a floppy wide-brimmed hat, he made a convincing Sancho Panza. He had purchased big phony bunny ears and fastened them to the headstall of Dolly's bridle, making her appear somewhat like a donkey. The little bay mare didn't seem to mind the apparatus flopping around her real ears as long as Wiggens provided plenty of the carrots he had stashed in his pockets.

Since having Sally the sheep following them around would be quite un-Quixote-like, Old Bowels had suggested they hitch Sally to a small cart and he would walk alongside and be the pooper scooper. Expecting a sheep to pull a cart was a little over the edge even for the Geezers, but since Sally followed the horses everywhere, they thought the idea just might work. Old Bowels had busied himself fashioning a two-wheeled cart out of a little trailer for a garden tractor and Sally stepped into the traces as though she had pulled a cart all her woolly life. Old Bowels dressed like a ragged peasant and carried a pitchfork over his shoulder.

"Hey, you guys," Yank-um said as he put one foot in the stirrup and pulled himself onto Teddy's broad back. "What do you think about going around behind the meadow and coming into the Faire through the woods rather than the main entrance?"

"Sure, that'd be fun. Nobody would expect anybody to come in that way."

"Yeah, we can say we're looking for windmills or some such nonsense. Are you ready, O.B?"

"You bet! Lead the way, Sire! Your noble sheep and poop scooper are ready to roll!"

So off they went, with Sally and Old Bowels rattling along behind, out the stable yard and along the Camp Sherman Road away from the Faire site meadow. They turned down Tamarack Lane which would lead them through the forest and around behind the meadow. The dirt lane briefly paralleled a gravel forest service road, number 1216. Yank-um suddenly pulled Teddy to a halt. He had spied through the trees a dusty truck parked alongside the forest service road. The truck looked ominously like Luke Dozler's.

"Cal, look! Do you think...?"

"Holy crap!" Wiggens then glanced at Old Bowels who had his eyes shaded with his hand.

"That sure does look like Dozler's truck!" Old Bowels exclaimed, re-membering how quickly Dozler had passed him on the highway outside of Bend. "Isn't that him out there in the woods? With his back to us? It looks like he's taking a leak."

Yank-um said, "Cal, before he spies us, run back and warn the others that Dozler has arrived. If I gallop, my armor will all fall off. We'll try to stall him."

"Okay! Come on, Dolly," Wiggens said to his little horse as he dug his heels into her sides and turned her around. "If you ever wished you were a racehorse, now is the time to live the dream!"

Wiggen's heels into her ribs surprised the usually sleepy Dolly and she took off like a shot, her bunny ears streaming back from her head. In turn, Dolly's Quarter horse quickness surprised Wiggens and he grabbed his hat with one hand and clasped Dolly's mane and the reins with the other. Soon he was able to smoothly follow the movement of his horse's body as they galloped back out Tamarack Lane. Once they had reached the Camp Sherman Road, Wiggens turned toward the festival grounds, knowing it was there he could find the police. As they sped along the shoulder of the road, he noticed Cyril Richmond leaving his office in the fire station. Wiggens sat down hard in the saddle and Dolly slid to a dusty stop.

"Cyril!" Wiggens was as out of breath as his horse. He shouted through the dust, "Dozler! Luke Dozler's out on Road 1216! I gotta... gotta go warn the Geezers!"

Wiggens spun Dolly back towards the river and still holding onto his hat, raced down the trail that cut through the woods from the Fire Station to the Camp Sherman Store. They clattered across the bridge over the Metolius and shot down the lane to Wardwell's cabin.

The Geezers were milling around in the cabin's clearing, laughing, chatting, taking pictures and admiring each other's costumes when Cal Wiggens, like a scene out of *The Man of La Mancha*, galloped up on Dolly with the news that Luke Dozler had been spotted.

This set the Geezers into a frenzy, all talking at once as to what to do. They decided they needed to get to the festival grounds as soon as possible and try to act normal so when Luke showed up, he wouldn't know they were wise to him. About the time they were scrambling around and trying to figure out who would go in which car, a tired Annie Dozler calmly walked out of the woods.

❧ CHAPTER 26 ❧

"ANNIE!!" AUNT PHIL yelped as soon as she realized who had stepped into the clearing. "Come on, we've got to get you disguised. Luke's here!"

Before Annie was fully aware what was going on, Aunt Phil and Emily had hustled her into the cabin and were helping her into a tunic and floor-length cloak.

Emily explained, "Cal Wiggens told us he and Yank-um saw Luke and his truck on a forest service road not far from here. There is a big Renaissance Faire going on and everyone is in costume. With this garb, you'll fit right in. Just keep your head down, your hood up, and stay close to us."

"The festival grounds are crawling with police," Aunt Phil noted. "I'd be surprised if Luke makes it past them. Just stay in the background and maybe he won't notice you."

"But I don't want any of you to get hurt," Annie pleaded. "That's why I came back."

"There are so many cops here, if anybody is to get hurt, it's not going to be any of us... or you. You gotta trust us on this one, Annie!"

Conrad came to the door and said, "Come on, girls! We have to go! We don't know how much time we have before Luke shows up."

With Annie concealed in her cloak and hustled into the back seat of the Volvo flanked appropriately with guards Mick and Dave, the Geezers all took off for the festival grounds.

❧

YANK-UM PULLED THE hood of his tattered grey cloak over his head until it covered most of his face. In a bellowing voice, he commanded Luke, "Halt! Who go-eth there?"

"What the hell?" Dozler zipped up his pants and peered through the forest at what he thought must be an apparition. A ghostly grey figure on a large horse stood some distance off into the trees, a grey hood obscuring the rider's face. It was something unlike anything he had ever seen. Was it wearing armor? Really? It moved slowly from dappled sunlight into shadows and often disappeared altogether but would then reappear, but never from where Luke thought it should.

"I say, Peasant!" Yank-um loudly addressed Dozler. "Reveal thyself and explain why you doth venture into the realm without proper escort!"

Luke shook his head and blinked twice. Realm? Really? Had he stepped into a time warp? He looked around himself as though to confirm what he was seeing was real. He remembered what Annie had said about Camp Sherman being a real-life Brigadoon. That's nuts!!

"I'm looking for Camp Sherman," Dozler hollered back to the apparition. "My damn phone won't work in these woods, and I've gotten lost."

Yank-um stayed half hidden in the trees but kept Teddy moving slowly about as it seemed to be confusing Dozler. Old Bowels remained unseen behind a huge Ponderosa pine. He watched Luke looking this way and that, obviously unsure of what he was seeing. Yank-um was doing an effective job of bamboozling Luke Dozler.

Yank-um again hollered, "You must leave this land and with great haste for the Queen's soldiers shall soon be here. Woe be to the stranger who lingers!"

"But I'm lost!" Dozler pleaded. "There must be a dozen roads through these woods and somehow, I got on the wrong one. How do I get to Camp Sherman?"

"There are many roads which lieth herein our fair land but there is only one road which will lead you there," Yank-um said in riddles. "You must find it or forever be lost! Go back whence you came and turn right. Turn right yet again. Drive 'til you can drive no more. That is all I will tell you.

As for the dangers that lurk in yon wilderness... beware!" Turning Teddy away, Yank-um said over his shoulder, "I must go now. Be gone with you!" Yank-um purposefully walked Teddy behind a large thicket of pines and brush, hoping they would conceal him and his horse.

Dozler scrambled into his truck, fired it up, and hastily turned it around, scattering dust and gravel in all directions. He didn't know what kind of a nutter that guy was, but the experience gave him the creeps. He was going to get the hell out of here!

Old Bowels left his hiding place behind the Ponderosa, tugging on a reluctant Sally who had amused herself nibbling on a huckleberry bush. "That was an awesome performance, Yank-um! There should be an Oscar for scamming crooks!"

"It was kind of fun, actually," Yank-um exclaimed. "I was rather surprised that it worked!"

"You realize that you sent him up towards Jack Creek and Sheep Camp."

"Yes, it will take him quite a while, without GPS, to sort himself out, if he ever does."

The dust Luke stirred up still hung in the air when Wiggens returned on Dolly. Both Wiggens and his horse were dripping sweat from their gallant gallop through the woods.

"Hey, Cal!" Yank-um called to his friend. "You looked like Paul Revere when you charged out of here. I didn't know Dolly had that in her."

"Neither did I," Wiggens replied, wiping the perspiration off his face. "Now I know what Dolly's origins were... she must have been a cutting horse. She just about sent me flying off when we spun around after telling Richmond about Luke. I found Cyril at the fire station. Then we ran through the woods to Wardwell's. You were such a good girl, Dolly!" Wiggens bent over and stroked his little mare's silky neck.

"Well, I see she didn't lose her rabbit ears," Old Bowels said, as he patted the horse's nose. Dolly, in the way of horses, seemed un-fussed by all the fuss.

"Yeah, and guess what?" Wiggens continued. "Annie's back! She came into the clearing just as I was telling the Geezers about Luke. They put a cloak on her and took her with them to the festival."

Old Bowels said, "Let's get out of here before Luke realizes he's been scammed and sent on a wild goose chase. Should we come into the festival the back way like we had planned?"

"Suits me," Wiggens agreed. The three friends continued until Wiggens spied a cloud of dust coming their way.

"Uh, oh! I hope this isn't Luke!"

They all paused breathlessly and then sighed in collective relief when they saw it was a Jefferson County Sheriff's truck. Cyril Richmond came to a stop and leaned out the window.

"I've driven the length of 1216 without spotting him," he reported. "We have two more deputies crosshatching the roads in the basin between Camp Sherman and Lower Bridge. He must come out somewhere."

"We sent him towards Jack Creek. For now, he thinks that's the way to Camp Sherman."

"He can thrash around those roads for a week, but we'll find him eventually. Between our deputies, Black Butte Ranch Police and Deschutes County Sheriff, we have the Faire covered. Most of those guys are volunteering their time. Dozler will be toast before the end of the day."

"What can you get him on, Cyril. It was just our say-so about him going into that warehouse."

"We were able to obtain a warrant based on info Port of Portland Police obtained from those goons at the warehouse. They quickly got a plea deal by incriminating their suppliers. Luke is just one of many."

"Sweet!"

Richmond put his truck in gear and said, "Okay, you guys, good work!

Keep your eyes open but your heads down. We know those people also dealt in assault rifles. We don't know what Dozler is armed with, but we're going to prepare for anything." With that, Cyril Richmond took off and soon disappeared in his own dust.

A BLACK BUTTE School six-grader dressed as a medieval page and blowing a trumpet heralded Sophie's grand entrance into the Renaissance Faire. Her hand rested on the proffered arm of Conrad, the Duke of Wardwell, who proudly walked beside her. She was accompanied by her Lady in Waiting, Lady Beth, and the guards, Mick and Dave. The little procession made its way through the row of tents where the Camp Sherman residents, now medieval merchants, dutifully bowed to their queen as she regally passed by.

They settled in a pavilion set up next to a make-shift arena where, a bit later in the day, local wranglers from Black Butte Ranch would be putting on a tongue-in-cheek jousting demonstration. Wiggens and Yank-um had persuaded the wranglers to participate in the faire. The wranglers' experience with the beguiling old doctors made it impossible for them to resist.

Meanwhile, Aunt Phil occupied her "Madam Gorgonzola-Fortune Teller" tent. Besides the bustier, she was wearing a flowing dress with a multitude of scarves trailing from a pointed hat as well as from gawdy bejeweled bracelets on both wrists. She had rigged a goldfish bowl with a sparkly scarf stuffed inside to mimic swirling mist. The bowl was then inverted onto a card table covered in a floor-length dark blue cloth with stick-on gold stars. Due to the uneven ground where the tent was pitched, she had to move the table around. Like a mother goose fussing with a nest, she rearranged the table several times. When she sat in the chair, she nearly slid out of it because the ground under the chair was also uneven. Finding a good place for the chair was harder than for the table so she moved the chair, then sat and wiggled her fanny and repeated this task until she was positive the chair wouldn't dump her onto the ground.

Finding this process mystifying and somewhat distressing was Fido. The diminutive long-haired chihuahua-dachshund mix, sporting a court jester collar complete with little bells, did his best to stay out of Aunt Phil's way during her fussing about. When she was finally situated, he expressed his relief by wagging his tail furiously. He put his front legs on her dress, wanting to be picked up. She was happy to oblige and snuggled and kissed him.

"You are such a good little helper," she cooed to the dog.

"Hey, can I get a hug and a kiss if I'm good?"

Aunt Phil looked up to see a huge Viking warrior filling the flap opening of the tent. She let out a little yelp of surprise at the hairy and fearsome creature until she recognized between a bushy beard and horned helmet the twinkling blue eyes of Deschutes County Deputy Greg Leese.

"Of course, you can!" she hooted, clasping her hands together. "You don't even have to be good! Come 'ere, you big hunk!"

Leese bent at the waist and enveloped Aunt Phil in a burly hairy hug. She planted a smooch on the end of his nose, the only part of his face other than his eyes without hair.

Leese said as he turned around to show her all sides of the costume, "How do you like this? I got it online for a hundred bucks." Besides the black wig and beard, he wore a belted tunic, a phony animal hide cape and furry boot covers that came to his knees. He carried a huge sword and a large round shield which on Leese, looked small.

"It's great! I have to admit, at first I thought you were Sasquatch, but the horned helmet gave you away."

"Dang! I should have thought of that. How are things going in here?"

"Fine. I'm just getting settled. No customers yet. Are all you police people in costume?"

"Yes, we're Vikings of some sort or the other. We thought that might be appropriate, guarding the village, so to speak."

"Or plundering it."

"Just the food booths."

Aunt Phil asked, "Any sign of Dozler other than on the road where Yank-um and Wiggens found him?"

"No. Cyril reported that he had found Wiggens, O.B., and Yank-um and they're okay. They told him they had sent Dozler up towards Sheep Springs. We have some deputies out there looking for him."

"Thanks to all you guys for doing this. Most of you volunteered your time, right?"

"Yes. We have to catch this guy. We're wrapping up the loose ends after raiding those growers and dealers. That was a huge haul!"

"Did anybody tell you Annie is back?"

"No! Really?"

"We put a cloak on her and told her to keep the hood up and her head down. She's going to stick with the Geezers."

"Okay, that's good advice. Well, I better get back to work. I'm to look mean and snarly."

"I'll tell people that I foresee they are going to meet a mean and snarly Viking who gives great hugs."

They both laughed and then Greg Leese disappeared out of the tent.

❧ CHAPTER 27 ❧

LUKE DOZLER WAS indeed lost. He had done exactly what the strange figure on the horse had told him to do. He had gone back to the first intersection, turned to the right and then, shortly, turned right again. Following what he perceived as the main road, he passed many intersections with gravel roads as well as with unimproved four-wheeled drive tracks which disappeared into the trees and brush. However, he doggedly kept going straight ahead until he ran out of blacktop. The subsequent gravel surface then soon faded into a dirt track.

At that point, a reasonable person would have deduced this was certainly not the road into Camp Sherman and would have reversed course to the main highway, seeking directions from the first sign of civilization. Dozler's manner of thinking never factored being reasonable. Instead, he became angry and as he stubbornly plowed forward on one primitive track after another, he swore he'd strangle that apparition, whatever it was, if he could get his hands around its scrawny neck.

Dozler's fumbling around in the Metolius Basin led him to a little used track which led to the trailhead of Jack Creek. The road soon deteriorated, leaving rocks and ruts in the volcanic soil. As the track steepened, he finally decided to go back. If he had gone another fifty yards to the trailhead, he would have had plenty of room to maneuver. As it was, he attempted to turn around his extra duty supercharged monster of a truck at a particularly narrow and steep portion of the road. Those dual wheels unavoidably slipped over the edge. The truck then slid quite un-monster-like backward and sideways into Jack Creek. It finally became jammed against a huge pile of fire-scarred trees swept downstream in a long-ago downpour. Dozler repeatedly applied power to the engine but accomplished nothing more than digging the wheels deeper into the creek. Finally, with barely a whimper, Luke Dozler's macho machine gave up the fight with Jack Creek.

The truck had come to rest at a peculiar angle, nearly on its right side with the bed and rear wheels awash. Dozler's mood did not improve when he angrily flung open the driver's side door only to have gravity immediately slam it shut. Neither did grappling around under the seat for the stolen Sig Sauer and extra clip of ammunition. He had to nearly stand on his head to fish out the gun and then again push mightily on the door to extract himself from the cab.

The vehicle's raised suspension system, like a crazed playground climbing structure, gave him means to lower himself to the ground. He then scrambled up the bank to sit exhausted in the dirt. Puffing from exertion and thoroughly pissed, he sat looking at the wreckage of his truck. His eyes narrowed into dragon-like slits. Oh, yes! That character on the horse was going to pay! Luke Dozler then got to his feet and brushing the dust from his backside, began to walk back down the road.

AUNT PHIL HELD court as Madam Gorgonzola for most of the day.

For five dollars, patrons of the festival could get their fortune told. For an extra three bucks, they could get a Tarot card reading. With Fido on her lap, the little dog's chin on the table and his buggy eyes fixed upon the fishbowl, she'd make a big deal out of swirling her scarves, moving her bejeweled hands over and around the fishbowl, and shuffling the cards. The fortunes and card readings were all generic and blatantly bogus, but they generated enough laughter that the experience was worth the investment.

"I see money in the future. It's not yours."

"A statue will be made of you some day. Meanwhile, be kind to pigeons."

"There is a new romance in the future. Not your future, but someone's future."

"The cards say in order to be taken seriously, you must avoid being seen with Muppets."

Outside Aunt Phil's tent, Tommy Jax and Oliver stood laughing and joking with several of their neighbors from Black Butte Ranch. When their neighbors heard that the big man and his partner were going to the festival as Robin Hood and Little John, the neighbors busied themselves putting together costumes of Hood's Merry Men along with a few Maids Marion. With Arthur as the Sheriff of Nottingham and Adam as Friar Tuck, the happy group from the fictional Sherwood Forest walked together through the festival grounds and were now giving kids lessons how to use a bow and arrow, the arrows, of course, were tipped with suction cups.

Deputies from both Deschutes and Jefferson Counties, in their scruffy Viking garb, roamed the grounds and took turns directing traffic where parking was allowed in the woods. They all had descriptions of Dozler and his truck. If he were to come to the festival grounds, he'd have to park his rig somewhere. The Black Butte Police volunteers, also costumed as Vikings, patrolled the back side of the festival grounds. Their eyes pierced the dense foliage for a glimpse of Dozler as they strode along the dusty roads, their swords and shields clanking but effectively disguising their real weapons and bullet-proof vests.

Yank-um and Wiggens, as Don Quixote and Sancho Panza, crisscrossed the grounds. Dolly and Teddy plodded along and often stopped for children who wanted to pet the horses. Old Bowels and Sally followed behind the horses and were a hoot with the crowd. Annie, in her tunic, hooded cloak and hiking boots, acted like a second pooper scooper. She carried a shovel commandeered from Dave's shop and humped along beside Old Bowels. Despite Luke's possible presence being a threat, she found herself enjoying the charade, laughing along with the crowd at O.B.'s barrage of poop jokes.

Capping off the day were the wranglers from Black Butte Ranch. At Wiggen's suggestion, they put together a hilarious spoof on a medieval joust and brought down the house. The makeshift arena was lined with bales of hay for folks to sit on. Once the crowd had gathered, a lavishly costumed rider, wearing an elaborate plumed hat, belted tunic and heavy boots, cantered into the area on a splendid pinto horse.

With a booming voice, he announced, "Lords and Ladies! Welcome to the first annual Camp Sherman Renaissance Faire! Are you all having a good time?" The audience responded with cheers and applause.

"Alright! We want to demonstrate to you how soldiers of yore displayed their prowess at war. Let me introduce today's two contestants."

Riding draft horses from the herd at Black Butte Ranch, the two knights entered the arena. They were dressed in outrageously phony armor fashioned out of Amazon packing boxes complete with the smile. Sir Laffalot and Sir Gallopsnomore were then introduced to the crowd. They were instructed to line up at separate ends of the arena and to charge at each other on opposite sides of a barrier called a list. Sir Laffalot galloped; Sir Gallopsnomore plodded, his horse's huge furry hooves scuffling along in the dirt. When the two knights reached each other, Gallopsnomore deftly ducked underneath Laffalot's lance. Laffalot acted totally bamboozled, did a double take over his shoulder at the other knight and in so doing, fell off his horse. Back in the days of real knights and jousts, to duck a lance would be an automatic disqualification and noisy scorn from the spectators, but no one in the audience apparently knew or even cared about authenticity and roared with laughter.

Sir Laffalot lay flat on his back in the dirt. His dutiful squire, really the wrangler's teenage son, ran out onto the field and revived his knight by dumping a bucket of water on him. This did a real number to his cardboard armor but drew belly laughs from the crowd.

Sir Gallopsnomore dismounted and drawing a sword, engaged Laffalot in a mock sword fight. They swung at each other in an obviously choreographed battle but the crowd, knowing the whole thing was phony and the wranglers were volunteers, cheered them on. Laffalot took the brunt of the beating. In the Queen's pavilion, Mick quipped to Dave, "I don't think he's laughing much."

In the end, Sir Laffalot, his soggy armor dropping off his body in gooey blobs, was helped from the arena by his squire. Sir Gallopsnomore was awarded a phony sack of gold coins and a kiss blown from the queen. He left the arena waving to the cheering crowd.

While patrons from Bend, Sisters, Tumalo, Black Butte Ranch and other communities in and around the Metolius River Basin enjoyed the festival, Richmond, his security force, plus the Geezers had their eyes peeled for Dozler. Anybody who remotely resembled him was surreptitiously scrutinized. Cyril Richmond was constantly on his phone, directing one or another of the "Vikings" to a certain spot on the grounds where someone was spotted who resembled Dozler.

However, the real Luke Dozler was miles away, still thrashing around in the woods. He had followed the Jack Creek Road back to an empty campground and continued to a three-way intersection where he stood bewildered as to which way to go. A cloud of dust was approaching from the fork to his left. Knowing the police all over the state were probably looking for him, he dashed into the forest and crouched behind a large Ponderosa pine tree. A Deschutes County Sheriff's deputy stopped his Ford Explorer at the intersection. While the deputy carefully scanned the woods in all directions before continuing, Dozler remained in hiding, hoping to all that is holy that the deputy wouldn't exit his truck and step into the woods to pee.

Once the deputy was gone, Luke continued until the road was crossed by a well-traveled trail marked The Metolius-Windigo Trail. He decided that the trail was a safer way of travel since it appeared the police were patrolling the roads. Still not sure he was headed toward Camp Sherman, he hitched up his pants and struck out on the trail.

Dozler shuffled through the shadows of early evening. Dust raised in puffs behind his weary feet. He was hot and hungry. He had never spent much time in the woods and was now getting nervous that he wouldn't find Camp Sherman before dark. He didn't. As the sun sank behind the Cascade Mountains, it sucked the last bit of warmth out of the day. Sweat under his shirt started to feel like ice. He knew soon he would be chilled.

With every step he took, he was getting more anxious about being out in the woods after dark. He picked up his pace in order to hurry to wherever the trail would lead him. Up to this point, his bravado depended on bullying the small and weak. The wilderness presented a world larger than he was. On some primitive level in Luke Dozler's unsophisticated mind, he was aware he was the only small and weak thing out here. The realization was equal to knowing your plane was going down.

The challenge of being outdoors overnight struck a distinct contrast between Luke Dozler and Annie. She was at home in the woods. All her life, she had sought the forest for solace and protection. As she had gotten older, she marveled at the plants and animals that made the forest their home. She always felt like a welcome guest in their world. Luke, on the other hand, treated the woods as merely a place to pee. So, as the night closed in around him and things in the shadows turned into the spooky unknown, he remembered what the apparition said about the dangers which lurked in the woods. Luke soon became overwhelmed by fear.

There were bears out here... cougars even. Maybe wolves too. Are there lions and tigers in the Oregon wilderness? He didn't know. He never bothered to have any interest. Now, he was keenly focused. Every rustle, crack, or swoosh he heard in the underbrush startled him. He finally pulled his handgun from his belt and pointed it ahead and swung it around him, ready to shoot anything that moved.

The forest became so dark that Dozler was convinced he needed to stay put. He would wait until daylight before moving on. He sat down with his back to a tree and held the Sig Sauer in both hands, his ears tuned to any little sound. Other than the wind murmuring through the trees, he heard nothing and dozed off and on until a loud thumping and cracking of undergrowth brought him wide awake, and his eyes became like saucers.

The sound was behind him. He spun around the tree and pointed the gun in the direction the sound had come from. In the starlight, he could barely make out what appeared to be a large and dark shape. Terrified, Dozler emptied his Sig Sauer into the shape and then took off running.

As he ran, he ejected the empty clip from his gun and jammed home the spare carried in his pocket. He stumbled through the forest as branches of trees and brush whipped at his face and tore at his clothes. For the first time in his life, he felt his entire being fill with the fear he loved to see on Annie's face.

❧ CHAPTER 28 ❧

CYRIL RICHMOND BOLTED from his bed as though, like Sir Laffalot, he'd had a bucket of water thrown on him. *Gunshots! What the hell?* He was grabbing for his pants when his phone lit up.

"Cyril! This is Yank-um! Someone is shooting up the woods! Not right here on Tract O. I can't tell for sure where, but to the west of here, I think. It's hard to tell 'cause stuff can echo off Green Ridge. It woke me up."

"Okay. I heard it too. I don't know what is going on, but keep your doors locked and your lights out. Stay away from the windows. I'm going to get some guys together and investigate."

Richmond hung up and immediately received a similar call, this time from Cal Wiggens, who owned a cabin not far from Yank-um. Richmond repeated his advice and answered yet another call. This time it was from his sheriff, Gary Larkin.

"Cyril!" Larkin barked. "What the hell is going on over there?"

"You could hear those shots from Madras?" With his mind still foggy from sleep, Richmond was momentarily flummoxed.

"I'm a policeman, Cyril. I sleep lightly and have ears like a bat." Larkin paused for a beat then added, "I'm at Emily's."

Ah! Richmond, while pulling on his pants, was holding his phone to his ear with his shoulder. Even though an active shooter in Camp Sherman was a dire situation, his mind's eye pictured Larkin also pulling on his pants in Emily's cabin. The thought made him happy. The feeling was fleeting. He was instantly serious when he said, "We have to assume it's Dozler because we have no reason to think he ever left the area."

Larkin replied, "Let me call Eric at Black Butte. They have a drone and a police dog and can get here faster than anybody from our county. Meet me at the store."

JUST AS A pre-dawn sky was turning cobalt blue, the Black Butte Police arrived at the Camp Sherman Store parking lot in two rigs: the Chief's cruiser and a special canine unit SUV. Sliding out of his cruiser to greet and shake hands with Larkin and Richmond was Chief Eric McElroy. He was a burly bull of a man with a full head of black hair greying at the temples. Piercing dark eyes revealed the smattering of Indian blood in his heritage. He had over forty years of law enforcement under his belt. Entrenched well into his seventies, McElroy had no plans to quit any time soon.

Accompanying the Chief was Officer Andy Evans. Red haired with an eager, smiling face, Evans also volunteered for search and rescue missions. Earlier that summer, he had accompanied Richmond into the mountains to look for the remains of several missing hikers on the Pacific Crest Trail. Officer Evans had become proficient at operating a drone and brought along the device.

The K-9 officer was Sergeant Jayden Martinez. He and his service dog, Lola, played an integral part in the Black Butte Police Department's crime fighting, safety and public relations functions. Lola, an Olde English Bulldogge with a big goofy grin, stayed in the SUV and steamed up the windows.

After introductions, Richmond briefed the Black Butte officers on who Luke Dozler was and why he was suspected of being at large in the Metolius Basin. "We think he's trying to find his ex-wife, Annie. She filed a restraining order against him as well as a petition for divorce and has been hiding in Camp Sherman with the help of several residents. There is a warrant out of Multnomah County for Luke Dozler's arrest for the transportation of illegal substances. He was confronted yesterday on FS1216 and when he asked for directions to Camp Sherman, was sent on a wild goose chase up towards Jack Creek Campground. He may have even gone as far as Sheep

Springs although when I talked to the folks up there yesterday, no one recalled seeing him."

"That wild goose chase," McElroy asked, "was that on purpose?"

"Yes," Richmond answered, straight-faced.

"I'd bet my boots on Geezers," Larkin said.

"You got that right," Richmond replied. "Dozler has a distinctive rig: a black Dodge 3500 super cab, dual rear wheels and with a raised suspension system, roll bar, black package, the whole nine macho yards. His ex-wife informed us that he does have a handgun. So, until we know otherwise, we are to treat him like he's armed and dangerous. Two residents of Tract O called me this morning to tell me they thought the gunshots came from somewhere to the west of them. I suggest that's where we'll start. Let's go down to the Allingham Bridge and find an open spot for the drone."

Once the lawmen reached the Allingham Bridge, they crossed the gurgling river and pulled over into a flat, fairly open area and exited their vehicles.

Larkin asked, "Andy, what kind of range does that drone have?"

"Up to nine miles, Sheriff," Evans replied. He had knelt on one knee and was setting up his machine. "However, once the battery reaches sixty percent, the machine will fly back to where it started from. So, if we don't have to go out very far, we can stay up longer. Plus, we'll have to go high because of the trees. The drone gets its signal from the controller by line of sight." Evans stood and stepped away from the drone, the controller in both his hands. He said, "Okay, guys, here it goes."

With a whirr, the drone lifted off. Evans continued, "We can feel fairly certain he didn't go as far as Sheep Springs, right? So let's start our search at that point as the furthest north... for now. We'll use the Metolius as an eastern border and cover the rest of the forest in segments."

Larkin, Richmond, and McElroy watched the controller's readout over Evans' shoulder. Martinez had Lola out of the SUV and was walking around the area where the other men were standing, watching the forest and seeing if the dog picked up a possible unseen human presence.

Lola snuffled the dirt, her wide face at ground level and occasionally she lifted her head to look around. Olde English Bulldogges were, ironically, developed in the United States. In the 1970's, a Pennsylvania breeder crossed traditional English Bulldogs with Bull Mastiffs, Pit Bull terriers, and American Bulldogs, developing a dog larger than Adam's two couch potatoes and with amazing speed and strength. When Martinez would be teased about having a squatty bulldog for a police canine, he would reply, "You don't have to be concerned about how fast Lola can run; just how fast *you* can run."

"What the hell is that?" Evans pointed to a dark image on the screen.

"It could be Dozler's truck," Richmond commented. "Can you get the drone closer?"

"Not much because of the trees."

"Oh yeah, it's the line-of-sight thing."

"Right. Let's see just how close we can get by zooming in with the camera."

After the image was magnified, it was clear they were looking at a black pickup truck with dual rear wheels, laying askew across the creek, it's left front tire hanging impotently in the air.

"Lugnuts!" Richmond exclaimed.

"Huh?" McElroy asked.

"That's what Portland PD calls him."

"The guy gets around."

Larkin asked Richmond, "Which creek is that?"

"Jack Creek... I think," Richmond looked off into the trees. His mind's eye trying to orient where the creek on the screen really was. "Yeah, that has to be Jack Creek."

"How the heck did he get there?" Larkin asked.

HOW THE HECK he got there was a good question and what the lawmen pondered as they stood looking at the wreckage of Luke Dozler's truck. They had hiked up the dirt track from Jack Creek Campground and found the vehicle. They checked it out for anything the man would have left but found nothing. Footprints in the creek bank revealed his scramble to the road from the truck and his subsequent walk back towards the campground. Richmond took a photo with his phone of the footprints leading from the truck to the road. Dozler had been wearing athletic shoes which left a distinctive print in the soft volcanic soil.

"Let's see where this bastard went."

Dozler's tracks led the lawmen back to the intersection with another primitive road where they had left their rigs. There they lost the trail in the tire tracks of the intersection. Martinez, with Lola leading the way, crossed the intersection and picked up the distinctive tread pattern of Dozler's shoes in the dust at the far side of the road.

"Here he goes!" Martinez announced to the rest of the group as he pointed to the continuation of the tracks. "He's headed down 1425."

"Wait a sec, Jay," Larkin cautioned. "Let's get the drone in the air again before we start down that way."

"Good idea!" Martinez had to shudder at the thought Dozler could be hiding where he could watch the lawmen. Their bullet proof vests wouldn't protect against everything.

"Should we cancel today's Renaissance Fair?" Richmond asked. He squinted into the sun as the first rays of morning fell upon his Sheriff's broad shoulders. The buck always stopped on those shoulders, Richmond thought. He didn't know how Larkin stood it.

With the weight of worry etched onto the Sheriff's face, he said, "I'd hate to have to do that, but we will unless we can find him first. What time does it open?"

"Ten. The merchants get there around eight or nine."

Larkin looked at his watch. "That gives us a couple of hours until the merchants arrive."

Officer Evans had the drone in the air again and was following the assumed path Dozler would have travelled had he stayed on FS1425. With a back-and-forth motion, Evans scanned the entire area while they slowly proceeded to follow the footprints.

They soon found where Dozler had turned down the Metolius-Windigo

Trail. They hadn't gone another fifty yards when they stumbled across signs where he had spent the night against a tree. Scrambling marks in the dirt led them into the brush behind the tree and to the massive trunk of a Ponderosa pine which had fallen sometime early in the last century.

"Whoa!" Richmond knelt when he spied a spent 9mm bullet casing. Looking around the area at the other casings scattered about, it was easy to see what caused the gunfire early that morning.

"Wow!" Martinez replied, as the other officers gathered around. He then looked at the stump riddled with bullet holes. "Boy, that's one big scary stump!"

WHILE THE LAWMEN were still scanning the woods, the Geezers were getting into their costumes. They had risen early and wanted to hurry to the Faire site to make sure the grounds were ready for the day's festivities. Crowded again into Mick's cabin were all the guys. They came bearing armloads of costuming, swords, boots, helmets, and other medieval paraphernalia. The rustic great room of Mick's cabin soon looked like the aftermath of a game of strip poker played at King Arthur's Round Table.

Mick suggested to Dave they switch costumes to see if anybody noticed.

Dave replied, "Nah! They'll know it's me because of all my muscles." He pronounced the word, *musk-ells*.

Mick answered, "You mean the ones between your ears?"

Conrad, after grunting into his blue tights and then getting help from Arthur donning the elaborate and poofy doublet, said, "You guys are nuts! Those costumes are identical and they're the same front and back. You look the same coming and going."

Mick and Dave pointed to each other and said, "Like ghosts!" They both raised their arms over their heads and said to Conrad, "Boo!"

"Come on, you Neanderthals," Arthur laughed, "let's get this show on the road. We need to pick up the girls."

Mick asked Dave, "Did he call us Neanderthals?"

"Just you, you dweeb."

"Klutz."

"Fooface."

Finally, the troop was appropriately garbed. Clomping and clanking in armor and heavy boots, the men filed out the cabin door. Conrad had to turn sideways to get his wide doublet to clear the narrow doorway. Arthur's sword nearly took out the door jamb.

Soon they had the women and their expansive skirts stuffed and tucked into Arthur's Dodge Ram, Wardwell's Volvo, and Adam's Explorer. In a cloud of dust, they were off to the Faire site.

Aunt Phil was excited for another day as Madam Gorgonzola. She had had fun laughing and joking with members of the public. Fido had the day off and remained in the cabin as the tent had become very warm in the afternoon.

Everyone was looking forward to seeing which booth took in the most money. They would win four tickets to the hugely popular Canterbury Renaissance Faire held in Silverton with overnight accommodation at The Oregon Garden Resort. On behalf of the fund raiser for the Sisters-Camp Sherman Hasty Search and Rescue Program, Dr. Mazie Odom, the tracker and resident of Silverton, had procured the winnings from the two businesses.

The booth which sold the curly fries would be stiff competition for the prize. The Geezers, by themselves, had consumed enough of the greasy, salty fries to put the booth in contention.

Once at the festival grounds and after parting from the rest of the Geezers, Aunt Phil ducked her head to enter her tent. Asleep in a heap on the floor was Luke Dozler. He was filthy, rumpled, scratched and bruised from his flight through the woods. Realizing who he was, she let out a shriek.

Dozler struggled to his feet and pulled the Sig Sauer out of his belt. Pointing it at her, he growled, "Shut up, you fucking old bitch! One word outta you and I'll blow you away!"

Aunt Phil, as a criminal defense attorney, had enough experience with killers to know she was facing one. Luke Dozler had the cold hard eyes of a predator. There was something else that flickered in his expression, and it was rage. Things had obviously not gone his way and she knew he was a hairsbreadth from pulling the trigger. People like Dozler couldn't accept misfortune was their own fault and freely took out their frustration on anybody else. The best she could do was throw the hate back at him with a look that could stop a train.

As Dozler backed away from Aunt Phil and toward the tent opening, a pair of black gauntlet-clad hands reached into the tent. The hands, belonging to Arthur, grabbed Dozler by the shoulders and flung him out of the tent and against a tree. Adam, Oliver, and Jax then jumped on him to wrestle away the gun. Backed by his considerable weight, Jax dropped a knee into Dozler's mid-section and knocked the wind out of him while Adam and Oliver went for his gun hand. Oliver, with strength that belied his frail appearance, slammed the hand over and over against a tree root. Adam clasped Dozler's fingers, pried them away from the gun and then grabbed the weapon when it fell out of the now mangled hand.

Tommy Jax then grasped Dozler by the shirt, stood him up against the tree and growled mere inches from the man's face, "The first time you knocked Annie to the ground, you mortgaged your soul, asshole. Now, it's payback time."

Dozler, a long-time gangster admirer, looked at Tommy Jax, at his size, at his huge hands and said, "You're not..."

"Yeah, I am, and I know some of the most brutally cruel people in the deepest, darkest corners of organized crime. But nothing is lower than someone like you who would hurt a defenseless person whose only fault was entrusting in you her love and willingness to devote her life to you. You chose to take evil to an unfathomable dimension. That deserves punishment on a scale law enforcement can't even get close to."

Jax pulled Dozler toward him by the shirt and then slammed him again against the tree. "If I hear anything...*anything* remotely suggesting you approached Annie or tried to re-enter her life in any way, and believe me, I'll hear everything, you won't live long enough to beg for a second chance. Someday, you'll get out of prison, and I suggest when that happens, you start running. Keep looking over your shoulder because organized crime has a dark web out there and it has eyes and ears everywhere!"

Luke was horror-struck. Clasping his ruined hand, he looked all around him, as though he was looking for an avenue of escape. Then he noticed Oliver. Oliver may be a thin man, but he looked formidable with his hands on his hips and a glare in his eyes that froze Dozler's blood. Dozler then looked behind Oliver and Jax to see Dave and Mick standing side by side, legs spread, arms folded over their chests like a barrier. He spun around and saw Arthur behind him. Arthur looked huge and imposing dressed as the Nottingham Sheriff. Flanked by Conrad and Adam, Aunt Phil stood with her hands balled into fists like the grandmother of all battle axes. Geezers were everywhere, standing among the trees like a force, not saying a word but making a huge statement.

Deputy Greg Leese had now arrived with a backing of several Viking-clad police officers. The lawmen swarmed Dozler, cuffed his hands behind his back and took him into custody. As they led him away, they hauled him past Yank-um and Wiggens. The two old duffers, again dressed like Don Quixote and Sancho Panza, had trotted up to the scene in front of Aunt Phil's tent and now were sitting astride their horses watching Dozler being taken into custody. Old Bowels and Sally peeked around Teddy's ample rear end.

Dozler spied Yank-um, did a double-take, then glared bullets at him. Yank-um, leaning casually on the horn of his saddle, looked at Dozler with no expression other than his glued-on mustache giving the slightest of sneers.

Once Dozler had been taken away, Annie, deer-like, stepped from behind the trees and said, "T.J., thank you!" She then extended her hand to him, not to shake, but as though she was giving it to him. He took it in both his huge paws, gently drew her in and wrapped his arms around her as though she was an injured bird. In a way, she was. Letting her cry, he held her against his chest for a long time as if by doing so, he could protect her forever.

❧ CHAPTER 29 ❧

THE DAY AFTER the Renaissance Faire, the Black Butte Resort home of Tommy Jax and Oliver was in busy, happy, pandemonium. Tommy Jax and Annie were in the kitchen, putting the finishing touches on an enormous buffet dinner. Sophie and Aunt Phil were setting the huge dining room table for fourteen. Outside, Oliver and Adam were firing up a barbecue where the two men would cook hot dogs, hamburgers, and ribs. Mick, Dave, Arthur, and Old Bowels were putting up several portable picnic tables and chairs under the trees. Emily, Wiggens, and Beth were spreading table-cloths and unpacking several cartons of rented plates and cutlery to be used outside. George the cat watched it all from a perch on the fireplace mantle.

This affair was a "Thank You" to the various law enforcement agencies, their officers and families who provided protection during the Renaissance Faire. Jax and Oliver's neighbors also were included as a courtesy. Their kids were busy setting up a badminton net in the cul-de-sac.

Because of the parties Jax and Oliver had thrown for their neighbors, Jax's cooking had become legendary at Black Butte Ranch. For a member of law enforcement, to dine on a feast prepared by a former organized crime figure was too tempting an experience to miss.

When the guests arrived at the party, it was a virtual swarm of police and their families which descended upon the house like an incoming tide. Upon watching the spectacle, one would wonder who was minding the store.

The male members greeted each other and Jax, Oliver, and the Geezers with manly shoulder slaps, fist bumps, and handshakes. The women did what women do everywhere, they hugged.

With lots of laughter and talking, people lined up for Jax's lasagna, hot bread, and a host of salads. The group then moved outdoors for Oliver and Adam's array of ribs, hot dogs, and burgers. Kids gobbled the hot dogs and burgers and then ran and played games set up on the lawn which were supervised by the older kids.

Once the meal was nearly over, Sheriff Larkin gave a short speech of gratitude for the cooperation among the three agencies to protect the public and apprehend a dangerous criminal. He also gave a hats-off to the Geezers for their share in that endeavor. He then introduced Sergeant Will Barclay and Officer Kayla Harvey of the Jefferson County Sheriff's Office and explained a new mission. Barclay and Harvey will be bringing together the law enforcement agencies of the Jefferson County Sheriff's Office, Deschutes County Sheriff's Office, Redmond Police, Madras Police, Bend Police, Jefferson County and Deschutes County District Attorney's Offices in a multi-agency operation to apprehend domestic violence offenders.

"These are crimes that happen quietly in too many homes," the Sheriff went on. "Sergeant Barclay and Officer Harvey will be developing a task force to investigate reports of domestic violence in our two counties and periodically make compliance calls on the victims of these cases to assure that their abusers are honoring the conditions of restraining and no contact orders.

"We appreciate the ongoing commitment of local law enforcement and our social service partners to hold accountable people who commit domestic violence and to help those impacted by these crimes.

"We encourage any of you looking for more information or to volunteer for this task force to contact Sergeant Will Barclay of the Jefferson County Sheriff's Office."

After Larkin spoke, Annie was shyly at the center of attention. She was approached and gently greeted by each officer. Some took her hand; some took both her hands. Others just smiled and said a few kind words. She was impressed by the grace and devotion of these people who daily put their own lives at stake to protect others. Had she given them her trust long ago, how different her life may have been!

Inside and outside Jax and Oliver's home, a massive cleanup operation then ensued, outdoor chairs and tables were folded, and the games disassembled and stuffed away. A garbage can and recycle bin groaned with the debris of a party well enjoyed. People expressed their gratitude and said their goodbyes. Cars and trucks pulled away and the neighbors drifted back to their homes on the cul-de-sac. Soon the forest regained its peaceful quiet.

After the other officers and their families had left, Cyril Richmond, Dave, Mick, & Old Bowels were folding the last of the picnic tables. Cyril said, "Mick, your pickup tire tread leaves a very distinctive pattern, and you know, I *am* a detective." Richmond paused with a grin. "I noticed that tread pattern in the dirt at Suttle Lake. O.B., when you came to my office that afternoon, I noticed the seat of your pants was dirty...really dirty! Not likely you would get that way, as you said, chopping wood, but more like sliding down a steep trail on your rear. I've done that plenty of times myself. Anyway, it was pretty damn clever of you guys disguising Annie's trail. Even Mazie Odom never caught on. The sheep..."

"Sally."

"Yes... Sally... stole the show. I could hardly hide my smile when we saw the sheep tracks with those of the horses on the Old Summit Trail and it dawned on me what was going on. No other sheep on the planet would follow horses."

"Cyril, if you suspected we knew where Annie was, why did you call in a tracker?"

"At first, we weren't sure what was happening with Annie Dozler. We even considered she could have been murdered and her husband's report of her missing was a ploy. Then we got word of the trespasser at the Santiam Ski Lodge. Our own Hasty Team was busy at Big Lake, so we had to do something about the trespasser, whether it was Annie Dozler or someone else. Dr. Odom was willing to come.

"You guys did a bang-up job of hiding Annie from Luke... and from us." Richmond paused then said, "To be perfectly honest, Larkin and I agreed, if we weren't wearing police uniforms, we would have done exactly the same thing."

Richmond flashed a wink in their direction and walked off. The rest of the Geezers then hovered together as Mick, Dave, and Old Bowels relayed what Richmond had said. The group then discussed the possibility that Larkin and Richmond purposefully led them on to find Annie and it was an elaborate scheme on the part of the lawmen to protect her from Luke.

"They could have just left a flyer at the store and then been done with it," Mick reminded everyone.

"But Richmond came and talked to us specifically, didn't he?" Dave noted.

Arthur answered, "Yes, but even if the police did find her, they couldn't protect her."

Sophie said, "They knew their hands would be tied until a violation of a restraining order occurred."

"And in domestic abuse cases, a violation can often be a fatal one," Beth added, sadly.

Conrad said, "They knew Luke Dozler's history better than we did and anticipated that's the way he would react."

Aunt Phil added, "They also knew that most likely, Annie wasn't going to trust the police... and she didn't. But they placed their bets on her trusting us."

"And knew that we'd keep her safe," Old Bowels added.

Adam noted, "A big city police department couldn't get away with doing things that way. 'Way too much bureaucracy. A remote county like this one could possibly be a bit lax where procedures are concerned. This may have been something that Richmond and Larkin cooked up on their own."

The Geezers looked around at each other until finally Conrad said what they were all thinking, "Well, I'll be damned!"

Tommy Jax then interrupted the crew and asked Aunt Phil and Conrad if they would wait a few minutes before taking Annie back to their cabin.

"Oliver and I'd like to talk to her a bit. You're welcome to join us."

The rest of the Geezers then said their goodbyes and dispersed to their respective rigs to return to Camp Sherman. Jax and Annie, followed by a somewhat bewildered Conrad and Aunt Phil, went to the deck behind the house where Oliver had set up five Adirondack chairs. A carafe of freshly made decaffeinated coffee and five mugs waited on a small wooden table.

Once everyone had settled, and those who wanted coffee had been served, George the cat tried out each lap and finally settled on Annie's. When viewed in retrospect, this action on the part of the cat was prophetic.

Oliver said, "Annie, T.J. and I have been talking, and we'd like to invite you to come to Seattle with us. We have a huge house. You can have all the privacy you need."

Jax added, "I cook. Oliver runs the house. We volunteer at a local homeless shelter. You're welcome to join our mission there or not. That's up to you. Other than that, we come to Camp Sherman to help the Geezers. That's our life." Then, with a laugh, he said, "How much safer could you be, living with two gay guys and three Dobermans?"

Annie looked at both their kind, friendly faces and she broke into a genuine smile, a smile free from the underlying anxiety she had lived with for oh, so long.

Aunt Phil and Conrad shared a look that communicated pleasant albeit surprised approval. The five friends then chatted about the day's events and the possible motive behind Richmond and Larkin's asking the Geezers to look for Annie. Meanwhile, the western sky lit up with glorious color as the sun sank behind the ancient volcano, Three Fingered Jack.

❧ CHAPTER 30 ❧

ANNIE DOZLER'S NEW life began that night on the deck of T.J. and Oliver's house at Black Butte Ranch. The next few days were spent by T.J. and Oliver packing up and readying the house to be left for several months. The Bentley's trunk was stuffed with items the men liked to take back and forth to Seattle. Annie's things consisted of only a small suitcase containing the clothes and a few toiletries Aunt Phil and Sophie had purchased for her on their shopping spree in Sisters.

Their last day started by saying goodbye to neighbors and friends, both at the ranch and at Camp Sherman. At Wardwell's cabin, the Geezers shared hugs and goodbyes with Anne. Cyril Richmond was also there and when he shook the hand of Tommy Jax, he felt a new appreciation for this big man with the easy smile. Richmond was one step closer to believing that, just maybe, gangsters can be trusted to leave a checkered past and start anew. When the Bentley finally pulled away from Wardwell's cabin, the Geezers and Deputy Richmond waved goodbye. There was a tear or two. Annie also sniffled and shed tears for these old people who had taken ownership of her peril and finally freed her from a horrible existence with Luke Dozler.

Oliver and TJ had realized Annie had never been out of her immediate surroundings in neither Baker City nor Madras, so they decided to give her a tour of some sights along the trip. Their first stop was at Timberline Lodge on Mt Hood. Just the ride up the steep road from the pass at Government Camp to the Lodge seemed to bring Annie wonderous joy. The above timberline view of the Cascade Mountains stretching to the south and fading into a blue haze was something she had never seen before nor could have imagined. As they approached the parking lot for the lodge, Annie asked why the trees were so small and crooked.

"These trees spend the winter months underneath several feet of snow and ice," Oliver explained as he piloted the big car up the twists and turns of the road. "The growing season is short and by the time the cold comes again, the new shoots get deformed by the weight of snow."

"Are they the same kind of tree that grows tall at pass level?"

"These are sub-alpine species. Firs mostly, Noble and White fir. They are very resilient, these trees."

"Like I'm going to have to be," Annie said, smiling shyly at Oliver.

"You have already proved you are," Tommy Jax said from where he sprawled on the back seat.

Twisting so she could see him, Annie remembered how Jax had taken the starch out of Luke. She said, "You have no idea how much I appreciate this... all of it."

"Nothing to it," Jax grinned in his usual casual, jovial manner. After a pause, he changed the subject. "You may find you like the big city. It can be an exciting place. There are lots of contrasts in a place like Seattle. As beautiful as the city is, there are needy folks on the streets. You'll meet them at the shelter, if you wish to do so.

"Governments don't want to spend money to institutionalize the mentally ill nor trod on their rights even though they can't care for themselves. And there is only so much we can do to help people who are addicted to drugs and/or mentally ill and sometimes it seems like anything we do is just a Band-Aid. It can be frustrating, so expect no pressure from us to participate in what we do. This is your opportunity to spend your time doing anything you want to."

At 6,000 feet, the expansive parking lot of Timberline Lodge was nearly full of cars, even in late summer. Skiers and snowboarders took advantage of the remaining glacier high on the mountain. Hikers with their kids and dogs also helped to fill the parking lot. A space was available close to the lodge and Oliver nosed the Bentley up to the ragged remains of a snowbank. As they walked toward the gaping doorway of the building, Annie's mouth hung open in awe of the iconic stone structure. Once inside, the massive rock fireplace and huge wooden beams of the lodge spoke of a bygone era but presented a solid permanence. To a little girl born into a life of profound insecurity, perhaps it was the sturdiness of the lodge which Annie found so captivating.

The walls of the second story lobby were adorned with photos showing the building of the lodge and ski area. The pictures told the lodge's story from its conception on the desk of President Franklin D. Roosevelt and his Civilian Conservation Corp to becoming the United States' longest ski area at 4,540 vertical feet and the only year-round training ground for the US Olympic Ski Team.

Annie wandered about the lobby, with T.J. and Oliver following. She gazed out a huge picture window which revealed the top of Mt. Hood, a mountain she had only seen from miles away. Now it seemed as though if she could reach outside, she could nearly touch the venerable peak.

The hand-carved figures of forest creatures which graced the newel posts of the staircase also fascinated her. She gently ran her fingers over the carvings as though by doing so, she could somehow connect to the long-ago artisan whose skills created the masterpieces. Without the employment the Civilian Conservation Corp provided, the carver's incredible talents during the Great Depression could have been lost to a life of hunger and poverty.

They had lunch in the Cascade Dining Hall. Jax and Oliver made sure Annie was seated where she had the best view. From their table, they were able to see Mt. Jefferson looming in the haze seventy miles to the south. Annie looked a long time at the soft crests of the foothills to the east of the mountain, trying to pick out where Camp Sherman and the Geezers might be.

All too soon, it was time to leave. If they were going to pick up the dogs before nightfall, they needed to return to the highway. Highway 35 took them through the bountiful Hood River Valley where harvest time for early apples and pears was in full swing. Once they reached the Columbia River, they traveled west on I84 and stopped for a bathroom break at Multnomah

Falls. Annie commented she had never seen a falls so beautiful. Again, she was fascinated with the lodge built in 1925 of stone and timber in the rugged Cascadian style.

They crossed the Columbia at Portland on the I205 bridge and headed north on I5 into Washington State. At Highway 504, they traveled east along what was left of the Toutle River channel after the eruption of Mount Saint Helens in 1980. Their destination was the Mount Saint Helens Science and Learning Center. Once at the center, they poked around the displays showing the devastation surrounding the eruption and the aftermath of healing to the forest, its wildlife and to human interests.

With time again running thin, they were soon on their way with a promise to return some day and spend more time. Late afternoon brought them into the green oasis that is Maple Valley. Roughly thirty miles from Seattle, Maple Valley is a wooded bedroom community of nearly thirty thousand. The Bentley turned off Highway 18 onto a rural road which wound into the hills. Occasionally the forest parted to reveal pastures cut out of the woods for the few small farms which dotted the area.

They soon came to a gravel lane marked with a sign *Hadwin Animal Hospital and Sanctuary*. The lane led uphill and was lined with fenced pastures on both sides. Annie caught a glimpse of a horse as its tail swished and the animal turned to watch the car go past. Standing behind the horse was a donkey. Its ears, like overblown, daffy antenna, turned and twitched as though to fine-tune what its eyes were seeing.

"What is this place?" Annie asked.

"Home, farm, and clinic for our vet, Dr. John Hadwin," Jax explained. "He boards the dogs when we travel. He has a veterinary clinic attached to his house. He also takes in animals that, for some reason, nobody wants. You know, ones where the owner doesn't want to spend the time or money to keep. They might be old or sick or something."

"Oh, my," Annie said, thoughtfully.

"Yeah, he's a nice guy. You'll like him. We won't stay long. I texted him that we'd be late."

In the clinic's parking space, Oliver pulled the Bentley to a halt to a chorus of barking dogs. The pack of mixed breeds, including Jax and Oliver's three Dobermans, had happily run, along with a few chickens, from all reaches of the little farm. Wading through the wagging tails was the doctor himself, tall, slender, sandy haired with a touch of grey at the temples. He was carrying a Golden retriever puppy.

"Jax! Oliver! I was about to send out the gendarmes for you." The smile which lit up John Hadwin's middle-aged, rugged face spoke freely of the man's good nature.

"Sorry we're so late, John!" Oliver said as stick-like, he pulled his lanky body out from behind the steering wheel. Shaking the doctor's hand, he said, "As T.J. explained in his text, we have a guest, and we wanted her to see some things along the way."

"I can understand! We live in a beautiful part of the world."

"Let's introduce you," Jax grunted as he got out of the car. He quickly closed the car door to keep George the cat inside. The cat, who was uncaged, now had his front paws on the windowsill.

Annie had exited the car and was soon up to her waist in dogs. Smiling, she passed her hand from one furry head to another as she made her way to where the men were standing.

She extended her hand to Hadwin as Jax made the introductions. Annie then pointed to the puppy and asked, "Who is this little guy?"

"Archie," the doctor answered, gently bouncing the little dog in his arms and stroking its head, "His people are also on a trip. I thought the other dogs might bowl him over running to greet you." He then put the puppy on the ground and said, "Come on up to the house. I thought you might be hungry, so I put together a little dinner for us."

"Gee, John, you didn't have to do that," Jax responded with a laugh. "You know us, we always have plenty of stuff in the freezer."

"Nah! Come on in. I'd appreciate the company." Hadwin led the way to his clinic, then stepped back so Annie could enter first. Once everyone was inside the white walled, immaculate facility, Hadwin stepped around the counter and said, "Come this way into the house."

Hadwin's home was an old farmhouse which had clung to the hillside for over one hundred years. They entered the kitchen, a large and airy space which sported an original farmhouse sink, Victorian cupboards, a pie safe, and sideboard along with modern appliances. In the front corner of big windows, a round solid oak table was set for four. The room smelled warmly of corned beef and cabbage.

During their hearty and welcome dinner, Jax, Oliver, and Hadwin caught up on news and happenings since the time last spring when Jax and Oliver left for Camp Sherman. Jax mentioned that Annie was going to stay with them in Seattle and perhaps help at the homeless shelter. Knowing Hadwin might have questions regarding this arrangement, Annie surprised all of them and told him her story.

"I'm very lucky, Dr. Hadwin," Annie went on. "T.J., Oliver, and the Geezers of Camp Sherman took very good care of me. I might not have survived without their help."

"Well, sometimes angels come in different forms than we would expect," Hadwin said.

After dinner, Hadwin asked Annie if she'd like to see the rest of the farm. She answered with, "I'd love to!" Then she said to Jax and Oliver, "Do you guys mind? Do we have time?"

"Of course, we don't mind."

"Not if we get to come along."

Again, with Jax and Oliver trailing, Annie got a quick tour of Dr. Hadwin's facility, from the clinic to the barn with its pens for critters in different stages of healing. Then, with the sun sinking low towards the western horizon, Hadwin told everyone to pile into a John Deere Gator.

Tommy Jax gave the vehicle a skeptical eye that Hedwin could not help but notice. He laughed, "Don't worry, T.J., it'll haul all of us. No sweat!"

"The man says, 'No sweat!'" Jax exclaimed with a laugh as he heaved himself aboard.

"Hang on now," Hadwin ordered as the vehicle lurched up a narrow lane which led into the woods above the house. "We're going up there." Hadwin pointed up the hill to a pasture barely visible through the trees. "That is where I have farm animals and riding horses so old or crippled that they were rejected by their owners. They get along fine up there," he explained. "In the mornings, they come through the woods for a little grain. The older ones get supplements appropriate to their species. I do head counts to make sure they are all still okay. Sometimes a deer will come down with them in the mornings. This year it's a little buck, a yearling. After grain, some stay for a pet or two, then they leave for their own private world up there. At any one time, I'll have cows, goats, sheep, donkeys, horses, and mules. I just let them live out their lives, you know, as nature intended without any demands put upon them. They've earned their rest. You'll love it up there! It's very beautiful."

Beautiful it was! They broke out of the trees into an expansive pasture dotted with thickets of trees and brush, the vine maples turning red in these longer nights of late summer. Mt. Rainier hovered in the distance with alpenglow on its 14,410-foot peak. Hadwin turned off the Gator and let the quietness of the evening take over. A small pond nestled in a low spot. A pair of Mallard ducks cruised the surface. Two horses and a goat looked up from their drinking to stare at the humans. One horse whinnied in recognition. Under a large fir tree, two mules stood with their heads together like old friends.

Annie was the first to speak, "It's really lovely, what you do for these animals."

Hadwin responded, "It's not hard, really, anybody would do it."

Jax and Oliver shared a look when they noted Annie's compliment brought a bit of a blush to the doctor's face.

Annie turned to Jax and Oliver. "I remember what Aunt Phil once said to me about humans being equal with animals. And because we are capable of taking care of them, we have an obligation to do so."

"Your aunt is a wise woman," Hadwin said then added, "you called her... Phil?"

"It's Phyllis and she's not my real aunt," Annie explained, "but as close to one as I'll ever know. She's a wonderful woman. She's one of Camp Sherman's Geezers." Annie went on, "You know, when I was on my own out in the woods, I crossed paths with all sorts of creatures. They never bothered me but would look at me curiously and then would go on their way, as I went on mine. Ever since I was little, I've felt that humans and animals are on an even plane, sharing a planet and the same journey through time. In the greater scheme of things, one isn't any better or more important than the other."

"That's a very beautiful and good way to look at life," Hadwin replied, looking at Annie.

Now it was finally time to go. Dr. John Hadwin stood in his driveway and watched the Bentley drive off, carrying a woman whose softspoken grace had taken his breath away.

❦ CHAPTER 31 ❦

WARM FALL DAYS quickly turned to early winter chill. Snow again blew into Camp Sherman from the mountains. The Geezers nestled in, stockpiling firewood, groceries, and toilet paper. The winter crawled along as winters do, one frigid day after the other. On Sundays, Aunt Phil, Conrad, Mick, Dave, and Old Bowels would enjoy a leisurely, late breakfast together at Wardwell's cabin. Occasionally, other Geezers would pop in to say hi and to share the phenomenal comfort of their friendship.

One Sunday in late February, the fireplace in Wardwell's cabin was burning with a cheery glow. Conrad sat in his chair, reading the Bend Bulletin over the top of Fido's fuzzy head. The little dog was warmly ensconced on Conrad's lap.

Mick, spilling a box of puzzle pieces onto the dining table, asked, "Conrad, what does the stock market look like today?" He sat down and started to spread the pieces out, turning them all right side up. His dog, Buddy, was under the table, his head on his paws.

Shuffling the newspaper to a different page, Conrad answered, "Well, let's see...out of six arrows, three are up, two are down, and one is sideways."

"That's good enough to make it worthwhile getting out of bed, don't you think?"

"That and having to pee."

Giving the front door a quick courteous knock, Dave came in and brought a blast of cold air with him. Carrying a box of cinnamon rolls he'd picked up at the store, he said, "Sorry I'm late. I had a longer than usual workout at the gym this morning."

"How so?"

"Getting extra exercise throwing people off the machines I wanted to use. You know, when they'd set up camp."

"Good for you!" Aunt Phil crowed. She was in the kitchen putting on coffee to brew. "What a tough guy!"

Dave curled his biceps and snarled, "Aargh!"

Mick said, "You sound like a pirate with gout."

Taking the box from Dave, Aunt Phil said, "Back in the day, I used to go to the gym and when people would park on a machine, I would get really pissed! I'd go do the rest of the machines and come back and they'd still be there! They would be looking at their phones, or their navels. Sometimes it's hard to tell the difference. I admit, my experience at a health club consisted mainly of trying to find a machine I could lie down on." She plopped the box on the kitchen counter and said, "Oh, yummers! These are still warm! Belly up to the bar, gentlemen, before these get cold."

Mick and Dave each took a roll and a helping of a fruit salad Aunt Phil had tossed together. Mick, always the doctor, encouraged Dave to take more than the measly amount of fruit he had spooned onto his plate.

"Come on, Dave. Dish up! It's good for your bowels, being old and all."

"Speaking of old bowels, where is he? Old Bowels, I mean," Dave said around a chunk of pineapple.

"He'll be along. He's helping Cal and Yank-um move hay," Mick answered, as he sat at the table, carefully moving puzzle pieces out of the way.

Conrad said from behind his newspaper, "That's hard on the back...or so I've been told as I've never bucked a bale of hay in my life. Something bad can happen when you're doing stuff like that. If you don't do anything, nothing bad will happen. Therefore, I stay in my chair."

"That's right! If you were standing up when you croaked, you could fall down and hurt yourself," Dave offered, chuckling. Licking the icing from his fingers, he took a seat at the table with Mick and the puzzle.

"All the more reason to stay in my chair...with the exception of eating cinnamon rolls." Conrad folded his paper, gently placed Fido on the floor, left his chair and went into the kitchen.

The rolls were consumed and with the puzzle well underway, Conrad announced he was going to the Post Office. "We didn't go yesterday. Anybody else want to go along?"

"I'll go," Mick answered, "I haven't been for a couple of days, and it's a good chance to air out the dog. Buddy, ready for a walk?" At the sound of his name, Buddy stiffly stretched and groaned and came out from under the dining table. With huffs and tail thumps against the table, chairs, and human legs, the old Labrador telegraphed that he was clearly ready.

After donning all sorts of winter gear; gloves, earmuffs, parkas, and scarves, Conrad and Mick left. Fido was on a leash since he had a propensity to impulsively pursue his own ideas of fun. The cold, crisp air filled their lungs in a not unpleasant way and their footsteps made squeaky noises in the snow. They made their way down the little lane which led past other cabins alongside the Metolius River. A few cabins were warmly lit with beams of light coming through mullioned windows and woodsmoke curling out chimneys. Other cabins had that dark, cold, clapped shut look of a dwelling put away until a warmer time.

The Camp Sherman Store parking lot was busy with the comings and goings of the few residents who stayed the winter. During winter months, the store was open only from Friday through Sunday. After Memorial Day, it would open full time for the summer. Mick and Conrad skirted the vehicles and approached the little post office attached to the far end of the store.

Stamping the snow from their boots, the men entered the building's tiny vestibule. To the right was a small lending library. To the left were post office boxes for all Camp Sherman residents. The men pulled accumulated mail from their respective boxes. Conrad exclaimed, "Oh, my! What's this?" It was a fully stuffed envelope addressed to "Conrad and Phyllis Wardwell and Geezers." The return was T. Jax with a Seattle address.

Conrad looked at Mick and said, "It's from T.J., but Oliver is not on the return. You don't suppose something has happened to him, do you?"

"Open it and let's find out."

Conrad reached into his pocket for a Swiss Army knife he always carried.

He found that the small tool often came in handy when your dwelling is a log cabin in the woods. He slit open the envelope and unfolded a letter containing several sheets and after a brief scan, announced, "No. It's about Annie. Let's take it home and read it to Phyllis and Dave."

BY THE TIME they returned to the cabin, Old Bowels had arrived, smelling faintly of hay and horse barn. As O.B. munched on the last cinnamon roll, Conrad dropped into his chair and told them about Jax's letter. The rest gathered around as Conrad began to read Tommy Jax's expansive scrawl:

FROM THE DESK OF TOMMY JAX

Hello Conrad, Phyllis, and all other Geezers!

Rather than call and have this info repeated from Geezer to Geezer,

I thought I'd just write it all down. Everything is fine here. In fact, we have good news to report about Annie Dozler!

Upon arriving in Seattle, we offered the entire third floor of this old brewery cum our residence or she could pick any guest room. She decided on the third floor and settled right in. It's like an apartment with its own private bath and Pullman kitchen, although she takes her meals with us. She fit right in with us and our crazy schedule. If we couldn't find the dogs or George, we knew they'd be up there with Annie. I've never seen animals take to a human quite like they do her.

On the days we volunteer at the homeless shelter, she started coming with us. She dug right in, and no task seemed too much for her. Whatever needed done, Annie would be right there, whether it was cleaning, laundry, or helping in the kitchen. The compassion she showed for the clients was extraordinary! We bought a laptop for her and Oliver showed her how to wade through the websites of social services for housing, addictions, citizenship, whatever was needed. Soon, she and Oliver could process twice as many clients as before. Where she really excelled was in connecting people, both men and women, to resources within the police department and DA's Office for protective services.

It was understandable how easily she could pick out people who were fugitives of abuse and encourage them into doing something positive about their situation. She was on their wavelength. Otherwise, many of those folks wouldn't know what to do and their fear would keep them running, just like she did. I'm sure her experience with you guys, Emily Martin, and the Jefferson County Sheriff's Department helped her help other people.

On her own, she found a part-time position at the local YWCA doing basically the same thing she does at the shelter with respect to connecting people with services. She does other odd jobs for them too, I'm not sure just what but it pays her a little "walking around money." She has used it to pay for online courses in veterinary sciences with a goal to get certified as a veterinary technologist.

Herein lies the heart of this letter! Our vet, Dr. John Hadwin, out in Maple Valley, offered to let Annie intern with him. We were driving her out there two days a week for about six weeks while she studied and got her driver's license... in the Bentley! That was a hoot! You should have seen the examiner's eyes pop out of his head. Then, she put some money down on a small car and now drives herself three days a week out to John's.

A little background on John, since you don't know him: he had married while he was still in veterinary school. A mutual friend told us his ex-wife stated she wanted to marry a doctor, she didn't care what kind or who it was! She was interested in the type of lifestyle she thought she would get. When she found out a country vet couldn't supply that for her, she split, but not without first causing John a lot of heartache.

John once confided in us that he expected to be single forever because he would never lose his heart again. He had been single for twenty years before he met Annie. They met when we picked up the dogs last fall on our trip home from Camp Sherman. Both Oliver and I noticed that John was somewhat taken by Annie's thoughtfulness and her sweet nature. Who wouldn't be? Now, you can tell by the way he looks at her that he worships the ground she walks on.

As for Annie, she didn't expect to fall in love with John. After her experience with Luke, she told us she could never again romantically trust a man.

It didn't take long for her to realize John Hadwin is clearly no Luke! In fact, their appreciation for each other has developed into a relationship beyond our wildest expectations for either of them.

So, they are getting married on the last weekend in June! They are planning an outdoor wedding, so we are hoping for nice weather. She wants all of you to come and invitations will be forthcoming. She told us she really doesn't expect you to come this far. The trip would be hard on you because of your ages, etc., etc. However, we would be thrilled if any of you could be here.

As you know, our Annie is a very special girl, and we are so very happy for her and John. We adore them both and wish them the happiness they have long been denied.

With fond regards,
T.J.

AND SO IT was, that Dr. John Hadwin and Annie Dozler were married on a sunny June afternoon in the high pasture of Hadwin's Animal Sanctuary. Annie wore a flowing yellow gown and flowers in her hair. She was escorted to the altar by both Tommy Jax and Oliver. In the audience among friends and colleagues of John Hadwin was also a contingent from Central Oregon; Sheriff Gary Larkin, Emily Martin, Cyril Richmond, Adam and Sophie, and the Geezers, every one of them.

THE END

Tommy Jax's Veggie Lasagna

2 Cup thinly sliced zucchini

1 ½ Cup thinly sliced carrots

1 Cup thinly sliced fresh mushrooms

1 medium onion, diced

2 ½ Cup thinly sliced Japanese eggplant

1 (14oz) can crushed tomatoes

1 (8 oz) can tomato sauce

1 (6 oz) can tomato paste

¼ Cup sliced fresh basil

2 cloves garlic, minced

1 tsp. salt

½ tsp. ground black pepper

1 (8oz) package cream cheese, softened

¾ Cup ricotta or cottage cheese

1 large egg, lightly beaten

8 oven ready, "no cook" lasagna noodles

12 slices provolone cheese

2 Cup shredded mozzarella cheese

Parmesan cheese to taste

Combine crushed tomatoes, tomato sauce, tomato paste, basil, garlic, salt, and pepper in a medium saucepan. Bring to a boil, reduce heat, and simmer 20 minutes. Give it a stir now and then.

Combine zucchini, carrots, mushrooms, onion, eggplant with water to cover in a large saucepan. Bring to a boil over medium-high heat; reduce heat and simmer 10 minutes or until vegetables are tender. Drain well, and reserve.

Preheat oven to 350 degrees F.

In a medium bowl, combine cream cheese, ricotta cheese, and egg. Stir together.

Spread 1/3 of the sauce evenly over bottom of a 13X9X2 baking dish. Place 4 uncooked, oven-ready lasagna noodles on top of sauce. Do not overlap noodles. Spread ½ of cream cheese mixture over noodles. Cover cheese mixture with ½ of the vegetables. Cover with 1/3 sauce, and top evenly with 6 slices provolone cheese and 1 ½ cups mozzarella cheese. Repeat layers with 4 noodles, rest of cream cheese mixture, vegetables, sauce, and remaining provolone and mozzarella cheeses. Top with a sprinkle of Parmesan cheese to taste. To Tommy Jax, that means lots of Parmesan cheese.

Bake 35 minutes until hot and bubbling. Let stand 10 minutes before serving.

To appease those who dislike onions, Jax will leave out the onion and make up the difference in volume with more of any or all the other vegetables or will add a generous cup or so of sliced yellow crooked-neck squash or sweet pepper.